THE REDEMPTION OF DAYA KEANE

THE
REDEMPTION
OF DAYA
KEANE

GIA GORDON

HARPER TEEN

An Imprint of HarperCollinsPublishers

Library of Congress Control Number: 2023944091
ISBN 978-0-06-331837-3

Typography by Chris Kwon
24 25 26 27 28 LBC 5 4 3 2 1

First Edition

for E
with my whole heart

One

HOUSE PARTIES

Walking into Justin Tadeo's house party Friday night is like diving into the deep end of a pool—except this pool is full of empty beer cans and not-quite-empty plastic drink cups and vomit and a few disembodied flower leis all broken apart and various articles of clothing floating on the surface like ocean debris.

I'm not antisocial, but there are plenty of places I'd rather be on a Friday night than here. I barely know Justin, and it doesn't matter if his parents are out of town, because at the end of the day, we still live in tiny Escondido, Arizona, and trust me, there's nowhere to hide in this town—not even when the name itself means *hidden*.

Girls like me don't usually come to parties like this. Girls like me are more likely to chill at the field hockey captain's house while *her* parents are away for the weekend. But the last time I went to a party there, one of the sweepers, I think her name is Naomi, cornered me and tricked me into dancing with her for a minute. Maybe-Naomi was nothing but grip and grope that night, and truthfully, I'm not into that either—the whole hookup thing, where you get with someone you barely know just because you're at the same party and the music sizzles against the steam in the air. That's Stella's game, and man is she good at it.

"Hey," Stella says, crashing into me. Some of the beer sloshes out of her cup onto my T-shirt, but she just goes, "Don't worry, it won't stain. It's *Lite beer*." She snort-laughs at her own joke.

Stella Avila is my best friend. Nothing ever seems to faze her. That's not me—I'm struggling just to breathe in this sea of bodies, this amorphous current of faces, where pushing through the crowd feels like fighting a riptide everyone just peed in all at the same time.

"Daya, listen, you love me, right?" Stella says.

This is code. She knows it. I know it. We've been best friends since we were still in single digits. I know all her tells. Like right now? Her neck is flaming red, the way it gets whenever she's near her newest crush.

"Of course I love you," I say, shaking my head against her offer of a sip of beer. "What's the favor?"

"I need you to distract Edgar Garibay."

"So you can . . . ?"

We slide our gaze in tandem toward a pair of French doors that open out to the back, and there she is. Yasmin Barroza. I should have known. Stella has been dropping her name into conversation for nearly a week, just because she likes the sound of it. Stella sees a line and looks for a curve, and tonight, she's convinced Yasmin's line will bend her way. That's the whole reason we're here.

She goes, "I just need five minutes with her."

"What should I say to him?"

"Tell him your car broke down. And you need a ride."

"I'm not getting in a car with him, Stells. He's so shit-faced, he can barely stand up."

"No, it's not about the ride, dude," she says. "There *is* no ride."

I'm trying hard to be a good wingwoman because that's my one job here, but I'm definitely having a hard time tracking this plan of hers. My brain is still on compute as Stella pulls me this way and that way like she knows exactly where she's going, which she probably does, because Stella Avila has never been anything but absolute. From her take-no-shit attitude to her give-no-shit wardrobe. She knows how to work a room. And that girl always gets what she wants.

She is my polar opposite.

A heavy bass beat pounds out of these massive speakers and ricochets off the walls, puffing up the floor-to-ceiling curtains on the downbeat. But as we walk through the living room, everything slows to a cinematic crawl, from the curve and sway of dancing bodies all the way down to the dust particles floating in beams of colored light.

Because against one wall, Beckett Wild is sitting on a long, crushed-velvet sectional.

Technically, she's on Cason Price's lap, while Cason—her boyfriend—is kicked back on the sectional. Beckett has her legs thrown across his, laughing, multicolored hair slow-flipping like the surf spray of an ocean wave for a shampoo commercial filmed in Hawaii.

The couch is blue.

I can totally relate.

My eyes are locked on Beckett Wild as Stella pulls me toward the backyard. My eyes have been locked on Beckett Wild since eighth grade. Three years is a long time to hold a secret, illicit crush. Because super-Christian, über-straight Beckett Wild is the most unavailable girl in school.

3

At least, unavailable to a girl like me.

The second we hit the patio out back, Stella flashes a smile. Not *a* smile. *The* smile. She's never used it on me, of course. It's not a best friend smile.

"There's Edgar," she says like a ventriloquist, still smiling in Yasmin's direction. Yasmin seems to notice Stella watching her. *"Go, Daya."*

She nudges me with the tips of her fingers, inching me closer to where Edgar and Yasmin are standing near the massive outdoor grill. I shoot another nervous look around the backyard, at all these faces I recognize from school but don't really know. Except for B'Rad Anderson, who's sitting on the diving board, dangling his feet into the pool, chatting with a couple of guys bobbing in the water. Back in ninth grade, when he asked me to dance with him at the Fall Fling Dance, he was still going by Brad. Now he calls himself B'Rad, says it's his new "brand." Not sure why someone like B'Rad needs a brand, but that's all him.

B'Rad sees me, lifts his hand, separates his fingers into a live-long-and-prosper configuration. I kick him a nod and smile back. I'd switch places with those guys in the pool in a heartbeat. Ten bucks says B'Rad's a much better conversationalist than Edgar will ever be, drunk *or* sober.

Stella gives me another push. *"Go."*

"Okay, okay."

I walk up to Edgar, squeezing between him and Yasmin so Stella has an opening.

"Hey, Edgar," I say, pushing the hair away from my eyes. They say guys like it when a girl touches her hair, not that it matters to me personally. Besides, mine just keeps falling back over my face.

He goes, "Hey, um . . . ?"

"Daya."

"Daya. Yeah."

He has no idea who I am. In fact, he's so drunk, he'll probably never remember we had this conversation. If you can call it a conversation. I blank on what to say next.

"So, that car out front? The, um, red one? That's yours, right?"

His smile slurs together with his words as he says, "Yeah. You want a ride in my red car?"

I look over at Stella. Whatever she's got going on, she's working hard for it. Yasmin looks like a tough sell.

I'm still thinking of what to say next when a puff of breath ruffles my hair from behind.

"*Boo.*"

I spin around.

Sweet Jesus, it's that girl from the field hockey party over spring break.

I clear my throat and go, "Hey . . . uh . . ." Is it *Naomi? Natasha?* "I mean. Hey."

Edgar Garibay seizes the opportunity and slides away from me. I try to call him back, but maybe-Naomi jockeys into his spot, and all I know is, I'm sucking at this wingwoman thing right now.

"I'm surprised to see you here, Daya," she says through a smile. "This doesn't seem much like your jam."

I don't want to talk about my jam with maybe-Naomi. I turn to look for Stella, but she's gone. Yasmin's gone too. I'm alone. Alone with maybe-Naomi.

"I'll be honest, it's not mine either," she says. "I was supposed to go to that party up at Cara's tonight, but you know how those things go. Plus, I promised Justin's mom I'd be here. Y'know. Just to make sure he doesn't let things get too out of hand again."

"Justin's mom?"

"My aunt. Justin's my cousin, so."

"Oh."

"Yeah, not everyone knows that. *I* sure don't advertise it."

My nod is no match for the awkward silence as maybe-Naomi's gaze singes its way down the entire length of me.

"So . . . uh." I scramble for something to say. "Are you thirsty? I'm thirsty."

"Yeah. I'm *thirsty*. Why don't we pick up where we left off at Cara's last time?" She hooks her fingers into my belt loops. "I can sing 'Nowhere, Girl' in your ear, just like that night—"

"You know what? I'll be right back with two . . . uh . . . yeah," I trail off as I back away from her.

"Limited-time offer," she calls after me as I spin around, hoping to find somewhere there's a sink—I need to splash some water on my face or something. Maybe-Naomi has me in an uncomfortable sweat.

I head into the house and down a long hallway, looking for a bathroom. I'm not expecting a door to fly open and Beckett Wild to step out into the hall. We both look equally surprised to see each other standing there as she closes the bathroom door behind her.

She goes, "Oh. I'm sorry. I hope you weren't waiting too long?"

"No, it's . . . it's fine. Are you okay?" I ask because she doesn't look okay. Not like she did when we got here, anyway.

"Everything's fine, yeah, it's just . . ." She tries to play it off by rolling her tear-puffed eyes. "Drama, y'know?"

I nod, wishing I could laugh or something, but not in a way that's dumb or creepy. I run my hand through my hair, push my bangs away from my eyes.

"Do you need a drink?" she says.

"A what?"

She points at my hands. "No cup," she says. "I was just wondering if—"

"Oh," I say. This time I do laugh, just a little. It's not dumb or creepy, but it does read sort of nervous. "No, that's okay. I don't . . . I mean . . ."

She sighs and goes, "Me neither. I'm not even supposed to be here, technically." This time, she tries to laugh it off. "I . . . don't know why I said that."

It's none of my business what she does on a Friday night, not that I haven't wondered. Still, I fake like I'm clueless, and ask, "How come you're not supposed to be here?" even though I'm pretty sure I know why Beckett's not supposed to be at a house party on a Friday night.

"Because *technically*," she says, "I'm supposed to be at youth group."

There it is. Youth group. Otherwise known as the Escondido chapter of The Great Wait. That's what they call our district-mandated sex-ed program. Which is a joke, because they only talk about straight sex, and they only tell you not to have it. And they never use the word *sex*, which is also weird. Even weirder is that The Great Wait isn't just a sex-ed program—it's this whole way of life in our backward town, thanks to the influence of one megachurch in particular: Grace Redeemer.

Beckett finally speaks into the awkward silence.

"Well . . . I don't mean to keep you from . . ." She nods in the direction of the living room. "Whatever you were doing."

"Oh. No." I twist halfway around before turning back. "You're not. I just got bored, and . . . decided to look around, I guess."

She starts walking, and for some reason I follow her—not in the direction of the party, but in the direction of the sweeping stairway just inside the front door. Beckett leans up against the wall that forms the side of the staircase. I put my hands in the front pockets of my jeans, then take them out again. Shift my weight from one leg to the other. Let my gaze trail up the long, curved stairway. I don't know where to rest my eyes, any more than I know where to put my hands. I just know that looking straight at Beckett Wild would be like looking directly into the sun. This girl leaves a trail of color and light wherever she goes.

She incinerates me.

"Thanks for coming out here with me," she says. "I'm not ready to go back inside right now."

"How come?" I ask.

It takes her a moment to answer.

"Sometimes, when Cason's at a party . . ."

She blinks a few times, makes a face that's hard to interpret.

"He's not supposed to be here either," she pivots. "He's definitely not supposed to be drinking."

I'm not sure why she's telling me any of this—maybe because all her real friends are at Bible study.

"Can I ask you something?" I say before I chicken out.

"Sure."

"Why are you at this party when you're supposed to be at youth group?"

Beckett lifts her hand like she's not even thinking about it, reaches for a delicate gold cross on a delicate gold chain at the base of her delicate throat. She pulls the cross back and forth along the chain as she stares into nothingness, and I can only guess she's thinking about how to answer a question like that in a way that wouldn't invite judgment. Or maybe I'm projecting my own shit onto her, since I constantly worry that everything I do in this town invites judgment. Because that's the world *I* live in. I watch her hand as she stands there thinking, her long slender fingers, her nails—cut short and painted lime green, all except for her ring finger, which is painted sky blue. She wears a thin gold band on that finger.

"You know what sucks about striving for perfection?" she blurts.

I'm not sure how this is an answer to my question, but she definitely has my attention.

"What?" I say.

"Failure is literally the only option. I fail my parents every single day, sometimes in ways you would never even believe. There's no way to be perfect."

"So, then, you're just here to . . ."

She shakes her head so hard that the wild splashes of color in her sun-bleached hair dance around her face. When she stops, her expression is still kind of squinched up, like she's trying not to think about something.

"I'm just a person, Daya," she says. "Just like you. I'm just like you." She whispers this the second time she says it, almost like she needs to convince herself it's true.

I feel kind of sad for her, but the real truth is, she's not like me. She's nothing like me. She lives in Greenville, in a big house with two loving parents and a dog. I know, because I've low-key stalked her Instagram a little. She sails through an easy kind of life, taking honors classes, making straight A's. She has a *boyfriend*, for fuck's sake. Nothing's ever hard in Beckett's world, and I know I shouldn't even be standing here talking to someone's perfect Christian daughter when all I've thought about for the last three years is what it would be like to kiss her.

And that's what makes her *not* just like me—because Beckett Wild would never think about kissing me. In fact, I'm pretty sure if she knew how I felt about her, she wouldn't even be *talking* to me right now.

"Why are *you* here?" she asks, grabbing the wrought iron banister and swinging around it until she's sitting on the staircase a few steps up from the bottom. "At a party like this?"

I wait a few beats before coming over and sitting next to her. Not right next to her, but one step below her.

"Truth?" I ask.

"Definitely," she says.

"I'm here as Stella's wingwoman."

She stares at me for a few seconds.

She goes, "Stella?"

I nod.

"That girl you came in with?"

Adrenaline rips through my bloodstream.

"You saw who I came in with?"

"Well, yeah, I mean . . ." Her hand goes to the cross again, only this time she just touches it. "She's your girlfriend, right?"

"Uh, no." I force myself not to laugh. Stella's like the sister I never had, but even if she wasn't, we'd never be each other's type. Stella always goes for girls who drip glam and exude rizz. I need someone more internal, who looks at the world and sees a kaleidoscope—the fractals, the broken bits, the lines and shadows. The negative space. Someone who sees something more than what the world appears to be and wants to dive deeper into it. Someone like . . .

Beckett nudges me with her shoe. "Come on. I see the two of you at school—you're inseparable."

"On the real—best friends, yes. Girlfriends, never in a million years."

Her mouth pulls to one side.

"So, what's with the smile?" she says.

"I'm not smiling, you're smiling."

Beckett's cheeks go kind of pink as she says, "I'm totally not smiling."

I'm totally not either. I *am* half smiling, but I'm also half not-smiling. And I'm all the way confused. Because this feels like flirt when I know it isn't, and it feels like heat when I know it can't be.

It can't be.

I'm at a straight party with the straightest girl in school—a straight girl who just put her hand on my shoulder while saying I wasn't making her smile, when I totally was.

So . . . what is *that*?

Beckett leans forward, just a fraction, just enough for me to register the warmth coming off her. She reaches out until her hand is almost touching my leg, and says, "Did you change clothes after school? Cuz these aren't the same doodles from earlier."

I look down at my jeans, at the series of line faces I drew in Sharpie on my right leg as I waited for Stella to get ready, and try to play off the fact that Beckett noticed I'd changed from what I had on in class today.

"Guilty as charged," I say.

"I love these. Seriously, you're so creative."

"I'm kind of obsessed with Picasso's minimalist vibe right now," I say.

Then I hear my actual words.

"Okay, was that too nerdy, or . . . ?" I laugh a little, and so does Beckett, so I add, "That was pretty nerdy."

Her smile twists a little as she drags out the word: "Maybe."

"I just feel like his surrealist stuff is almost a prototype for modern street art." She doesn't respond to that, so I add, "Who's your artistic crush, I mean . . . you do seem like a bold-color person, that's for sure."

She touches her hair. "I don't know. Jackson Pollack? Keith Haring? Did you know if you do a search for *which artists should every aspiring artist know*, it's like ninety-nine percent male?"

This surprises me, coming from her.

"With the notable exception of Daya Keane," she adds, "who uses her jeans like a canvas." She leans playfully into my shoulder. "I love seeing what you come up with every day."

I tip forward, let my hair sway over my face to block out any signs of embarrassment on it.

"Thanks," I say.

"So, you don't get in trouble for drawing on your—?"

Before she can finish asking, Stella comes whipping around the corner, all breathless.

"There you are!"

She swings from me to Beckett.

"Hey, it's Sister Mary Margaret. Didn't expect to see *you* at a party."

A blaze of red shoots up from Beckett's chest into her face.

"We just stopped by for a few minutes," she says, sitting back up at a ninety-degree angle and smoothing her hands over her hair.

Stella goes, "Yeah, well, I just saw your boyfriend inside, beer ponging for Jesus, so."

Beckett twists a chunk of her hair around one finger, stalling like she's trying to decide something.

"I guess I better go get him," she says without moving.

Stella winks and goes, "Better take his keys too. Just sayin'."

I look up at Beckett, and Beckett looks down at me, and she's totally not smiling anymore, and I don't even know what's real right now.

I need to get out of here.

"You ready to roll?" Stella asks.

"Definitely," I answer.

"Good. Let's do it. They're expecting us over at Cara's."

Beckett slides up the wall. Her face has gone back to the way it looked when she came out of the bathroom.

"See you Monday, Daya," she tells me, skipping down the three or so steps to the bottom before disappearing into the living room. She doesn't look back.

My chest feels tight as I watch her walk away.

"Did I interrupt something?" Stella asks.

I shake my head, and she waits a beat or two in case I have more to say about that.

When I don't, she says, "Good, then. Let's bounce."

"You know what, Stells? I don't feel like going to another party."

"*What?* Daya—"

"No, you go. Have fun. Do your thing. Get laid."

"Okay, you're starting to sound like your mother now—like Joanna 2.0."

I make face at her. "Dude. What the fuck?"

"Not the get laid part, obviously, but y'know . . . *My name is Joanna and life is hard, and that's why I'm so bitter.* No, Daya, I'm not going to let that happen to you. Friends don't let friends turn into their mothers. Come to the party."

Before I can even accuse Stella of being too drunk to make sense, B'Rad Anderson cruises around the corner and goes, "Daya!"

"Fuck me," Stella mumbles under her breath.

He nods at her without a greeting, not that it matters. She'd ignore him whether he greeted her or not.

"I was looking everywhere for you," he tells me. "Edgar said you might need a ride home?"

I lift an eyebrow at Stella, like *See?*

"Fine," she says. "I won't need a wingwoman at Cara's, anyway."

"You never need a wingwoman," I say as she leans in for a hug. "You do know that, right? Girls throwing their panties at you and shit."

Stella just goes, *"Pffft!"* before flipping us both off.

B'Rad waits until Stella's gone before saying, "I don't know why she doesn't like me."

I know why Stella doesn't like him, but it's not mine to get into. They'll work it out someday, or they won't. For now, I'm so grateful he's here, I thank him profusely for the get-out-of-jail-free card.

"Trust me," he says as we walk toward his weird little yellow VW wagon. "It's a mutual assist tonight. Coming to your rescue gave me a solid reason to leave."

He doesn't elaborate, just unlocks and opens the car door and makes sure I'm all the way inside before closing it.

We pull away from the curb onto the tree-lined street, and B'Rad turns the radio on to Christian rock music—the one station that comes in halfway decent up in Greenville. The station starts to ghost out as we head south, and the vibe shifts, too, the farther away we get from Greenville. You always know when you're hitting the Flats at the south end of town. The houses get smaller, the streets get narrower, more potholes, less shine. It's easy to see where the money stops and life gets harder. Parts of Escondido can definitely be a little sketchy sometimes, especially at night. Not the part where Justin Tadeo and

Cara Morasco live. But for sure the part where Stella and I live.

"You looked kind of miserable tonight," B'Rad says as we drive. "Or am I making that up?"

"House parties aren't really my thing," I say.

"Same."

I turn from looking out the window to looking at him.

"What are you talking about? You looked right at home out there in the pool."

He does this kind of snort-laugh. "There's only one reason a guy like me gets invited to a party like that, and it's—"

"Here," I cut in. "Turn on Cortés."

He swings right and I point to the third house from the corner.

We pull up in front of my place and sit there for a few beats, the soft sounds of the night coming through the open windows of his car. I'm not sad that I left Justin's party so early, or even that I didn't go to the other party with Stella. But going home is its own kind of ache.

"Thanks again for doing me a solid," I say.

"Anytime."

I wait for his weird little car to sputter away before easing into the kitchen through the back door and going inside. The house is dark except for a chunk of light coming from the living room. Joanna calls out to me from where she's most likely sprawled on the sofa in front of the TV. She's watching *Murder by Design*—I can tell by the sound of the narrator's voice. And she's drinking wine. I can tell by the sound of hers.

"Daya," she calls again.

"I'm not late," I call back.

"No, I just need you to set an alarm so we can be out of the house early."

I groan, knowing what this means for my Saturday.

Before I go to my room, I detour into the living room, where Joanna's exactly as I pictured her: stretched out on the sofa in front of the TV, an empty wineglass on the coffee table. I pull the crocheted blanket off the arm of the couch and cover her up, pick up the wineglass with one deep-purple drop curled into the bottom of it. That wineglass wasn't always a fixture, but it is these days. Along the way, it became part of the sequence of events. Somewhere between Joanna finding out about my dad and my dad moving out. Or my dad moving out and my mom having the breakdown that cost her her job at the salon in Oviedo. Somewhere in all our shared sadness, that glass of wine showed up and never left. *Like a blanket*, Joanna calls it. *To soften the nights.*

I go to my room and set the alarm for her. We used to have fun thrifting together for things like home decor or kitchen utensils. Clothes for both of us. Toys sometimes, when I was a kid. Now Joanna is more interested in oddities, things with weird or morbid backstories. Anything with some tragedy attached to it is high on the list. Maybe it makes her feel better knowing that other people's stories are sadder than hers, but honestly? I'm afraid one day she'll break again under the weight of all her carefully curated trauma.

I pull out my phone, text Stella.

U solid?

Better than solid. She adds a few winky emojis, hearts, and four-leaf clovers, plus a pair of kissy-lips at the end. Something tells me

Yasmin Barroza is already a distant memory, and that some other lucky girl is making Stella's neck turn bright red right about now.

Good on her. Stella got lucky in love. And I got lucky avoiding that second party, plus scoring a ride home from B'Rad.

I stretch out on my bed and set my brain to autopilot. The memory dial moves straight to the staircase at Justin Tadeo's place, on what was arguably the weirdest Friday night I've had in a while. It replays every nanosecond of my conversation with Beckett Wild at a house party she wasn't supposed to be at.

She smiled. At me. At things I said. Genuinely smiled, more than once. Girls like me don't make girls like her smile.

Girls like me come home and cover their mothers in quilts made by other people's grandmas, and go to bed dreaming about girls like her until the alarm goes off and reality cracks with the dawn.

Two

ESTATE SALES

The alarm rips me out of a deep-dream sleep at five thirty a.m., so groggy I can barely find it, much less turn it off.

I zombie-drag myself into the hallway, pound Joanna's bedroom door with the side of my hand a few times.

"Mom. Time to get up."

I hear the squeak of the mattress as she turns over, hear her breathe out heavy a few times. But she doesn't answer.

"Mom."

"Put on a pot of coffee, Daya," she calls out. "I've got a migraine trying to break through."

On my way to the kitchen, I stop to fold the crocheted blanket back up and toss it over the arm of the couch. The brew I set up before bed last night is already going, so I pour myself a bowl of cereal and eat standing up, waiting for it to sputter to a finish.

As soon as the smell of coffee hits the air, Joanna's bedroom door creaks open. We pass in the hallway, mumbling *good morning* at each other as I slip into the bathroom. I don't need to pee, I just don't want to be in the same room with her. Not yet. There's not a lot of space in this house for privacy, and I'll be a captive audience in the car with her for what could be a few hours. I need to hoard my solitude—like carb-loading before a race—just to get me through.

I close the bathroom door, flick on the light, stand in front of the mirror as I brush my teeth. Stare at my reflection after I rinse my mouth out. Lift my hand, fluff up my bangs. Touch the scar on my cheek that I wish maybe-Naomi hadn't noticed that one time we danced. The scar that's been part of my face for over half my life. I can almost forget it's there, at least until someone says something about it or stares at it too long. Then I stumble right back into a memory of the day I told my mother I wanted to marry my first-grade teacher, Miss Zuñiga. I didn't know that was a no-fly zone at the time. Eventually, I learned to keep that baby-dyke shit to my six-year-old self, but not soon enough. That day, I just wanted to understand why my mother said I couldn't marry her.

"Only a boy can marry Miss Zuñiga."

The answer made no sense to me, so I pushed. I kept asking: *But why?*

"Because it's a *sin*, Daya," she finally said. "God didn't create you for that. You were created to fall in love and marry a boy, like I did with Daddy, so He could bless your marriage and give you children."

But I didn't want to fall in love with a boy. I wanted to marry my teacher, because she was kind and pretty, because she knelt down next to my desk and looked me in the eyes when she talked to me and smiled a lot, and she never raised her voice at anyone. Wanting to marry Miss Zuñiga didn't *feel* like a sin. It felt like love.

That's what I told my mother, and that's when something inside her snapped.

She said, "Do you want to be a boy, Daya, is that it? Is that why you want to marry Miss Zuñiga? Okay. *Let's see how you like being a boy.*"

She went and got the scissors—not the good ones from her beauty salon box, but the dull ones from the junk drawer that she used for cutting up cardboard boxes and opening hard plastic packaging. It scared me. I wriggled as she sawed through my hair, fought to get away from her as she held my face with one hand and cut with the other. I only have camera-clicks of memory from that point—her fingers clamped on to my cheeks, me fighting against her, the sharp pain biting into my right cheek as the broken tip of the scissors caught me in mid-squirm. More camera-clicks, this time of Joanna, sweeping my hair up off the floor as she apologized to me.

"I'm sorry. I'm so sorry, Daya. Mommy's just tired. I don't know what I was thinking."

Trying to clean the blood off my face and shirt before my dad got home.

My dad, livid at the sight of me, asking, "What the hell did you do to her, Joanna?"

A look of fear on her face that was different from the fear on mine. Hers was made up of things I couldn't see or understand at the time.

"She cut her own hair behind my back," my mother said. "I was just trying to fix it."

What the hell did you do to her, Joanna?

I've thought of her as Joanna ever since.

"Daya, hurry up!" she calls from down the hall.

I snap off the light and go meet her by the front door.

❖

The sun is climbing over the edge of the desert rock as we head out to the first estate sale. Sunrises in Arizona can be pretty extra sometimes—all that earth-toned drama and big beams of sunlight shooting out, casting long shadows off the rocks and saguaros. My grandpa taught me to see shapes in those shadows, the way most people look for shapes in the clouds.

The first estate sale is a bust, even though we get there pretty early.

That one is in Greenville, the same bougie neighborhood where Justin Tadeo's party was last night, where the houses are majestic and they give away full-sized candy bars at Halloween. Joanna always likes to start where the rich people live. Everything there is bigger, even the yard sales. Houses made of brick or stucco, with grand archways and elaborate wrought iron fences and even more elaborate gardens out front, full of plants that need more water than the native succulents do, in spite of how arid it can get here during the dry season. None of the houses in Greenville have blue tarps on them to keep the rain from leaking through holes in the tiled roofs. Blue roof tarps are as common as front doors on the houses in my neighborhood.

The churches in Greenville are bigger too. As if rich people deserve a more glorious God than the rest of us.

As we leave Greenville, and the big stucco houses get smaller and smaller in the rearview mirror, Joanna says, "Rich people might have better stuff, but poor people have better stories."

We get stuck at the tracks as we head to the west side, to sale number two. Joanna taught me to count train cars when I was little, whenever we'd get stuck at the tracks. My grandpa taught me to appreciate the graffiti on the train cars as they went by.

22

This estate sale looks like a win, at least on paper. The couple had been married for sixty-two years before dying five days apart.

But my mother isn't interested in a love story with a happy ending. She doesn't believe in them.

In the living room, Joanna inspects a hand-quilted blanket that I pray she doesn't bring home. It looks old enough to have been a wedding present when the couple were newlyweds.

"I guess I just have different taste," she whispers.

I'm pretty sure that's code for: She's ready to leave.

Back in the car, Joanna consults the GPS on her phone as we head toward sale number three. It's pretty desolate out this way—flat and dry and rocky, without some of the trees we have in town, but still. It only takes a second of distraction to plow your car into one of the huge boulders off the side of the road if you're not paying attention.

Not to be all morbid.

"You shouldn't look at it while you're driving," I tell her.

"I just want to make sure we're going the right way." She swipes between screens a couple times. "It's taking us out near the electric towers."

"Let's just go home," I say. "There's no rule that says we have to hit all of them."

But I know she won't go home until she's gotten her sad story. She just keeps taking her eyes off the road like she doesn't trust it. Like she knows better than the GPS.

The directions take us onto a long dirt driveway. At the far end is a beat-up house to the right, a beat-up pontoon boat to the left, and a sprawling yard in the middle filled with so much junk, a dozen or so rickety tables can't contain it all. As we slow to a stop, I spot a rusty, mustard-yellow VW wagon that looks suspiciously like B'Rad's. That would be funny if he and I showed up at the same estate sale.

"This looks promising," Joanna says once she's out of the car.

I sweep my gaze in a panoramic arc across the yard, on the lookout for B'Rad, yes, but also wondering about the word *promising*.

"What could you possibly be looking for that makes *this* look promising?" I ask.

She picks up a glass vase with a chip in the rim and inspects it. "Your aunt told me to get something to finally put Grandpa's ashes in."

I drop an open stare on her. "I think she meant from the funeral home. Don't you get a discount?"

"It's not Walmart, Daya," she says, like *I'm* the one who's out of touch with reality. "There is no employee discount at the funeral home."

I lean up against the car and cross my arms. Joanna can pick her way through every table and pile on the property. I'm not moving.

"Greetings, earthling!"

I spin around. B'Rad Anderson is right behind me.

The dude is all smiles, as usual.

"Greetings," I say. "What are you doing here at this ungodly hour?"

"I live here."

The shack behind him dials into focus—cracked stucco falling off the exterior in patches, warped wooden lattice where the windows should be.

"Oh," I say. "I didn't . . . I had no idea."

"Most people don't even realize anyone lives out this way."

He pushes his glasses up by the nosepiece. He doesn't seem awkward about living someplace like this, the way a lot of people might. B'Rad doesn't seem awkward about a lot of things. That time we danced together, he actually dive-bombed me as we pretend-swayed to a Maya Xanadu song at the end of the night. It wasn't a good kiss, but I'm not sure how much that had to do with him being a bad kisser and how much was about me one hundred percent not being into guys.

I follow B'Rad over by the house as Joanna sorts through a table at the far end of the yard. A low hum overhead makes my head feel weirdly heavy. It's probably from the electrical towers nearby, but it's the kind of sound that can drive a person insane over time.

He looks up. "You hear that?"

"Yeah. What is it?"

"Electricity running between towers. I block it out, for the most part."

It would take a mind of steel to block out that low-grade hum.

"So, whose stuff is all this?" I ask him.

"It's my granddad's."

Shit. I take another slow sweep around the yard, and say, "Damn. I'm sorry for your loss."

"Oh, he's not dead." B'Rad runs his fingers through the patch of hair on top of his head.

I go, "Wait . . . so . . . this is your grandpa's stuff, but he's *not* dead?"

"No, he's fishing."

"But . . . this is an estate sale," I say, leaning against the wrought iron railing. I realize quick that it's too wobbly to hold me up.

He goes, "Yeah, that's what I'm calling it. Drives more business out this way."

I nod, but I don't completely get it. B'Rad seems to sense this.

"It's simple economics. I work twenty hours a week on average, only it's never enough because the old man literally won't pay for anything. On the other hand, there's so much shit in this yard, and he doesn't do anything with it. Hell, he doesn't even know what's here anymore. So occasionally, if I'm in a pinch, I'll just . . . sell some of it off."

My disbelief turns into a strange sense of admiration.

"That's very enterprising," I say with a smile.

B'Rad smiles back. "I know, right?"

I peek over at Joanna, edging toward the back of the yard. I know she's looking for something specific. And I know he's trying to earn some cash. So, what if . . .

I swallow my better judgment and lower my volume a couple of clicks.

"If you can hook her with a really sad story, you can probably get her to buy something."

He leans back, nods knowingly.

"Gotcha," he says, nice and quiet. He starts to make his way over.

I carefully follow him to the table where Joanna is sorting through a collection of dusty tin canisters.

"Good morning!" He greets her like a guy who was born to sell shit.

She shades her eyes with her hands, says *good morning* in that tone of mistrust, like she's afraid he might steal her purse and then try to sell it back to her.

"Looking for anything in particular?" B'Rad asks.

"Not really," she tells him.

"Aren't you looking for an urn or something?" I say.

Maybe it's not cool of me to chuck my own mother under the bus, but B'Rad did do me a solid last night. I feel like I need to return the favor.

"Yes," she says. "That's right. I was keeping an eye out for something that would hold my father's ashes—"

He snaps his fingers. "I have just the thing."

He starts digging around in a pile of what looks like spare car parts and old cooking utensils and a bike wheel with no tire but the spokes still intact, and the bones of a basketball hoop, and just when I'm convinced he's going to pull up a rattlesnake next, he resurfaces holding—

"Wait, you have an actual *urn*?" I blurt.

"I have two," he says. "Actually."

I'm a little weirded out by this, but he could work it to his advantage if he's smart about it. From behind Joanna's back, I point at her and make an exaggerated sad face.

He pushes in closer.

"This one belonged to my mother. My father killed her when I was nine, and then he killed himself. That's who the other one belonged to."

Man, he went *all the way* there, zero to sixty.

Joanna touches the urn. "That's . . . awful."

"It is. I won't sell my father's, though. I never want to set his bad energy loose on some unsuspecting person, you know? After they died, it took us a few months to go through all their stuff, and that's when we came across my mom's handwritten will and testament. She said if anything ever happened to her, she wanted her ashes scattered into the Grand Canyon, so. We finally just got around to doing that last summer."

I shake my head at him.

Too much, man, too much! Pull back!

He pushes his glasses back in place and I watch as he recalculates, like a GPS when you take a different route from the one it says to.

He goes, "Well, anyway. That's why I'm selling hers now. It's classic pewter. We never even got it engraved."

"That must have been so hard for you," Joanna says.

B'Rad nods back like one of those bobblehead dolls.

She goes, "How much are you asking?"

"I can let it go for twenty."

"I have fifteen," she tells him.

I know she has more than that, but Joanna reaches into her bag and pulls out a ten and a five, swaps them for the unengraved pewter urn. She rolls it gently between her hands a few times, turns it over, looks at the mark on the bottom.

"Nice," she murmurs.

As we leave, I throw B'Rad a look over my shoulder and flash him a peace sign. I hope that fifteen bucks makes things a little easier for him. Life looks kind of hard out here.

He lifts a hand as he watches us head down the driveway.

The urn is the only thing Joanna ends up buying today.

On the way home, we stop at Fool City, the main grocery store on our side of town. It's really called Food City, but the curve of the *D* burned out sometime around fifth grade, and they've never fixed it. Stella and I have called it Fool City ever since.

Joanna doesn't like grocery shopping, never has, but around the time she got her job at the funeral home with its unpredictable hours, we settled into an unspoken routine where she'd do the shopping once a week, and I'd cook some form of a dinner most nights. When I was nine, that mostly looked like reheating something out of a can or a box.

Tonight, it will look like chicken Caesar salad.

When we get home, she sets the urn on the bookshelf in the living room, but she doesn't clean it out or put my grandpa's ashes inside. They're still in a plastic baggie, in a plain wooden box at the back of her closet. She hasn't taken them out once since my grandpa died— that would mean having to deal with her feelings about it. She can't even deal with her *memories*, much less her feelings. That's why we have a house full of other people's memories. Their stories, their losses. I guess for some people, it's easier to grieve what isn't theirs.

Joanna sits at the table while I make dinner. She has her day planner open like when she's working, but I can tell she's scrolling on her phone, stopping every now and then before swiping on.

"Oh, look. Nicole got her hair done," she says. "I love it curled like that. Pretty."

"Yeah, I . . . I don't follow my cousins online."

That's only half the story. Because not only do I not follow them, I've always walked the other way whenever I've seen them at school.

"Well, it was on Suzanne's Instagram." She swipes again.

I stop for a second, hover over the cutting board with the knife.

"You follow your sister on Instagram?" I say. "I thought you didn't like her."

"I like her." She keeps scrolling. "It's the whole, *Nicole had her first date on Friday. Gabby made cheer squad this year.* It can be a bit too much sometimes."

I go back to chopping lettuce and biting my tongue. What can "be a bit too much sometimes" is Suzanne always telling my mom what she should do. That's been true since they were kids—my aunt has always had this weird power over my mom. Less like an older sister and more like a surrogate mother. Suzanne is the queen of "should." As in: *You should make Daya grow her hair out. You know, Jo, if you're going to keep paying for Daya's clothes, you should monitor what she buys. Less T-shirts and jeans, more dresses.* I even coined a secret phrase for it: *bull-should.* What's "a bit too much" for Joanna is that my mother has no cute-new-hairstyle or new-outfit pictures of me to show off. I'm not the youth group treasurer, not dating the captain of the football team. What's "a bit too much" is that Suzanne always asks her what's wrong with me or when I'm going to start coming to church instead of how I'm actually doing, and that conversation must get stale for Joanna after a while.

My mother has stopped scrolling again. She's staring at something on her phone from point-blank range.

As I scoop the grilled chicken into the salad bowl, she pitches back and goes, "Where were you last night?"

I look up from bringing the bowl to the table.

"At a party you said I could go to."

"With who?"

My throat goes dry. She knows I was with Stella. Even though I know she doesn't like Stella, I don't lie about hanging out with her.

I set the salad bowl on the table.

"You know who I was with. I told you."

"What kind of party was it?"

"What's this about? Why are you asking me all these—"

She flips her phone around, shows me a grainy picture of me and Stella from Justin Tadeo's party last night. It looks like it was taken when we were conspiring for me to distract Edgar Garibay away from Yasmin. We're leaning against each other in a way that could be totally misinterpreted by someone who wanted to. And plenty of people around here would want to misinterpret a photo like that, just so they'd have something to talk about.

I take the phone from her.

"Where'd this come from?" I ask.

"Your aunt got it from one of your cousins."

It had to be Gabby—Nicole graduated last year.

"What was she doing at a party?" I ask.

Joanna's face twists at the thought. "She wasn't at a party—"

"Then where did she get it?"

"She saw it on someone's Instagram from school." Her arm flops into her lap. "Daya . . ."

"Okay, so . . . ?" I pull my chair out slowly, keep my eyes on her as

I sit. "It's not like it's a picture of us making out or anything."

"People will see this and think it means what it looks like it means. They won't know you're not . . . together."

"So what? I know we're not together. *You* know we're not. Right?"

She leans back in her seat, eyes glued to the photo. "Things like this . . . they add fuel to the fire. Everything you do—all the time you spend with Stella. Letting her cut your hair off—"

"Why are you still on that?" I say. "Are you mad because I let her talk me into it, or mad that I didn't let *you* cut it?"

"That's not fair."

Joanna puts her phone down, but she never takes her eyes off me. She taps the screen.

"You know how these things go, Daya. Someone sees you at a party, takes a picture, puts it online, gossip spreads like wildfire—"

"Okay, but it's not like someone snapped a nudie of me. I don't get why you're freaking out about this. I was at a party you knew I went to. I wasn't sneaking around. And I wasn't doing anything wrong."

She can't decide what to do with her hands. She picks up her phone again, puts it down, runs her fingers up and down the side of her water glass.

"Should I be worried about you?" she finally asks. "Suzanne says I should be more concerned about the influence Stella has on you."

Oh gawd. "Mom—"

"Daya, people like Stella can be hard to resist. If you're not careful, you could end up doing things you regret and . . . you know how vicious kids can be."

I know how vicious adults can be. I've seen it firsthand, how rumors can chew through a person's life in this town.

Escondido ate my mother up and spit out everything but her guts. And I know how long it's taken for her to come back from the near death of what that did to her. I know why she's worried. But Stella's not the problem, and I don't know how to convince Joanna of that.

"I don't know what to do for you," she says.

"You don't need to do anything. Just . . . try not to freak out again. Okay?"

Joanna picks at her dinner, excuses herself without finishing, falls asleep on the couch in front of the TV not long after I finish doing the dishes. The episode of *Shunned Nuns* she's watching is so loud, I have to turn the volume down just to hear myself think.

As I pull the quilt up over her, I spot the urn she got today on the bookshelf across the room. A used urn she bought based on a made-up story that was bad enough to hook her. That's what's so messed up about this town. I didn't have to get caught having an actual lesbian moment with my best friend at a party last night. Someone just had to make it look like I did. Snap one picture and the story takes care of itself.

Then there's Beckett, who tells her parents she's going to Bible study, but goes to a house party instead. And apparently, they trust that's where she was because that fits their perfect-daughter narrative. They'll believe she's at Bible study because they *want* to believe she's at Bible study. Another story that just takes care of itself. No questions asked.

Me? I have a lot of questions. About everything.

Especially Beckett.

And even though talking to her at that party last night was a blender-whirl of luck, chance, and confusion, I'm still hoping with everything in me for one more opportunity to talk to her. Just talk. Maybe bask a little too.

That's not too much to ask, is it? The chance to linger in Beckett Wild's sunlight for a few seconds?

Because I know that's all it can ever be.

Three

CHURCH

Three firm knocks on my bedroom door pop me out of a hard sleep way too early Sunday morning.

"Daya . . . ?"

"No. Go away," I mumble, hopefully not loud enough for her to hear.

"It's time to get up."

Get up . . . ? The words haven't fully clicked in my brain when Joanna opens the door, and all I can see is her blurred silhouette in my squinty vision.

"What's wrong?" I ask.

"Nothing's wrong. I just want you to go to church with me this morning."

She backs out of my room, and I track the sound of her footsteps down the hall.

I force myself all the way awake before rolling out of bed. Joanna's in the living room, bent over the coffee table, picking up her wineglass and the crumpled remnants of the snack she had last night.

"Why are we going to church?" I ask, trying to keep my voice even.

"I go to church every Sunday," she says.

I follow her into the kitchen.

"I know but . . . why are *we* going?"

She moves to the sink, runs water into her wineglass, swirls it around, adds some soap. She does all of this without answering me.

"Is this because of what we talked about last night?" I ask.

"It's because we need God in our lives," she says. "It's that simple."

But it's not that simple.

Not for me.

I have God in my life. But in my way, not hers. Or should I say, not Suzanne's.

"The thing is . . . I don't feel like I need to go to *church* to be with God."

"How so?" she says, looking skep as fuck.

I jump in to help her put away the clean dishes.

"I mean . . . God is everywhere, right? So, we could even . . . go out to the lake, and . . . and connect with Him there."

She takes out her Sunday travel mug, a gift from the church to all new congregants, and pours her coffee into it like she's done every Sunday for the past six or seven months. It says *Made New* on one side and *Welcome Home* on the other. But I can't shake the feeling that Grace Redeemer won't make me anything, least of all "new." And I doubt it would feel like "home" for someone like me.

"Daya," she says, like she's reading my mind. "This place is different. It's not like St. John's, it's . . . it's hard to explain. I just . . . I'd really like to share this with you."

I don't get it. She had no need for church after my dad left. Zero desire to go or to make me go. In fact, our old church, St. John's, had become a big ouch for Joanna. Still is, probably. So I have no idea how weird it was for her to step foot into Grace Redeemer after Suzanne pressured her incessantly for months. I only know that the God I connect to doesn't seem like He'd hang out exclusively at a place like that.

As I look at Joanna looking at me, one thing becomes clear: I can't refuse. Because that's what my dad did to her. First, he rejected the church. Then he rejected Joanna. Then everything fell apart. Any feelings I have about not wanting to go slide backward down my throat. It's funny how guilt and regret tend to switch places with even our best-laid arguments.

Neither of us says much on the ride to Grace Redeemer. I stare out the car window as street after street rolls by, watching the texture of Escondido shape-shift as we cross from the rough and splintered south side to the self-consciously manicured north side of town. Grace Redeemer is the uncontested crown jewel of the north side, where there are smooth, straight sidewalks in front of the houses, and the wrought iron bars in fancy shapes on the windows are more for decoration than for safety.

From the drone shot above Escondido, you'd immediately see a collection of steeples that seems like overkill—even for Arizona, where the ratio of churches to people is already higher than average. But the one steeple that towers above them all is the one that rises above Grace Redeemer Church. Religion has always been the anchor of this town. But from the way everyone talks about it, this church is, like, next-level worship—and not just for us, but for people who come from all over the county and beyond.

As we roll into the parking lot, I see that *steeple* is an inaccurate description. There are three steeples, actually. Three tall, sweeping facades, made up mostly of blue-tinted glass, angled at the top like arrows pointing to heaven, with a looming cross rising over each one. I've never seen this place up close. I had no idea how massive it was.

By the time we find a spot in the bumper-to-bumper parking lot, my hands are sweating profusely. I wipe them on my pants before getting out of the car, while Joanna checks her hair and lipstick in the rearview mirror. As soon as I open my door, I hear a bass beat coming from inside the building.

Wow—this definitely isn't St. John's. This place is . . . *intense*.

Joanna says hi to at least a half dozen people as we climb the shallow steps to the entrance.

"From my women's group," she says.

"You're in a women's group?"

"Mostly virtual, but yes."

The wide glass doors open automatically as we approach, and a blast-wave of cold air and music and laughter pours out all around us. My eye-line goes vertical, up the towering wall straight ahead, to the floor-to-ceiling message in neon: MAKE ROOM FOR GOD.

Whoa. I've landed on an alien planet, where nothing makes sense. There's another, smaller neon sign over the doorway of a side room that reads MERCH! like it's a Beyoncé concert. Speaking of concerts, I'm totally peeping the crowded selfie station next door to MERCH! where a lot of people I recognize from school are taking pictures in front of a sparkly Great Wait logo. I'm definitely not surprised to see Lucy Davis taking pictures with her sometimes-but-not-always boyfriend, Javi Benitez. Also no surprise: our school's Great Wait president, Nestor Camarillo, waiting in line for his turn.

"I'll be right back," Joanna says into the side of my face, since I'd never be able to hear her otherwise.

She leaves me next to the gift shop and jogs up to a group of women she seems to know.

I turn and look through the gift shop window—I mean, the Merch! window. *Church merch*. I snicker at my own joke.

But the merch inside is no joke. Piles on piles of CDs. Bookshelves loaded with all the usual suspects, plus Christ-centered fiction and manga-style graphic novels for kids. Racks and stacks of clothes. Display cases full of jewelry—thin gold bands and slender gold cross necklaces. A row of travel mugs just like the one Joanna brings with her every Sunday.

It feels like Disney World in here. And it's not just the neon everywhere—it's the electric hum that practically pulses out of people. I've never seen anything like this in my life.

Joanna motions for me to follow her, and we end up at another set of huge doors. This is a trip, I swear. Considering we just walked through an actual Bible-themed mini-mall, I can't even visualize what's on the other side of this mammoth doorway.

A smiling usher greets us like he's known us all our lives as he pulls on the foot-long chrome handle. The door opens into a massive space that has serious concert hall vibes, all the way up to the balcony section above our heads. There's a stage up front—not an altar, like at

St. John's—flanked by some kind of scaffolding surrounding a giant screen. Off each side of the stage are two sets of colossal speakers you can practically see the music bouncing out of. The room is lit with beams of colorful lights that pulse and sway and swirl nonstop.

Seriously, this is not the stained-glass, marble-sculptured, gold-swept church I grew up going to every Sunday for the first six years of my life. I don't even know what to call this. It's an alternate reality.

Another usher escorts us to a row somewhere in the middle of the already-crowded church. He's wearing a T-shirt that says *Made New* in big, bold letters—same as the guy who opened the door for us.

As we take our seats, I look around on the stealth for my aunt Suzanne and my cousins, praying we don't end up sitting near them. I know they're here somewhere.

It's so loud, I can barely hear my own thoughts. But maybe that's a good thing. It means I don't have to talk to anyone if I don't want to, goddess bless.

Before long, the music from the speakers stops, and a live band onstage starts playing. I almost think I recognize it as a Coldplay song, until the words *Jesus* and *worship* fill the auditorium. The audience sings along, and since the lyrics ticker out simultaneously across the big screen, I mouth along too. I have to admit, this music is pretty fresh. If it was about something more relatable than surrendering my life to a less accepting God than the one I believe in, I might actually be into it.

A man in a baseball jersey and a faded denim jacket takes the stage. He welcomes everyone, tells us he's Pastor Mike. It takes me a minute to process this, because I've never seen a pastor who wasn't at least in a suit and tie. For sure I've never seen one wearing Jordans before. His voice floats smooth and easy through the open space as he leads the room in prayer. The band continues to play softly behind him, a soundtrack meant to tug at our emotions.

Pastor Mike praises God for the work He's doing both in the church and out in the world through His parishioners.

"Lord, I pray that You touch the hearts of every person in this room today," he says. "I pray that every one of you here today has an experience and an encounter with God."

All around me, folks raise their hands in the air. I'm probably not supposed to notice this because my eyes are supposed to be closed, but honestly . . . how could I *not* cheat a little? From the double-decker panorama of raised hands and tear-streamed eyes, to the murmurs of "Yes, Jesus!" and "Thank you, Lord!" a sense of near euphoria vibrates in every molecule of this air.

After Pastor Mike says, "Amen!" the giant screen behind him rolls out a video with two high-school-aged kids, welcoming us to this week's announcements.

"At the end of today's service," the girl says, "don't forget to stop by our *Merch!* shop so you can rep Jesus throughout the week!" She points to her *Made New* T-shirt that all the ushers are wearing today, while the dude with her shows off his *True Love Waits* shirt that's super popular around school.

Next is an invitation to all the ladies in the room to join Grace Redeemer's SHIMMER group. "My mom attends SHIMMER in person," the guy says, and the girl goes, "My mom keeps it virtual!" and in unison, they say, "Shine and reflect Jesus with SHIMMER!"

They give a shout-out to the Great Wait meetings kids can attend at all area schools.

They plug something called the Redemption Baptism Experience, coming in June, and also the Revive Alive Conference happening in July.

"Music, games, workshops, line dancing, BBQ, and more!" they say together.

There's a short clip about summer camp that looks more like a nonstop concert venue, with live bands, prayer tunnels, sports and games—even ax throwing—plus tons of awesome-looking food.

There's a QR code you can scan for more information.

Man. This isn't church—it's a whole separate, self-contained world. A biosphere, where everyone speaks the same language and each individual heart beats at the same communal frequency. The banner hanging from the balcony says WELCOME HOME, but in spite of the inclusive language, I still feel more like the extraterrestrial who doesn't quite understand where she landed.

The video ends, and the band bursts into an Adele sound-alike that everyone seems to know. I'm shocked that even Joanna knows the words to this song. She closes her eyes and lifts her hands and sings along, and I look away, vaguely mortified.

Pastor Mike's voice rolls gently over the top of the fading song.

"Friends," he says. "I want to talk to you today about honoring God's purest gift to us—His precious children—made in His likeness."

My gaze drifts to the guy playing electric bass in the band. He looks familiar, like maybe I saw him at Justin Tadeo's party Friday night. I think he was one of the guys in the pool, talking to B'Rad.

"To call into question the nature of what it means to be a man or a woman is to dishonor the nature of God's creation."

These words hook me back toward the stage.

"I don't want to offend anyone," Pastor Mike says directly into the microphone, "but I'm going to say that again. Questioning our identity *dishonors* God."

I'm locked onto Pastor Mike now. He looks like someone's cool dad. Like a guy who would coach his kid's Little League games and bring Happy Meals home in the middle of the week for no reason. He does not look like a hateful person. But what he's saying is just that. Hate, wrapped in the kind of cake-soft God-love people seem to crave.

"Friends, God did not create His children as an *experiment*." Pastor Mike lingers on this word. "He forged our precious little ones in the fire of His love and with *intention*. He knows what He calls each one of us to be, because He has made us in His image. Our job? Our job is to joyfully fulfill His plan! But there are those who would allow the children, created by our Almighty God, to question their *identities*. *This is dangerous. This* . . . is tantamount to letting our children play with fire. A fire that can burn their psyches. Fire that can harm them physically. These efforts . . . to allow our *children* to *question* the *very nature* of their existence . . ." He pulls a bandana out of his back pocket and wipes his forehead with it. "Friends, it just doesn't square with what God calls us to."

An echo of agreement ripples through the room, and my chest tightens.

"Lord," the pastor continues, closing his eyes. "For anyone who might be questioning their identity, may they know that their identity lies solely in *You*."

A collective murmur rises up, joining a sea of hands already lifted in praise.

"Let anyone searching, Jesus," he says, his eyes still closed, "let them know that whatever they search for lies only in *You*."

I look around to see if anyone else's bullshit meter is going off. Instead, I catch a beam of purple-and-turquoise light spilling across the row where Beckett Wild is sitting.

Beckett . . . in living color. Beaming the same light she does every single day.

Pastor Mike says, "God tells us, doesn't He, to love our neighbor?"

The crowd responds.

"That means our *gay* neighbor," he says, punctuating each point with a jab of his finger. "That means our *transgender* neighbor. God doesn't make exceptions about *who*. He tells us emphatically and unambiguously. *Love thy neighbor . . . as thyself*. We believe that God loves everyone. And He instructs *us* to love everyone. And so, we do. But sometimes . . . sometimes loving someone . . . means bringing them . . . to the *truth*." He pauses every few words for dramatic effect. "That what they *seek*, they shall *find* in *Him*!"

A current of shared electricity seems to pass from one set of raised hands to another, bouncing off every *Amen!* and ricocheting against every *Praise Jesus!* The crescendo of euphoria builds as the congregation absorbs Pastor Mike's words.

"God alone knows our true identity. Heck, God alone *gave* us our true identity. I'll say that again. Your identity is the one *God* gave you. Can I get an amen?"

The crowd does as he says.

"God tells us, you will seek Me and you will find Me, if you seek Me with all your heart!"

This resonates with the room. With my mother. With her out-loud "Amen!" of agreement.

"Praise Jesus," Pastor Mike says, dialing back his energy and his volume. "Praise Him for restoring the youth of this great state through The Great Wait, and through Grace Redeemer. Let us lift Him up in song."

The band launches into a tune that sounds something like J. Cole feat. J. Christ, while all the kids from middle school and high school rush the stage. They raise their arms, jump up and down with the music, rap along with the lyrics.

I follow the beams of light until I spot Beckett again. She's standing near the back of the group gathered up front. Swaying, not jumping, to the music. Singing along with the words.

As the song comes to a close, the band doesn't stop playing—they just ease into a series of aching chords, playing softly behind Pastor Mike as he takes center stage again. This time, he talks about abundance. He talks about giving abundantly, about how generously God gives to us in our daily lives.

"We need to meet God's generous abundance in all the ways we can," he says. "To water the seeds that will grow God's kingdom. To bring His truth out into this community and to every corner of the world."

The music changes as Pastor Mike shifts his energy, whipping the crowd into a near frenzy.

"My friends. Brothers and sisters in Christ. We need to make Grace Redeemer into a soul . . . winning . . . machine!"

The band jumps back on that J. Cole number as an image flashes, then stays on the screen. **Give Abundantly,** it says, and below that:

Cash or check; or

GraceRedeemerGives.net—select the God Gives Tab; or

Download the <u>Grace Redeemer Gives</u> app; or

Text any amount to 33415.

I'm stunned as Joanna reaches into her purse, pulls out her wallet. Some folks take out their phones. Everyone is reaching for something that will allow them to give generously to Grace Redeemer Church.

I look over at Beckett again; Lucy's next to her now. They're bouncing in time to the music, hands lifted in praise, or worship, or whatever it's called here, and suddenly Friday night seems like forever ago. Whatever it was I thought I felt from her that night . . . flirt . . . spark . . . ?

It was *nothing* compared to the way she lights up here.

At church.

Where all she has to do is bring someone like me to "the truth."

Four

O'RING

"We can stop for burgers on the way home, if you like," Joanna says.

We never stop for burgers.

"Um . . . sure," I say back.

I text Stella on the way there.

Just left church. Joanna's taking me for burgers.

Stella shoots back: **Not sure which sentence is more confusing. Don't take your eyes off your food tho.**

I send her an all-teeth emoji and she writes back: **If I don't hear from you in two hours, I'm calling Dateline.**

I snort as I key in: **And that's why you're my ride-or-die.**

Stella may be onto something, though.

I tell myself the weird feeling in my stomach isn't all edge.

I tell myself it's because I'm actually starving.

I tell myself lots of people go out to eat after church.

I tell myself sometimes a hamburger is just a hamburger.

At the same time, I've learned that Joanna isn't always consistent. Like I can never fully know which version of my mother is coming through the door at a given moment. When you break it open, I think that's what's making me so nervous about the whole stopping-for-burgers thing right now.

Our booth inside O'Ring overlooks the parking lot out front. Inside the restaurant, seats are packed with after-church crowds. Families with little kids. Teens in their school jackets or T-shirts repping their house of worship. Laughing. Chatting. This is what they mean when they talk about "fellowship" at church. It's like the endorphin high that got whipped up inside people during the service has followed them all the way into this restaurant.

I text Stella again after we order, when my mom ducks into the ladies' room.

9-1-1. Our universal code for *Help!*

Sorry, boo. I got Sunday plans that don't involve Jesus.

I put my phone away as my mom slides back into the booth, and the server comes in right behind her to bring our food. Cheeseburger basket for me. Grilled chicken for Joanna. I move in for a fry, but she takes both my hands in hers and drops her head.

"Lord, we thank You for this food, God, that it may bless and nourish our bodies."

Oh shit, we're doing this again. I look around to see if anyone's watching as Joanna goes on, but of course no one here would think anything of her saying grace before the meal.

"May all that we do be to the glory of You, Lord. We thank You for Your steadfast love. Amen."

I mumble a quick *amen* and pull my hands away.

We reach for the ketchup bottle at the same time, and she motions for me to take it.

"Looks like there's a youth group that meets on Wednesdays," she says, like she's been thinking about it ever since we left Greenville. "That could be fun."

I don't say anything as I hand the ketchup to her. My annoying cousin probably goes to that youth group thing on Wednesdays. If so, hard pass. If not, it's still a pass, just without the required anti-Gabby sentiment.

"You know, Daya . . . I think . . . it's been just the two of us for so long. You and me against the world. And it just seems like it's not . . . enough. Community is such a big part of our spiritual path, and—"

"It's part of *your* spiritual path," I correct her. The words feel tight in my throat, but I can't not say them. "I don't mean to be a jerk about it, I just don't want you assigning that to me."

"But our spiritual path—"

"*My* spiritual path is different from yours, so. I'm not really sure why all of a sudden—"

"It's my job to protect you spiritually," she cuts in. "Can you understand that?"

There's a shift in her tone. Like how she sounded the day before she asked my dad *Are you in love with that woman?* versus the day after.

I lean back, try to figure out where to go next. I had a bad feeling something like this was going to happen. And maybe it wouldn't hit such a nerve if it didn't sound like something my aunt Suzanne told her to say.

Joanna leans forward. "I need you to hear me, Daya. Our connection to God is *so* important." She clasps her hands together on the word *connection* to help her make her point. "But our *reconnection* after going astray is . . . it's a matter of life and death."

I watch her eyes shift back and forth, waiting for the light of recognition, of agreement, to flicker in mine.

"I didn't go astray," I tell her. "You did."

There it is. The line I'm not supposed to cross. I can see it all over her.

She clears her throat, recalibrates.

"We go astray when we don't seek God out," she says, her eyes just barely fluttering, like she's fighting back tears. "And we can't seek God out without help from the church."

"But it was fine when *you* didn't need church all those years."

She waits before speaking again, probably so she can count to ten, take deep breaths. Use the tools her therapist gave her to help her function again after her life imploded nine years ago. But she doesn't take her eyes off my face, even as her expressions shift between anger and sadness and something else. Hurt, maybe? I swear, I'm not trying to hurt her.

But I have my own relationship with God, and I don't have to go to Grace Redeemer to experience it.

It feels like an eternity before she half turns and signals the server to come over. Then she turns back to me.

"It wasn't fine. *I* wasn't fine."

The server steps up to our table.

"Two boxes, please," Joanna says. "And the check."

I'm as stunned by this as I was when she bowed to pray before our meal. If she wants to leave so we can really throw down over this, I'm not doing it. I don't want to fight with my mother about God.

"One box," I say, looking back at Joanna. "I'm going to stay for a while."

I hold my breath, wondering if she's going to give in or just take the gloves off right here. But that's not my mother's style. She wouldn't do anything that would open the door for people to talk about her again. To say she's a bad mother this time instead of a bad wife. She'll never let that happen. And I don't want that either.

But if I thought she'd let me have the last word, I'd be wrong.

"The first step your father took in destroying this family," she says, lowering her voice to just above a whisper, "was breaking away from God. That was the beginning of the end."

She swipes her plate off the table, walks it to the front counter, and packs up her untouched food while the cashier runs her payment. She swings out the door without looking back at me even once.

I watch her get in the car and drive off, blinking away the hot sting of tears as I follow her taillights out of the parking lot. I keep staring long after she turns at the signal and is gone.

I reach for my phone, thinking I'm going to text Stella. But instead, I open Instagram and go to the Grace Redeemer page. Scroll through their youth group photos. All those hands lifted in prayer. The tear-streamed faces. The laughter. The joy. I can almost hear the band playing their church version of Ed Sheeran as I scroll. That's the magic sauce, I think. That music, pulling you in, giving you such a rush of emotion, you want to keep chasing that feeling long after it's over.

I swipe a few more times, stop on a photo, zoom in close. It's a prayer tunnel, and Beckett's the one going through it. Eyes closed. Mouth pulled into a not-quite smile. Kids on both sides of her, reaching out, laying their hands on her shoulders and head as they pray.

I click out of Insta, grab my earbuds, jam them into my ears. Find "Nowhere, Girl" on my playlist and crank up the volume.

Why don't we head out to nowhere, girl....

I was only seven or so when I asked Joanna why we'd stopped going to St. John's. Too young to understand when she said, "Church is for broken people." But I knew on some level that she was broken. That we were broken. And I didn't know why we couldn't go back to the one place where we were always told we could be fixed.

Just hitch a ride to you-know-where, girl.
The only thing to hate is hate.
The only thing to love is love.

I put "Nowhere, Girl" on repeat and hum softly along with Cassie Ryan as I pick at my burger. It's not enough. C.Ry isn't working this time.

A knock on the other side of the glass window pulls me out of my headspace. With my earbuds in, I don't hear the knock so much as see it in my periphery, and for one ridiculous second, I think it might be Joanna.

It's B'Rad.

He swings his finger back and forth between my half-empty booth and him, like he's asking if he can join me.

I nod, popping my earbuds out.

"What are you doing here?" I ask as he slides into the other side of the booth.

"I was just meeting up with someone real quick."

He looks down at my plate.

"You know, Daya, in some contexts, sitting alone in a restaurant with nothing but a cheeseburger and fries between you and the great dark void, looking the way you do? It could be construed as a red flag."

I push the plate to the middle of the table. "I'm not alone, though. Am I?"

He smiles, takes a fry, eats it.

"So how *do* I look?" I ask, and without a beat, he goes, "Hella fly, in that button-up shirt. That's a good vibe on you."

I laugh. "No, I mean . . . you said *looking the way you do*, so . . . what way is that?"

"Like someone ate all your Fruity Pebbles."

I nod, thinking that's a pretty accurate description. We each drag a fry through the ketchup and eat it, and then another one, and then he goes, "So . . . who was the bastard that ate all your Fruity Pebbles?"

"Yeah, that would be my mom. Joanna."

B'Rad leans back, takes another quick assessment of my button-up shirt, leans over to peep under the table, sees that I'm wearing slacks, not jeans. He comes back up with an all-knowing nod and goes, "Ahhh, okay. It's Sunday. You're wearing clothes."

"I always wear clothes on Sunday."

"You know what I mean."

I stare out the window until the traffic light on the corner cycles red-to-green twice.

"I didn't even hate it, really, it's just—"

"You didn't *hate* it?"

"I mean . . . okay, it was Grace Redeemer, so the music was great, and that was most of the service. It's like going to see your favorite band in concert every weekend, right? But like . . . then they got into the whole, *Don't be gay or trans, or God will force us to remind you who you really are* kind of thing, and I just . . ."

"Ouch."

"And you know . . . if they could just hold the message at *Love thy neighbor*, I'd be totally down. That's a great message. So why do they have to get into the other stuff? You start out feeling like you're at a Green Day concert and end up in don't-say-gay Florida."

"Gotcha."

"And it feels like Joanna's going to start pushing me to do *all* the church things now."

"Is this a *new* thing? Is there Kool-Aid in your fridge all of a sudden?"

I smile, shake my head. "Yeah, no. My aunt got her to start going to this church about six months ago, and since then, it's like . . . like my mom's turning into a clone of her older sister. And she wants to turn *me* into *her* clone. Like, if I don't think how she thinks and act how she acts, there must be something inherently wrong with me."

"Great word."

"Thank you. I just . . ." I pick up the saltshaker, spin it across the table. "She's suddenly worried about my spiritual path without ever asking me if I even have one, and . . . I don't know."

"You *do* know."

"What?" I put the saltshaker back. "*What* do I know?"

"You know it's not going to be like this everywhere. Once you leave Escondido—"

I lower my eyes to skeptical-half-mast and say, "Dude. Where am I gonna go that isn't at least as messed up as it is here? Half the states in this country still don't have rights protecting people like me. More than half are banning books if they even *think* there's queer content. Or Black history. Because we can't teach teenagers about *actual history* or the world might end. And Florida? They're so anti-gay in Florida, they're ready to throw teachers and librarians in *jail* for shelving books with queer characters. You can't spit and not hit a state that isn't writing—*and* passing—anti-queer legislation, so. That's what I know."

His mouth bends into an empathetic smile.

"No . . . seriously. Where am I gonna go that's different?"

"Okay, but." B'Rad pushes his glasses back into place. "It won't be like that forever, right?"

"I don't know, man. It just feels like we're going backward. And then you go somewhere like Grace Redeemer, with their message of love and acceptance. And you have this really powerful emotional experience, right? And as soon as you're all open and vulnerable, *pow*. Now the message is, God commands you to talk gay and trans people *out* of their identities. And they make it all sound so . . . *acceptable*."

"And your mom's right there, in the middle of the sausage."

I almost want to laugh at the visual, but I can't. Not now. Instead, I start picking off little bits of hamburger bun into the shape of a flower.

"And now I get to go home and start up where we left off," I say.

"At least let me drive you," he offers.

I let him.

On the way home, I fire off another text to Stella.

What r u doing?

She says, **What do u think I'm doing?**

Perv. I put a wink emoji after it.

She sends back the kissy-lips emoji, then types:

So . . . church . . . pick up any cute girls?

Damn—that question hits too close for comfort.

Let's just say, it's been a weird day.

Dude, you better spill ALL the tea tomorrow!

On the way to school – I pinkie swear.

Meet me early, she writes. **I have to make up a quiz for Moore's** class.

Yer killin' me, you know that?

Stella's so anti-establishment, she still uses emojis. She sends me rock-star hands, followed by a middle finger, followed by laughing with tears.

When we pull up to the house, my mom's car isn't parked out front, goddess bless.

"Thanks again," I tell B'Rad. "See you tomorrow."

He flashes me a peace sign back and pulls away.

I jiggle the back door open, where the first thing I notice is a note on the fridge from Joanna.

Out with the gals from SHIMMER.

I pull the note off and throw it away. Just because I'm relieved she's not home doesn't mean anything has blown over. She's meeting with her women's group from church, right after we had a fight about church, so. That feels like logs on a fire, honestly.

I keep all the lights off in my room except the string lights across the ceiling. Put my earbuds in, fire up the whole C.Ry album with the songs on shuffle. And because I can't stop myself, I go back to Grace Redeemer's Insta page. To the picture of Beckett.

Eyes closed, walking through the prayer tunnel.

I wish I could read her face in that moment. Was she peaceful? Elated? Uncomfortable?

I could message her and ask. Not like sliding into her DMs but just . . . just a question. From a friend. At school. A church friend. No, a school friend.

I go to her Insta. Look at her newest pics before I message her. She posted after church, it looks like. Her and a bunch of other kids in someone's backyard. A beautiful swimming pool behind them. Her boyfriend Cason's there. So is Lucy.

Cason's clowning for the camera.

Lucy has her arm around Beckett's shoulder.

I go to the message window on Beckett's feed. Type something. Delete it.

C.Ry wails on track 7: "Blackened Red Flesh."

I swipe back over to her profile. To the picture of Cason and Lucy and Beckett. Take a swing at a new message. **Looks like fun.** Except I'm in her DMs. She won't even know what I'm talking about. Delete.

Track 4 comes on. "When You Called Me Baby." Its slow, haunting vibe calms me, so I put it on repeat and close my eyes. Try to regulate my breathing.

I guess it works, because I wake up to the sound of Joanna pushing the sticky front door shut. For a couple of disoriented clicks, I look around my room. Listen to see if Joanna knocks on my door so we can talk. She doesn't.

I should be grateful.

But time has taught me that silence doesn't always equal safety.

Too often, silence is the sound life makes just before the other shoe drops.

Five

CLUB MEETINGS

At seven fifteen Monday morning, I swing through the short wooden gate and knock on the front door of Stella's house.

Stella's hot mom answers.

"Good morning, Daya!" she says with a huge smile. Unlike Joanna, Stella's mom rolls out of bed gorgeous. My mom's lucky if she wakes up looking just this side of rough most days.

"Good morning, Mrs. Howell," I say.

"It's Avila again. I'm sure Stella told you?"

Stella did not tell me.

"I'll try to remember," I say anyway.

Stella comes around the corner with a triangle-shaped piece of toast sticking out of her mouth. She pulls it out long enough to say, "I wouldn't get too attached to that name either," before shoving it back in.

Ms. Avila playfully swats at her as she walks by, but Stella deflects, grabbing another slice of toast off a plate on the counter.

"Have a nice day, you two," her mom tells us on our way out.

Stella rolls her eyes. "Whatever."

The door closes behind us, and Stella drops her Notorious RBG skateboard onto the street and hops on. She holds the strap of my bag like a towrope.

"My mom's such a tool," she says as we pass the fancy new restaurant with the 3D mosaic sugar skull sticking out over the door.

"What makes you say that?"

"It's Avila again," she says in a mocking tone. *"I'm sure Stella told you."*

"Well, you didn't tell me, so she kind of had to. And I'm glad she did. I don't want to keep calling her by the wrong name."

"She changes it so often, what difference does it make?"

She chucks her last bite of toast into the gutter and toes her board up into her hand, and my early warning system kicks into high alert. Her energy's way off, like when the weather shifts suddenly right before a storm hits and the sky goes from blue to black in a matter of minutes. You can feel that shit coming from miles away.

"It does matter," I say. "It's no different than if you kept calling Mercedes García by *her* old name."

"That's not the same at all," she says.

"It kind of is."

"Daya—"

"No, Stells, be objective about this for one second. You would never use Mercy's deadname now that you know who she really is."

"That's about identity," she says. "It's a core thing, an essence."

"You really think your mom *identifies* as Mrs. Howell, though? After the horrible things your stepdad did—"

"It's not the same," she says.

I stare at her as we walk, but she's carved in stone right now.

"Why are you being an asshole about this? She's your mom."

"Right, Daya. Because you've never been an asshole about Joanna."

I feel a whoosh of heat shoot through me for a second. That's different. I want to tell her how that's different, only I can't because it's not that different, actually. I mean, I call my mother by her first name when she's not in the room. And, yes, it's true that some level of asshole with our moms *is* justified from time to time. I just don't think this is one of those times.

"Everyone defends poor little Gina Avila," Stella says. "Not because she's a delicate flower that needs to be defended but because she's a flower. Period." She drops her board onto the sidewalk half a block from school and says, "Face it, Daya. Beauty is its own kind of privilege."

I watch Stella roll in the direction of school without me, not even sure what just happened. But I don't think it's really about her mom changing her name back. I think Stella's still pissed at her for hooking up with that Howell guy in the first place. Some pretty shitty things went down with her stepdad—things Stella still hasn't shared with me. I know the basic shape of it, but not the details. She won't talk about those, not with anyone. I definitely think she should, though.

Campus is pretty sleepy this time of day, I notice as I make my way across the commons. It's not that I mind getting here this early, but once Stella's gone off to AP US History, I'm alone with nothing to do.

I wander a bit before turning down the 300 wing, where there's light pouring through the open choir room door. Even from this end of the hall, I hear talking coming from inside. I move closer, close enough to read the neon-green posterboard propped up on an A-frame partially blocking the walkway.

THE GREAT WAIT
TODAY @ 7:30 A.M.
FREE FOOD!!

A hit of adrenaline kicks against me, knowing Beckett's probably inside. Schrödinger's Beckett. Because right now, from where I stand on this side of this door, both versions of Beckett exist: the one from Grace Redeemer yesterday and the one from Justin Tadeo's party Friday night. Only the act of going inside will confirm for me once and for all which version of Beckett Wild is the real one. And whether my feelings for her would have any room to breathe, no matter where we both were.

A couple of kids push past me as I stand in front of the door, trying to decide if I want to go in and find out. Another guy starts to swerve around me but stops and says, "Sorry. I didn't mean to cut you off," and motions me ahead of him.

Before I fully process what's happening, I'm at a Great Wait meeting at seven thirty on a Monday morning.

And yes. So is Beckett.

She must have seen me before I saw her, because she's waving me over, and my heart does the zapateado, as Stella calls it. I edge through the crowd toward her.

"Hey!" she says, inviting me to take the empty seat next to her that was probably meant for Cason, only he's not here yet. "You know Lucy, don't you?"

I start to say "No," because I really don't know Lucy Davis, other than having junior honors English with her this year. We've never even sat on the same side of the room in that class.

But Lucy goes, "Yeah. I know Daya," and I'm not sure what to say to that, so I don't respond at all.

Beckett leans in close to me and says, "Seriously, it's so cool that you're here."

I smile as the heat from her arm melts into the rest of my body.

The chairs in the choir room curve in half circles that stagger up these short, wide steps, with a kind of stage area left open in the center. That's where Nestor Camarillo stands. He nods once to cue the acoustic band—two kids on guitars plus a drummer—to start playing. The guitar players sing in harmony on a song that sounds like Imagine Dragons but with salvation. They're pretty good, though.

The club officers, including the band, are all in matching sports-style jerseys I recognize from the *Merch!* shop at Grace Redeemer. Only instead of an athlete's name across the upper back, theirs have books of the Bible. Nestor's says *2 Timothy*, and where the jersey number would be, it says 2:22.

The music settles to a few hushed chords as Nestor calls for us to bow our heads in prayer.

I lower my eyes without closing them.

He thanks God for everything from helping Tina Morgan get to State Tennis Finals to the music boosters coming through with new clarinets for the marching band. Meanwhile, I try to pretend there isn't a smolder of energy between me and Beckett. Because there can't be. She's straight, for starters, plus we're in a room full of people who might be actively looking for evidence that someone is not.

After the prayer, Nestor and his vice president, Alexa, talk about prom committees and spending limits and task lists, and because none of this is relevant to me, I click out. Beckett's taking notes, at least that's what I assume she's doing, until she flips her notebook open to a blank sheet of paper and scribbles something on it. She nudges my elbow with hers.

My whole arm incinerates from the touch.

She wrote: *I'm really happy you're here.*

I slip the pencil out of her hand and write: *Same*—but only because she's sitting next to me, not because The Great Wait lights me on fire.

"Group leaders, raise your hands," Nestor calls out, pulling at the bottom of his Bible jersey, and before I give the notebook back to Beckett, I write, *Hey, can I ask you a question?* and show it to her.

She nods.

What's 2 Timothy 2:22?

It takes longer for her to jot down an answer than I would have thought. I look around the room as she writes, so it doesn't feel like I'm staring at her. It's way too easy to stare at Beckett Wild when I'm not being careful about it. My eyes catch Lucy's for a beat, but she cuts away quick as Beckett hands the notebook back to me.

"Flee the evil desires of youth and pursue righteousness, faith, love and peace, along with those who call on the Lord out of a pure heart."

This time I can't help it—I stare at her with my mouth open a little.

I scribble: *You know all that by heart??*

She smiles and leans in close enough to whisper, "They made us memorize it."

Having Beckett lean into me is a lot like stretching out on the hot sand on a warm beach, letting the sun heat up my skin, licking salt water off my lips, wishing I could stay in that one amazing moment forever.

I take the pencil again but not the notebook. I lean over instead, halfway into Beckett's air space, and write: *What about . . . ?* and signal the girl in front of us who's wearing a jersey with *1 Thessalonians 4* on it.

Our fingers touch as she slips the pencil from me and writes: *For this is the will of God, your sanctification; that is, that you abstain from sexual immorality.*

Holy crap. I always knew the purity stuff was pretty thick with The Great Wait, but . . . wow.

Beckett scribbles another note and hands it to me.

So does this mean you're going?

I look at her, confused, then write: *Going where?* and hand her the pencil.

Prom.

I scramble to figure out why she's asking me this, until Nestor says, "I just want to thank everyone for all the hard work you've put into making this year's Pure Prom the best ever."

Pure Prom?

Beckett's still waiting for me to answer, but I just shake my head like *I'm not sure,* because I feel kind of spun by the whole Pure Prom thing right now.

The band plays a few more songs that everyone sings along to, and they keep playing softly as Nestor closes out the meeting with a prayer. We're finally invited to come get donuts and cocoa from a table near the piano, and Beckett and I funnel that way along with everyone else. Everyone but Lucy. She stays put.

At the snack table, two Great Wait officers in those same biblical sports jerseys place a donut on a napkin for us with their gloved hands. Alexa pours warm water into tiny Styrofoam cups, hands them out with a cocoa packet, a plastic spoon, and a strip of paper with a Bible verse on it.

"Have a blessed day," she says, over and over again.

Back at our seats, I stir my cocoa into the warm water and eaves-drop as Beckett and Lucy chat about random stuff and giggle like besties. I think back to Friday night, the way Beckett sweated me about Stella and me being inseparable, and feel a wash of embarrassment that I'm kind of doing the same thing with her and Lucy right now.

But then Beckett says, "I'm going for more. Anyone want anything?"

Lucy shakes her head like the thought of a donut disgusts her. I give Beckett a thumbs-up as I inhale cocoa-scented air, trying to get the last few marshmallows unstuck from the bottom of my otherwise empty cup.

With Beckett gone, Lucy's stare becomes ninety percent challenge and ten percent curiosity. I don't know what the challenge part is about, but I'm pretty good at the staring game when I want to be. I put my cup down, pop the last bite of my donut between my lips, and lick my fingers, all without breaking eye contact.

"How was it?" she asks, twirling her thick braid around one finger.

I'm not sure if she means *How was the donut?* or *How was the meeting?* so I just say, "Fine."

"I'll be honest, Daya. I was a little surprised to see you walk in here."

"Were you?" I ask. "I'm surprised you have an opinion about seeing me literally anywhere."

"I saw you at church yesterday."

I don't know what's happening right now, exactly. But I'll keep playing along.

I go, "You must've seen a lot of people at church yesterday."

And Lucy goes, "I'm just saying."

She adjusts herself in the seat, leans toward me. She doesn't have a donut or even a cup of cocoa in her hand. She probably doesn't eat donuts. Maybe her mother doesn't let her. Maybe her mother has unrealistic expectations of her, and anything less than a perfect daughter won't cut it, and that's why every single strand of dirt-blonde hair is in place and her outfit is Pinterest perfect. I could relate to a mother with impossible expectations, even empathize with that, but honestly? I don't know *what* Lucy's problem is.

"What *are* you saying?" I finally ask.

"You might think it's funny to play someone like Beckett," she nearly whispers. "You follow her to church, you follow her to a Great Wait meeting, score some brownie points, maybe a free donut or two. But for *her?* This isn't a game."

"I don't think it's your place to judge me," I tell her. If she thinks I'll be intimidated by her, she can suck it.

But Lucy just lifts her hands like she's ready to back off.

"You're absolutely right," she says. "That's between you and God."

Beckett comes back, licking chocolate icing off her fingers.

She goes, "Did I miss anything?" But the homeroom bell rings before either of us can answer.

Lucy hops off the chair like it's wrapped in barbed wire.

"See you later, Becks," she says, crossing the entire length of the room.

Beckett's gaze ricochets from the door Lucy disappears through back to me. She gives my arm a little squeeze.

"Everything okay?" she says.

But everything is not okay. Everything is . . . it's Lucy, and Pure Prom, and my mom freaking out, and . . . no. Everything's kind of messed up, actually.

And I don't want to lie to her, so I just say, "See you in fifth, Beckett."

I can't get out of this room, away from Beckett, away from Pure Prom, from the whole Great Wait industrial complex, fast enough.

Six

LUNCH

I don't know why I wasn't dialed into it before. Maybe because I hate this time of year in general? But it's truly inescapable, if you're paying attention. All anyone talks about is prom.

Regular prom. Pure Prom. In class. Down the hall between periods. Walking across the commons toward my locker.

"Is it weird that my dress is purple and he wants his tux to be all silver? Does that even work?"

"What are you doing with your hair?"

"I'm having these three fingers done in gold chrome, this one done in burgundy chrome, and the pinkies will stay sheer with pink glitter tips."

I'm over it. Screw prom. Screw prom posters. Screw prom announcements piped into class through the loudspeakers. Now happening. Every. Single. Morning.

And screw people talking about tickets and dresses and tuxes and hair and makeup in every class too.

B'Rad spots me in the commons on my way to lunch.

He goes, "Where you headed?"

"I don't know," I tell him. "I might go over to Sonic. My dad just put some money in my account, so."

B'Rad doesn't move for long enough to feel like a hint.

"Want to come?" I add.

"I brought my lunch from home."

"No one will care," I tell him. "Come hang out with me."

Sonic is just across the street and down one block from school. When we get there, B'Rad nabs us a table while I place my order, and by the time I come back to join him, he's pulled a brown bag out of his backpack that's so well used it looks more like suede than paper. He dumps out the contents: a sandwich that looks mostly like ketchup seeping through two slices of doughy white bread, a store-brand juice box, and a handful of chips wrapped in a napkin that's twisted shut.

The patio quickly fills up with kids from school, laughing, shoving, throwing french fries and ice cubes at each other. B'Rad doesn't seem fazed by the chaos. He doesn't seem to notice the way some people stare at his food as they walk by. But I do. I'm not an aggressive person, generally speaking, and I'm used to ignoring the way people look at me a lot of the time. But I definitely want to kick some of these people in the tots for the way they side-eye B'Rad's lunch. I saw how he lives. Not everyone's dad can load allowance money onto a debit card so they can eat out once in a while. Not everyone gets to buy lunch at Sonic on a random Monday.

The girl who roller-skates my order out looks familiar, but she doesn't acknowledge me as she puts my food on the table and rolls away.

It seems kind of extravagant to eat this in front of B'Rad, under the circumstances.

"You want half my burger?" I ask.

"I'm good, thanks," he says, sinking his teeth into his sandwich. A huge gob of ketchup oozes out the side.

"Dude," I tell him. "I hate to say this, but . . . you got ketchup-spooged."

"Where?"

"Right there." I signal which side of his mouth to hit, and B'Rad snags one of my napkins so he can wipe it off.

"Did I get it all?"

"You did not. On the positive, nobody rocks this zombie-cannibal vibe better than you."

He snort-laughs, then goes overkill on the napkins to make sure it's all gone.

After a few minutes of eating in silence, he goes, "So how's the urn?"

I groan.

"Can we not talk about that?" I say, pushing my cheesy tots into the middle of the table. He takes one.

"How'd your estate sale go?" I ask.

"My granddad came home early, so . . ."

I'm hit with the image of B'Rad's grandpa rolling up to a bunch of strangers in his yard, buying all his shit, and I have to force myself not to laugh out loud.

"So, that probably didn't go over well," I say with a snort.

"Not at all. Yeah, that may be my last one for a while. Which sucks, because prom's coming up, and—"

"God," I groan, even louder this time.

"Wait, that's also off-limits?"

"Absolutely, completely off-limits."

"Okay, so no urn, no prom. What's still on the table?"

I stab three cheesy tots and shove them into my mouth as an answer, but B'Rad, being B'Rad, won't drop the subject.

"Why so bitter?" he asks. "No date?"

"No. Because prom is stupid, and it hasn't even happened yet and I'm already sick of it. Aren't you sick of it? Don't you feel like it's a lot of unnecessary pressure?"

He says, "Yeah," like he has to, not like he believes it. He stops talking long enough to take a few more bites of his sandwich, wiping his mouth every time now, just to be on the safe side.

"Would you *want* to go, though?" he asks. "If someone wanted to go with you?"

I stop chewing the bite of hamburger I just took and blink at him. He knows, right? I mean . . . he must know I don't date guys.

He goes, "I'm just asking because we've already gone to one dance together, so. It'll be like old times."

"Uh-uh," I say with my mouth full. "We did not *go* to a dance together. We *danced* together one time. And that was just awkward."

"Awkward how?"

"Dude, I was there with Coley Salazar and Araceli Guzmán, who—by the way—saw you kiss me and would not shut up about it for two whole weeks."

"That's not on me." He takes another tot from the paper basket. "I asked if I could kiss you and you leaned in."

"I leaned in because you said something, and I couldn't hear you."

"Damn," he says, chewing on that tot until it's nothing but a memory. "That *is* awkward."

"It's the actual definition of awkward."

B'Rad's glasses start slipping. He pushes them up and I see for the first time how the earpiece is attached to the frame with electrical tape. He's freaking MacGyver—that shit blends in so well, I almost didn't notice.

He finishes off his sandwich, checks in with me about the ketchup situation, then says, "At least the kiss was okay."

My head tips heavy to one side, but I try to keep my voice soft. "Dude . . ."

He flat-palms me and winces. "Don't do that, Daya. Not pity-face. Not from you."

At least he's still smiling.

Oh, B'Rad. Someday, some nerdy girl with a collection of unicorn-cat T-shirts and a cool retro gaming system will be the happiest person alive to have you as a boyfriend.

I pile up my trash, reach for his lunch bag, but he slips it out from under me.

"I got it," he says.

As I get up to throw my trash away, I catch him stuffing the paper bag into his backpack.

We make it back to campus within seconds of the tardy bell. But before heading off to fifth period, B'Rad turns to me and makes one last-ditch effort.

"Hey. If you change your mind about prom, let me know."

I point at him. "You'll be the first."

I head toward class with my unicorn-cat-T-shirt radar on high alert. I'm not above girl-scouting on B'Rad's behalf, for a prom date or otherwise.

"Escuchen bien, estudiantes."

Here it comes. Señora Muñoz is about to give instructions for our end-of-the-year project.

All in Spanish, she explains how we're supposed to give a presentation on a Latin American figure—who they are or were, and what their impacts on history and culture have been. Halfway through Señora's explanation, Beckett's hand goes up, and I smile in private, because of course her hand would go up before Señora Muñoz is even finished explaining. Beckett is a super-student. She crosses all her *t*'s, dots all her *i*'s, squiggles all her *ñ*'s.

"¿Sí, Señorita Wild?" Señora Muñoz says.

"Is this a partner thing? Can we pick our own partners?"

"¡Buena pregunta!" Señora Muñoz pulls a plastic cup off her desk, filled with crafting sticks that she's written our names on. She tells us, again en español, that yes, it's a partner project, and yes, we can choose our own partner if we like, or she can choose one for us at random using the sticks.

Gustavo Meza blurts out, "What if there's an odd number of people in class?" because that's what Gustavo Meza always does, and Beckett turns backward in her seat and looks at me. She smiles, flips her lime-green-tipped finger between us.

My heart does the zapateado again. I never fully understood it when Stella would say, "That girl makes my insides do the zapateado," until she tried to show me the dance moves once. The footwork was too fast and fancy for me to keep up. But I get it now. My heart is racing way ahead of my brain.

I stutter-nod a *yes* at her.

Beckett raises her hand again.

"I choose Daya," she says.

The word *choose* dances in my stomach.

Señora Muñoz scribbles our names in her plan book, and the guy behind me leans forward and makes kissing noises in my ear, just soft enough for the teacher not to hear.

An uncomfortable heat fans out across my face.

Once all the pairs are recorded, Señora Muñoz projects the rest of the information onto the board so we can copy it into our notes. I'm mostly finished when a folded piece of paper lands on my desk, and when I look up, Oscar Díaz tips his head in Beckett's direction.

"From her," he says.

She's smiling at me again. Or maybe she's smiling still, I don't know. Smiling comes so easy to her.

I open the note.

Talk after class for a minute?

She's watching me. Waiting.

I look around, wondering if anyone else will make kissing noises, before turning back to her. I give a single nod as my answer.

I spend the rest of the period counting the clicks of the second hand as it drags excruciatingly slow around the dial toward the bell.

When it finally rings, Beckett comes over to my desk. She sits in Oscar Díaz's empty seat as I pack up my bag.

"So that's cool," she says. "Right?"

"Definitely," I say, trying to keep from losing all my chill right in front of her. I know it doesn't mean the same thing to her as it does to me that we'll be working together for the next two weeks. She's just doing a Spanish project. I'll have to constantly remind myself that, once the project is over, it'll just be . . . over.

No one, especially Beckett Wild, will ever have to know how I feel about her.

"I'm really glad you're my partner, Daya," she says.

"Yeah?" I smile just enough to seem friendly, but not enough to let her know that her words are alchemy. That all I have to do is be near her and I'm transformed.

She nods, smiles even wider. "Yeah."

I tell myself not to be weird about it as I push the flap of my bag closed, realizing too late that the entire front of my bag is covered in feminist fury patches.

She doesn't seem to notice. She just goes, "So anyway, I kind of want to get started right away. Would that be cool with you?"

The question makes me smile. Of course Miss A+ in every class would want to get started right away.

"Yeah," I say. "Sure."

"Awesome." She pulls her phone out of her bag. "What time?"

I blink and go, "What time, what?"

"Should I come over."

"Come over?" I say. "Like, to my house?"

This time, Beckett smiles. "How else are we supposed to work on our project?"

My mouth goes desert-dry all of a sudden. "I just—I guess I

figured we'd go to *your* house. Because. I mean. You probably have snacks. And internet. All the modern amenities, y'know?"

"You're so funny, Daya." She throws a playful nudge against me. "We're just brainstorming ideas. We don't need anything for that."

She holds her phone out to me.

"Type in your deets," she says, and I reel between euphoria and dread as I key in my address and phone number.

"Great," she says. "I'll see you at three thirty."

I'll see you at three thirty. Beckett's words have been on repeat in my head since fifth period, but the closer I get to my house, the faster they spin. I shimmy the back door open, and hurry down the hall to my room to put my things away and straighten up a bit. If she's on time, I've got maybe ten minutes to pull myself together before she gets here.

And please God let Joanna work late tonight so she doesn't come home and crop-dust our study session with her negativity.

I hit the brakes crossing from the living room to the kitchen when I spot the used urn Joanna bought over the weekend. Something like that could freak a person out. My grandpa's ashes aren't even in it yet, so I pull it down and stash it in the front hall closet.

There are so many other things I wish I could change about our house before she gets here, but thanks to a rip in the fabric of the universe, Beckett Wild is ringing my doorbell right this very second. I take a deep breath and open the door.

She's standing there, smiling as always, radiating color and light. Man, how does she do that?

Over her shoulder, I see the brightly colored scooter she must have ridden here, plus the neighbor from across the street, who's pretending not to look our way as she checks her mailbox.

Beckett says, "Hey," real soft, and my gaze rolls back to her.

"Hey. Hi. Come in."

This is so surreal. Friday night, I was chatting with Beckett Wild at a house party, wondering if she'd ever willingly have another conversation with me. Now she's standing inside my house. She smells like flowers. Like the kind of flowers you'd find growing in an open field just off a hiking trail, not the bogus ones they sell in stores that smell like scented bathroom cleaner.

She drifts into the living room, taking in everything around her while my heart moshes in the pit of my chest. I wonder what she must be thinking.

But all she says is, "Cool."

And all I say is, "Yeah."

And then she says, "Anyway," and the air in the room coagulates for a few seconds.

"I'm kind of dying to know what your room looks like," Beckett finally says.

I feel like a helium balloon she's holding on to as we head down the hallway.

I open the door.

"Oh wow, this is cool." She stops to pick up a bronze statuette off my dresser. She studies it like it's going to be on the test. "Did you make this?"

"My grandfather did," I say.

I watch close as her fingers trace the lines and curves of the woman's skirt.

"He wanted to do a whole series of, like, rebellious women from history. But he only did two or three before he died."

"I'm sorry to hear that," Beckett says.

"Thanks. This one's an Adelita," I add, moving in a little closer. "She's a soldier from the Mexican Revolution."

Her eyes pivot from the figurine in her hands to me, then back again. "I don't remember hearing about women soldiers in the Mexican Revolution."

"Yeah, they don't like to teach us about badass women in history," I say. "But they should, because these women were amazing. Even the ones who didn't fight in battle, but especially the ones who did."

"Wow," she says again. The word floats, light and soft, into my room.

I look at the patinaed surface of the Adelita sculpture.

"That's what I loved about my grandfather, though. He shared those stories with me. He always told me how art should say something, and . . . he made me want to make art so *I* could say something."

I reach over, run my fingertip along the bandolier of bullets across the Adelita's chest, careful not to touch Beckett's fingers as she cradles the statue.

I take my hand away before that can happen.

"My grandpa had a lot of respect for women who fought for what was right," I say. "Especially when it was seen as not being their place at the time. I think he understood that kind of fight better than a lot of men. I mean . . ." I laugh. "The dude had a Joan of Arc quote tattooed on his arm."

I wish I could read her face, or her mind. I have no idea what she's thinking.

But all she says is, "Seriously cool," before she puts the Adelita back on top of my dresser and moves over to the bed.

My. Bed.

Of all the places in the universe she could be right now, she's on my DC Comics blanket, leaning back against my wall. She slips a pencil out of her backpack, then her notebook. She's fully prepared to start on what she came here to do.

I roll my desk chair out, but the seat part falls off like always, and I fumble for a few seconds to reattach it.

"Shit," I mumble, then realize what I said. "Shoot. I'm sorry." I tuck the broken-off seat bottom under my desk. "It happens all the time. It's fixable. I know how to fix it."

I'm rambling.

She goes, "Just sit here. I don't mind."

But I do. I mind. I don't want to be that close to her. I don't want to feel the warmth of her body just inches away from mine because that would make her seem real, and she's not real. None of this is real. This is Spanish class with a change of venue. Friends without benefits. Barely friends.

"I promise I won't bite," she says.

Jesus, my mouth is so dry. I ease down on the foot of the bed, the lower half of Wonder Woman visible between us, while the string lights across my ceiling catch the prism of colors in her hair. She smiles at me through her freckles, smiles with her eyes, not just her mouth. Beckett Wild belongs in a museum. She's an impressionist master-piece, a kaleidoscope of randomness. Only . . . not. Nothing about her is random, except for the fact that she's here.

The sight of her eye-line sloped in my direction snaps me back to reality. But it's not reality, because every time I breathe, I smell flowers. Just like in eighth grade, when she dyed her hair with blue Kool-Aid, and I asked our art teacher if I could move seats next to her. I made up a lie about why I wanted to move, because the truth was, Beckett Wild smelled like blue Kool-Aid and all I had to do to be part of it was sit next to her and breathe.

"You know what bugs me about Spanish?" she asks out of the blue. "I always feel like I'm doing it wrong because there's always a differ-ent way I could've said something. Like, why does every question have so many ways to answer when they only teach us one kind of formula?"

Beckett Wild has just summed up my entire life in a single, perfect sentence.

"I know what you mean," I tell her. "But . . . it's also true in every language. Y'know? There's always more than one way to say some-thing."

She leans back. "I get that. Language is definitely fluid."

"Yeah, but I mean . . ." Our feet touch, and I stare down at them as I add, "Everything is fluid."

Beckett pulls herself into a lotus position and looks around, stop-ping every place I've hung a piece of my art, and I feel suddenly self-conscious. I stretch my legs out, throw one over the other to keep from touching her again, but she's still so close. Too close.

Close enough for her to notice the doodles on my jeans. To touch them as she asks, "So, how come we haven't had an art class together since, like, junior high?"

"I don't know," I say, still tripping on the statistical improbability that Beckett Wild would ever be in my room, on my bed, and yet . . . here she is.

In the silence, things go awkward again. My eyes drift, trying to see things through her POV . . . my broken desk chair, the ceiling full of string lights, the figurine on my dresser. I pan in close on the Adelita's face. On the determination of her expression.

I go, "Hey, what if . . . ?"

She sits up tall, does her super-student lean-in.

"What if we did our report on la Adelita?"

Beckett follows my gaze to my grandfather's figurine.

"You already know a lot about her," she says.

"Actually, it wasn't really a *her*. It was a whole movement of women who cooked and took care of the men, and eventually fought alongside them. They inspired all kinds of music and art too."

Beckett's already got her phone out and scrolling.

"Adelita's bravery and revolutionary spirit are lost to the fatalism and insecurities of male soldiers who focused on passion, love, and desire," she reads. "Well, that's bogus."

I can't believe this is my life right now. Even if this moment just turns out to be one small patch of color on a giant blank canvas, it doesn't matter. Because we're here now.

She's here now.

And then she's gone.

After Beckett leaves, I stretch out on the bed, try to match my body to where her body had been. Stretch my legs where her legs were. Lean my head where her head was. I take a deep breath. My room smells like whatever she uses to wash her hair. I press back against my pillow, imagine Beckett and me, filling up that blank white canvas with an explosion of color.

Alone, in my room, I let thoughts of Beckett Wild take me somewhere else.

Somewhere bigger than here.

Where someone like her could be with someone like me, and no one would have anything to say about it.

Somewhere that's not Escondido.

And I wouldn't have to worry about what happens when my mother gets home.

Seven

THE HOUND'S TOOTH

I'm out in the living room when Joanna gets home because that's where the only TV in our house is. Cartoon Network plays in the background while I draw Beckett's face again and again in my sketch-book, adding her signature splashes of color into her hair while the TV throws splashes of color into the room.

The volume is low so I can hear Joanna pull into the driveway, and I swing my feet to the floor seconds before she comes through the door. She'd lose her mind if she ever saw me using her cheap estate sale coffee table as a footstool.

We mumble hello to each other.

"Homework all done?" she asks on her way to the kitchen.

"Yup."

I listen for the familiar thud of her purse being dropped onto the one dining chair no one sits in anymore. Bottles of mineral water clink together in the fridge as she pulls one out, the cap hissing when she twists it off.

The oven door squeaks open.

"Dinner smells good," she says.

"It's almost ready. You have time to shower first, if you want."

She always showers after work to wash off the smells of the

mortuary. She says death has a tendency to cling.

I start plating our food when I hear her move from the bathroom to the bedroom, so that by the time she comes back into the kitchen, dinner is on the table. She sets her mineral water to the left of her plate, and I set my tap water to the right of mine, and we simultaneously pull our chairs out. We have this choreography memorized by now.

"Did you bake this chicken?" she asks.

"Mm-hm."

She pushes the meat and vegetables around on her plate, like the elephant in the room might be hidden underneath a wayward bell pepper.

"I never thought to make fajitas in the oven," she says. "Clever."

"Thanks. The rice was from a box." I don't know why that seemed important enough to say out loud.

This time she doesn't take my hands but turns hers palms-up on the table and bows her head.

"Thank you, Lord Jesus, for this beautiful meal. Bless this food to our bodies, and our bodies to Your service. Amen."

It goes quiet again—nothing but the clink of forks against plates as we eat. The silence is too much after a while.

"How was your day?" I ask, just to break the tension.

"I worked on a ninety-year-old woman who passed in her sleep at the nursing home. We should all look that good at ninety."

"Cool."

I wait, half expecting her to ask me how my day was. But she doesn't. We've never even circled back to what happened at O'Ring on Sunday. But I want her to know I heard her. I hear her. I'm trying.

So I go, "There was a Great Wait meeting at school today."

"Mmm," she says without looking up.

"I went."

That gets her attention. She goes, "Oh? How was it?"

"They mostly talked a lot about prom coming up. Their version of prom. And I'm not interested in going to that, so . . ."

Her fork goes loose in her fingers. "Why wouldn't you?"

Uh-oh. That took a hard left. "I don't know. It's kind of late now—"

"It's never too late, Daya." She takes a bite of her chicken while I wonder if we're really talking about prom, or if prom is code in Joanna's mind for something else.

"The more opportunities you open up to," she adds, "the closer you come to getting right with God."

There it is.

And then . . .

"Sometimes, it takes a while to get comfortable with the idea that we need redemption."

"Why do I need redemption?"

"All sinners need redemption."

I push back against my seat.

"How am I a *sinner*?"

"Honey . . ." She shakes her head like I'm totally missing the point. "We're all sinners—"

"No, but you're saying it like . . . like you think there's something wrong. Like if I go to a couple of Great Wait meetings or whatever, it'll fix whatever's *wrong* with me."

"I'm not saying The Great Wait will *fix* you. I'm saying it'll bring you closer to God. And being closer to God gives you clarity in your relationships."

My *relationships*?

"The young people at this church are so full of light and hope."

"Yeah, but—"

"That's all I want for you. To let that hope and light lift the veil of confusion—"

"I'm not confused," I say. "I don't need to be fixed. I'm not broken."

With everything I say, she recalibrates, looks for a new way in.

"This soul we carry . . ." she says, forming the shape of an imagined soul with her hands. "It's so very fragile, and . . . things can sneak up on us when we're the least prepared for it."

"What things? What are you *talking* about?"

"I'm talking about choices, Daya. Even our smallest choices can get out from under us without our even realizing it."

The air in the room has a life of its own. Heavy heartbeats and thick breath that expand and contract around us.

"You don't really mean choices. You mean sin," I say. There's nothing subtle about her Grace Redeemer–charged subtext here.

"Yes."

"You mean *his* sin," I whisper. "*His* choices. The way *he* was broken."

For a moment, neither of us moves. I crossed the line again, bringing up my dad—I know I did. But I'm not wrong. I'm not.

For the longest time, she doesn't move. Not a fingernail. Then she gets up without a word, slips her purse off the empty third chair—the chair my dad used to sit in.

I follow her to the living room.

"Mom."

She ignores me. Gets her keys out.

"*Mom!*"

She turns at the door, her eyes blazing with anger and hurt.

"We're *all* broken, Daya." She shakes her head and adds, "The sooner you acknowledge that . . ."

It's the last thing she says before closing the door behind her. And she doesn't even finish the thought.

I stand in the living room, staring out the cracked pane of glass in the door that my dad was supposed to replace before he left. After a while, I go into the bathroom and wash the tears off my face. I clean up the dinner neither of us finished. I wander to my room. Stand just inside the door, look at the Adelita statue, at the bedspread where Beckett Wild sat earlier—where I fantasized about her after she left, without worrying if masturbating over a girl I can never be with is a sin.

Joanna was right. This house is full of brokenness. Broken promises. Broken relationships. Broken hearts. For the first time, I understand a sliver of how it must have felt for her these last nine years. Our house is a tomb. It physically hurts to be here.

I grab my messenger bag and my phone and let the back door slam behind me.

"Welcome to the Hound's Tooth, proudly serving the Hair of the Dog That Bit You. What can I get started for you this evening?"

B'Rad is Cheshire-Cat-smiling from his perch at the kiosk window.

"Are you ever *not* cheerful?" I ask.

"Not without good reason." He winks from behind his busted glasses. "You here to eat, or did you come to accept my prom offer?"

"Option C, actually."

"Oh yeah?" he says. "What's option C?"

I smile, hoping it's a good enough substitute for an answer. Option C should have been to call Stella, but she was in such a mood this morning, she may not be able to hear me around my Joanna drama right now.

"Is it okay that I just showed up here? I took the bus and everything."

He throws me rock-star hands and says, "Sounds like option C is a friendly face with a side of hot dog."

B'Rad motions for me to go around to the back of the kiosk. He opens the door, pokes his head out, waves me inside.

"Won't you get in trouble?" I ask.

"Doesn't matter. I'm the only one here. Plus, they freaking love me."

"Who loves you?" I say, hiking the three steps up into the kiosk.

"The owners. They appreciate my work ethic."

"Ah."

Once I'm inside, the first thing I notice is that it's stuffy as hell in here. The second is that everything is gunky if you make the mistake of touching it. The metal cabinets, the counters, even the floor.

A smoky tang hangs in the air, the unmistakable mix of hot dog, mustard, relish, and onions. If memories have a smell, this one brings me back to a little roadside hot dog stand on a trip to California with my grandparents and Joanna not long after my dad left. Joanna wasn't eating much back then—all she got was a Diet Coke. My grandmother just sat there shaking her head like she'd never eat anything off a food truck, least of all a hot dog. But I wanted my mom to eat. I wanted her to be happy again. I challenged my grandpa to a hot-dog-lightsaber duel, and we laughed as we battled it out. It still wasn't enough to make Joanna hungry.

"Wow," I say, sniffing back the memory. "Those onions are brutal."

"I must be immune," he says. "Hey, wanna learn how to make a Hair of the Dog That Bit You? It's our signature dish."

"Sure." I nab a couple condiment packets when B'Rad isn't looking and slip them into the side pocket of my cargos, next to the ones I stashed there at lunch earlier. Emergency relish. They always give you way too many ketchup packets at Sonic and not enough of anything else.

"So, what you have to know about making a Hair of the Dog That Bit You is—"

"Are you sure this is cool, though?" I ask.

He goes, "Daya. It's chill. Take a risk once in a while."

"Something tells me you do enough risk-taking for the both of us."

B'Rad leans back against the dinky metal counter and uses his hands to help explain the situation to me.

"Here's the dealio. If I make a mistake on someone's order, I have to log it in as waste and toss it, plus it comes out of my check. But if I'm *training* someone and they make a mistake, I can let them eat it. I don't know why. It's just company rules."

He smiles.

I smile too.

"But you're not training someone," I say.

His head tips to one side. "Aren't I, though?"

I look at him for a second, but he just stands there, looking at me right back. Nothing seems to throw B'Rad Anderson off balance.

"Okay, sure," I say. "Let's do this."

It turns out, a Hair of the Dog That Bit You bears a striking resemblance to Anything Daya Keane Likes on a Hot Dog, menu be damned. In this case, those ingredients include: mustard, ketchup, onions, and lots of shredded cheese. B'Rad says there's a fixed set of toppings for the Hair of the Dog That Bit You, but my version is close enough.

I'm genuinely salivating at the aroma of my Anything Daya Keane Likes on a Hot Dog, filling the tight quarters inside the Hound's Tooth Hot Dog kiosk. Meanwhile B'Rad's doing such a great job training me that he accidentally makes a second training dog.

"Here's a weird thing I just noticed," I say, looking up at the hand-written chalkboard menu. "There's something up there called To Thine Own Self Be True. It says *your dog, your way.* So how is that different from my customized Hair of the Dog?"

"Look, I know it's only your first day," he says. "But details matter. Try not to get overwhelmed with everything you still need to learn."

As B'Rad throws paper wrappers around the two "mistake" dogs he just made, I dip down to look out the service window. That's when I catch a glimpse of Beckett Wild leaving her dad's Vespa dealership across the parking lot.

She's right there, directly across a stretch of asphalt from me.

And she's carrying a bag from the Hound's Tooth.

My brain is trying to connect these unexpected dots. Beckett, placing that bag on the seat so she can strap her helmet on, throwing one long leg over the same scooter she drove to my house earlier. Giving the Vespa some juice before riding off into the literal sunset. I picture myself trading places with that bag tucked between her legs.

"She ordered the Jackson Pollack," he says. "Her dad owns this place too."

My stunned gaze drifts from out the window to back inside the kiosk, landing on B'Rad.

". . . She what?"

"The Jackson Pollack. It's a splattering of ketchup, mustard, and our famous sauce. I can teach you how to make the dog, but not how to make the sauce unless you really did work here. That's the only thing that would for real get me fired."

I stare at him.

I stare at the chalkboard menu behind him.

I stare at the words: *The Jackson Pollack—a splattering of ketchup, mustard, and Hound's Tooth's own best-kept-secret sauce.*

I turn back to B'Rad, who has the strangest look on his face, like he just got caught telling me the super-secret-sauce recipe.

He goes, "I had to sign a nondisclosure agreement. Are you okay, Daya?"

I can't get the image of her out of my mind, can't make myself stop thinking about her.

I'm all flame and no oxygen.

"You want to talk about it?" he asks.

"No."

The word hits the thick air a little too hard and quick.

"Okay," he says.

Something about seeing Beckett here has me twisted. She went from secret crush to in-my-house in the span of a few hours. Then, after her galaxy and mine comingled for a brief moment in time, after the fight with Joanna at dinner, after coming here, hanging out with B'Rad, having a good time . . . boom. Beckett. Again. Knowing her dad is B'Rad's boss. Knowing how I feel about her, what I've imagined doing with her. Things that would definitely shock Mr. Wild, not to mention the rest of the congregants at Grace Redeemer. It's all kind of messing with my head.

"I . . . I guess I should probably get going," I tell him.

"What do you mean? You just got here."

I don't know what I mean. There are too many thoughts in my head, all getting bottlenecked trying to find their way somewhere else.

"I got in a fight with my mom earlier, and . . ." I let the thought trail off, since I don't know where it's going anyway.

"I had a feeling it was something like that. Because of yesterday?"

"Kind of, yeah."

He looks out the window and we both watch as the lights go out at Wild Rides Vespa Dealership.

"I have a bold proposal. There's only about ten minutes left on my shift, so." B'Rad unties his apron and hangs it up on a hook near the door. "If you *have* to go home, can I at least drive you?"

"Are you sure? Don't you need to do some end-of-shift ritual or something?"

"It's been dead all night," he says. "No one will care if I close up fifteen minutes early."

"I thought you said ten."

He ignores me. "Gimme a hand putting things away. I'll wipe everything down real quick. No one will ever know."

"Isn't that what you said about your gramps just before he came back early from his fishing trip?" I ask, putting the lids he hands me onto the condiment trays.

B'Rad ignores me again, but he does it with a smile. He does everything with a smile. Only this smile has *famous last words* plastered all over it.

We spend a few fast minutes cleaning the kiosk, since it would take a chisel and a lot of prayer to fully remove the years of gunk on everything. Then we lock up.

B'Rad says, "See? Took half as long to close as when I do it myself. We should totally work together," he adds as we walk out to his car. "We make a pretty good team."

He manually unlocks the car doors, and I pull open the creaky passenger side of his old VW wagon and get in.

"Do you care if I eat my Hair of the Dog?" I ask. "I'm starving."

"Nah," he says. "Hand me mine."

"I love your ride, by the way," I say, mouth full of hot dog, as we head out of Greenville. "Looks like something out of your granddad's junk pile."

"I rescued it from the junk pile," he says.

"Seriously? Was it even running?"

"Nope." He turns onto the Strip that runs north to south through town. "I watched a bunch of videos online to figure out how to fix the engine, and voilà."

My mouth pops open. "You're shitting me."

"I shit you not."

"Man, you really are MacGyver. You're all that and a tank of Hound's Tooth's Best Kept—" Before I can finish, I go, "Hey, pull over real quick."

He whips to the side of the road with lightning-fast reflexes, and as we roll to a stop, I lean out the window.

"Stella. *Stells!*"

Stella looks up from where she's sitting on the curb.

I go, "Dude, what are you doing?"

"Shaving my legs," she says. "What does it look like?"

"Well, it *looks* like you're hanging out on a street corner waiting for your pimp, but that can't be right."

She pushes to her feet, bending over enough to see who's in the driver's seat. Her eyes do a whole three-hundred-sixty-degree rotation when she sees B'Rad behind the wheel, stuffing the tail end of a hot dog into his mouth.

"Goddess, give me strength," she mumbles.

"We can give her a ride, right?" I ask him.

"If she'll get in," he says.

I open the door for her, lean forward so she can climb in behind me while he puts on a smile like he's about to take her order at the kiosk window.

"I'm B'Rad," he says. "I don't think we've ever officially met."

"I know who you are," Stella says as she slithers into the back seat. "And, no, we've never officially met."

Just that fast, the air in the car changes, like when your hair stands up during a lightning storm. Something's off with Stella. Something's been off since this morning, when she went on that rant about her mom.

"Is she going home with you?" B'Rad asks me.

I'm not sure how to answer. Now that Stella's here, I don't actually want to go home.

"Can we crash at your place?" I ask her.

Her face twists up. "Fuck no."

Oh man. It's her mom—I'm one thousand percent sure.

I turn back to B'Rad. "Can we just chill with you for a while?"

Stella's breath fogs up the grimy back window, but she doesn't openly object.

B'Rad kicks another look at her through the rearview mirror.

"I'm not . . . I mean, I don't usually bring people home," he stammers.

"It's not a sex thing, Be Weird," Stella says against the window. "I'd be down to just go somewhere I can look up at the stars for a while, so I can erase any lingering doubt about how petty and insignificant everything is."

Yikes.

He looks over at me and I shrug back at him.

He goes, "We can do that at my place, I guess."

As we drive in the direction of the electric fields, the evening sky goes from robin's-egg blue to cobalt. When the sun dips below the horizon, it throws a rose-gold tint over everything in its path. Something about the color reminds me of Beckett.

Who am I kidding?

Everything reminds me of Beckett. . . .

If I were anyone else, I'd have grossed myself out about it by now.

But it's not my fault. Tonight's sunset is a near-perfect color match of her hair, which, please God no, don't let me become one of those pathetic, cream-filled, piney-eyed girls.

I shiver against the unsettled energy all around us. It's not just the crackle coming off Stella. Or the unstable air from inside my house earlier. Or the low-grade hum as we get closer to the towers flanking B'Rad's place . . .

I can't put my finger on it, but . . . it feels like dread. Like something about tonight wants to break loose and run feral around B'Rad's junk ranch.

The thought of it sends a shiver straight through me.

Eight

THE ELECTRIC FIELDS

The doors of the rusty yellow VW wagon grunt when we open them.

"Where the fuck *are* we?" Stella says.

I slide out of the front and let her out of the back. She stands there gawking as B'Rad gathers up his things.

"What is this?" she asks more directly this time.

"What is what?" He throws his messenger bag over his shoulder, manually locking the driver's-side door before shutting it.

It's warm out, but there's a chill punching through the air.

"I mean, what the hell *is* this? All of this," she says again, gesturing. "What is *that?*"

"It's a pontoon boat," he tells her, like it should be self-explanatory.

"Okay, but—"

"It's where I live."

"You live on a *boat?*"

"Depending on how bad monsoon season is," he tells her.

I didn't know about the boat either, but I'm not about to make a thing of it.

"So, who lives in that shitty house right there?" Stella asks.

"Nice," I say. "Real tactful."

"It belongs to my shitty granddad," he tells her, and that's when I hear it. That thing people do. That voice thing. Not really a lie, but maybe an omission. If you're paying attention, you can hear the space between half-truths that incubates secrets like a cocoon.

"So, your granddad lives in that house," Stella presses, "while you're out here freezing your sprouts off on this boat?"

"It's not that bad," B'Rad says. "I have a space heater."

"Safety hazard," she mumbles, following his lead by hiking herself up onto the boat's platform. She goes, "Where do you take a whiz?"

I mouth *I'm sorry* to B'Rad, but Stella just says, "I saw that, Daya. Don't assign an apology to me." She turns back to him. "I can actually pee standing up if I'm in a bind. Now *that's* a skill."

He pretends he doesn't hear her. He says, "There's a bathroom in the cabin, but it's not hooked up to anything."

"So, you do your business in the house, or what?"

He lifts his chin and signals a cluster of dry brush next to the boat.

"I just hang it over the side and aim for those," he says.

"Thanks for the visual," I mumble to no one in particular.

Stella nods knowingly, says, "Hmm. What about number two?"

"*Stel-la.*" I make face at her. "It's already been a weird night. I don't want to hear about anyone's shit habits right now."

"Fair game." She keeps walking around the boat, surveying it like it's a used car she's thinking of buying. "I just never heard of a dude living on dry land in a pontoon boat before, so there you go. Something new every day."

She leans against the rickety metal railing, stares out across B'Rad's granddad's junkyard. Some of the old bottles and jars, strips of metal, gas cans, and broken car windows gleam so deceptively in the moonlight, you'd almost believe you were on some kind of trea-sure island instead of a homegrown landfill.

B'Rad disappears inside the dinky cabin for a beat, roots around before coming back out with a couple sleeping bags and one of those space-age emergency blankets that makes you look like a to-go bur-rito wrapped in aluminum foil. He starts unzipping and laying out the sleeping bags across the deck, and I come over to help. Stella just stares out across the yard like she's floating away from the mother-ship, untethered.

Eventually, she pushes back from the railing to join us, and for a while, no one talks. It's actually kind of nice.

"You okay?" I lean in and ask after she drops next to me on the sleeping bag.

"It's dark out here," she says instead of answering.

"Definitely the best place to see the stars," B'Rad half whispers, like he's gone somewhere else too.

Stella lets out a deep exhale as she looks up.

She goes, "Damn. That's intense."

I put my hands under my head, and she rests her head in the bend of my arm, and thousands of millions of light-years above us, entire galaxies spread out like spilled sugar. All those stars and planets and solar systems, invisible to the bare eye, spinning their versions of days and years. Trusting us to believe they're out there, even if we can't see them.

"You wanted confirmation of how petty and insignificant every-thing is," I say as we look up. "There you go."

The soundtrack of frogs and crickets cues up cinematically.

"But also?" B'Rad says. "There are so many shooting stars out here, it's actually kind of cool. Like a magic show that goes on all night."

"You don't get any more shooting stars than anyone else does, Be Weird," Stella says. "You just see more of them because it's so fucking dark out here."

"Doesn't matter," I say. "It's all just a trick."

Stella shifts. "What do you mean?"

"They're not actually stars. They're bits of dust and rock burning up when they hit the atmosphere."

She goes, "Wait, so when we make a wish on a falling star, we're really just wishing on a rock? That's bogus."

"You have a sixty percent probability of seeing one if you watch the sky for just thirty minutes," B'Rad tells her. "That's not bad odds, if you think about it."

"It's terrible odds," Stella says. "Would you go to a concert if you only had a sixty percent chance of seeing the band?"

"Can we just talk about how all those rocks had a chance to escape earth's atmosphere, to get out into the universe and do something bigger, maybe become a planet someday, only to burn out because they tried to come back?"

Stella and B'Rad turn to me like a synchronized boy band.

Stella goes, "Dude. Where you been hiding that edge all this time?"

"And here I thought *I* was the only one filled with existential angst," B'Rad says. "What else you got swirling around in there, Daya?"

I look over at B'Rad, who's still stretched out flat on his back.

"You're the chillest dude I know," I tell him. "If you're filled with anything, it's a creamy center. Like a Twinkie."

"Happy people are the scariest people," Stella says. "They've got the most skeletons."

"Everyone has skeletons," B'Rad murmurs. "I don't care how happy or sad they are."

"See?" Stella says. "I told you. Bones—lots of 'em. They're probably all buried out in this yard too."

I think about the urn he dug out of this junk heap on Saturday, and shudder against Stella's words.

But B'Rad just keeps looking up, like the map of stars is more familiar to him than the landscape of junk stretched out around him, teeming with long-forgotten memories. Like if he could just lift off into the cosmos, he'd never have to think about whose stuff this all once was, or what memories were attached to any of it.

With Stella's head cradled in the bend of my arm, we both look up too. I don't know what's on her mind—probably some deep, dark existential meanderings. I'm just looking for shooting stars. Even though I know they're not stars. And they're not so much shooting as falling. But they're out there, doing all they can to be seen for a moment. To be known for what they are, even if most people want to make them into something else.

There's a loud crash inside the house that jolts the two of us completely upright. But B'Rad just lies there, looking up at the sky as a string of chilling utterances weaves through the lattice-covered windows and floats past us.

"Goddamn sonsabitches!" the old man inside hollers.

B'Rad slowly sits up, clears his throat, shoots eye-bullets against the side of the house.

"I can take you wherever you need to go," he offers.

Something lingering between his words makes leaving now the only option.

As we hop down from the boat, the shouting gets louder, more combative. Stella hustles ahead of us to the car. No wonder—she had way more than her share of belligerent screaming in the four years her mom was married to Richard Howell.

When she climbs into the back seat, I realize I never locked my door. B'Rad and I both start our *I'm sorry*s at the same time, but I stop, and he follows all the way through on his.

"Sorry about that. He's just . . . I mean . . . he's not—"

"It's cool. Really. I'm just glad we got to chill out here for a while."

"Right."

"No, I mean it."

I lean out the open window as we ease down the driveway. Look up. Think about shooting stars and space dust. I think about B'Rad's granddad, and the fact that B'Rad would rather live on a pontoon boat than in that house, where he'd have to listen to a drunken tirade every night. B'Rad talks about other places. About going somewhere different from here. I pray to God he never becomes a shooting star. I pray that B'Rad can be a comet—one of the rare ones that breaks free.

From the back seat, Stella goes, "Daya. Tell your mom you're coming home with me."

"I can't just *tell* her that," I say, twisting around to look at her.

"Why not?"

"That's more of an ask-my-mom situation."

"Why? She'll just say no."

"We go through this every time, Stells. It's a school night, for one—"

"It's not like you're asking her if you can smoke crack. You're staying over at my house like you've done a bazillion times. I don't get how that's an ask-my-mom situation."

"Because." I turn back around. "She's not *your* mom."

"Fine," she says. "Then *ask* her."

Stella messages her mom to let her know I'm coming home with her, while I text Joanna to tell her Stella's in crisis and ask if I can stay the night.

Five minutes later, she still hasn't written back.

You can call her mom, if you want, I add.

Three dots pulse for a few seconds, followed by:

Stella's always in crisis.

That's not an answer. I pull up a Google search, find what I'm looking for, then type it back to Joanna.

Okay, but even the Bible tell us to calm each other's burdens.

We're just about to turn onto Cortés when she types:

If that's what you feel called to, Daya.

Wow. That's a whole new approach for her. She didn't say yes, exactly, but I'm glad she didn't say no either. So why don't I trust it?

B'Rad lets us out with a wave. When we get inside, Stella's hot mom is painting her toenails in front of the TV. She's watching that movie everyone loves so much—*One More Time Around the Sun* or something. Stella refers to every movie in that genre as *Heteros in Love*.

"Hola, mi preciosa," she says. "Did you eat? There's some carne guisada in the fridge."

"Pass," Stella mumbles on her way to her room.

"Thanks anyway, Mrs. Howell," I say.

"You can call me Ms. Avila," she tells me with a dimpled smile.

Damn.

"I forgot again, didn't I?"

"No worries. G'night, you two."

"Good night, Ms. Avila." I turn and follow Stella into her room.

She shoves the door closed with her foot.

"You look like you wish that door was someone's face," I say.

"Starting with your friend Be Weird. Why are you hanging around that asshole, anyway?" she asks as I pull out the trundle from under her bed.

I sit down on it, taking a temperature check on the mood as she grabs a T-shirt and pajama pants out of her dresser drawer and tosses them to me.

"He's not evil," I finally tell her. "He may actually be one of the good guys."

"Good guys don't steal a bitch's girlfriend."

"It was eighth grade," I say.

"She was still the love of my life, Daya." Stella looks at herself in the mirror over her dresser, fluffs up her hair. "And don't come at me with any of that *if you love someone, set them free* bullshit either. I know how your mind works."

I snort. "What am I thinking right *now?*"

She turns to me and smiles. "That filth has no business in the sanctuary of this room."

Stella comes over, flops on the bed above where I'm stretched out on the trundle, drawing solar systems on my arms in fine-point Sharpie. She sticks her leg out, pushing it into the space between my hand and the pen I'm holding.

"Draw me and Valentina Orozco together," she says. "I'm manifesting."

I start on the fleshy part of her calf, sketching out the basic shape of Stella.

"So, why are you hiding from Joanna tonight?" she asks.

"Why were you sitting out on the street earlier?" I ask back.

Valentina starts taking shape next to her. She always wears a dress, so I wrap the skirt around Stella's calf.

"We're both following nature's mandate to have complicated relationships with our mothers," she finally says.

I go, "Man. That's some deep-rooted Psych 101 shit."

But I know how her mind works too. When she doesn't feel like talking about something, she makes jokes instead. I sneak a look at her, but she's somewhere else.

She pulls her leg up so she can look at the Sharpie tattoo I gave her.

"Damn, you're good," she says.

I watch her trace the lines of Valentina's dress with her fingertip.

"You want to talk about it?" I ask.

"Not really. I just kind of want to sleep it off." She flops back on the bed and pulls the covers over her head, and within minutes her breathing becomes slow and rhythmic.

There's nothing slow or rhythmic going on inside my head right now—just endless camera-clicks from a day full of cringe. Beckett, sitting in my room this afternoon, worrying about saying something the wrong way in Spanish while I'm worried about doing the wrong thing around her. Yesterday's fight with my mom that turned into today's fight with my mom. Sending questions into the universe tonight, but not getting back any answers. People seem to think God is *up there* somewhere, but in my experience, He's not. He's not at Grace Redeemer, or The Great Wait, or wherever Joanna thinks I'll find Him. Why is it so hard for some people to separate the idea of God from the idea of church? If you really drill down to it, religion and God are mutually exclusive.

This is the hamster wheel I can't get off right now.

This is what keeps me awake until almost dawn.

Too much confusion, not enough resolution.

And no way of knowing where the universe will spin me next.

Nine

FOOL CITY

The note on the door of the choir room Tuesday morning says: *Hanging flyers—see you there!*

I'm actually kind of relieved. I don't know what I was thinking, wandering toward the Great Wait meeting this morning, just because Stella and I got to school a little early. I start to walk away, but a few hallways over, I find a handful of kids in those *True Love Waits* T-shirts from the *Merch!* shop, hanging up mini-posters on every door. Cason Price and Lucy Davis are there, laughing and jabbing at each other. If I didn't know any better, I'd think *they* were the couple.

I hook a fast U-turn around the corner, where more mini-posters have been taped to the walls and classroom doors. I stop to get a closer look.

"Here," Beckett says from behind me.

I jolt at the unexpected sound of her voice in my ear as she hands me a flyer.

She goes, "You can keep it. We printed, like, four thousand of them."

I glance at the text.

JOIN US AT PURE PROM
A WHOLESOME NIGHT OF MUSIC,
DANCE, FOOD, AND GAMES!
YOU HAVE ALL THE FUN!
GOD GETS ALL THE GLORY!
LET THEM PRAISE HIS NAME WITH DANCING. PSALM 149:3

"Grace Redeemer is hosting it this year," Beckett says just as I look back up at her. "You should come."

"I . . . it's . . ."

I look at the flyer again because I don't know how to finish the thought.

She goes, "It's not boring, if that's what you're thinking."

"It's the same night as prom," I blurt.

Beckett's smile dissolves. "Oh. I didn't realize you were going."

Going . . .

"To prom?" I say. "Oh. No. I'm not going to prom, I just . . . it was an observation. That's all."

She nods excessively for a few seconds before saying, "It's the same night on purpose. So you can't go to both." She pulls a piece of tape off the dispenser and rolls it into a ball. "They say they're big on giving people the freedom to choose," she adds. "But . . ." She shrugs.

We stand there, pretending to look at the flyer taped to the wall. At least that's what I'm doing. Beckett's hand flutters toward me, comes to rest on my arm. I float as I look down at it, spiral as I come back up, into the gravitational pull of her intensely blue eyes.

"Seriously, though," Beckett says. "It would be so great if you could come."

This is not an invitation. I have to tell myself that. Inviting me to go to prom isn't the same as inviting me to go to prom *with her*. They even frown on that at the non-church version, not that it would ever matter anyway, since Beckett's currently with—

A pop of laughter bursts at the other end of the hallway.

"Hey!" Cason Price calls out through a smile aimed straight at his girlfriend. "I wondered where you went."

He eases up next to her and slides his arm around her waist.

I don't know why I turn away when he leans in to kiss her, and I don't know why I turn back a nanosecond later. Maybe I'm a masochist; I don't know. But it seems like if I'm never going to have the chance to kiss Beckett Wild, I might at least want to see what kissing her would look like.

For the record, Cason kisses her in black and white.

I'd kiss Beckett Wild in living color.

"I'll see you in class," I tell her as I back awkwardly down the hall and around the corner.

where ru? I text Stella at the beginning of lunch.

Locker – about to leave campus.

I type **wait up** as I scramble out of fourth to meet her.

She's quiet as we walk down the Strip toward midtown. She was quiet this morning, too, as her mom drove us to school. More than quiet—sulky. As soon as Ms. Avila dropped us off in front of the main office, Stella evaporated into the morning bus crowd. Sometimes when she's in a bad mood, it's better just to let it burn off her instead of trying to pressure-wash it away.

We cut a path for Fool City, and when we get there, she flips her board vertical with the toe of her shoe and carries it inside. We're barely through the door when some girl walking by a display of mangoes flashes Stella a neon smile.

The girl says, "Hey, you!" like she has Sour Patch Kids in her mouth—all pucker and saliva.

"Heya, cutie," Stella calls back.

Once that mystery girl is out of range, I turn and go, "*Heya, cutie?* Really—that's your line?"

But Stella just says, "I couldn't remember her name."

"So, how do you know her?" I ask.

"I met her at a party a few weeks ago."

"Met her?"

"You know. We danced." Her neck goes red.

We turn down aisle nine, and she slows her pace, runs her fingers along the cans.

"Y'know . . . there's such a thing as too much order in the world."

I'm not sure why she says this exactly, but the next thing I know, Stella's moving things around, sowing the seeds of chaos in the canned vegetables section.

"Alphabetical order is for chumps," she says, switching stewed tomatoes with peas.

"Seriously, though. How do you not remember someone's name?" I ask.

"She never actually told me her name." She hands me a can of okra, takes the candied yams I grab off the shelf and hold out to her. She spends a few seconds deciding where to put them.

"Hold up," I say, intercepting the next can Stella takes down. "They're seriously calling this *Mexicorn*?"

This is what finally cracks her. Mexicorn. Stella launches her atomic belly laugh as I hold the label up and pulse it at her, the bright yellow kernels swimming in a pool of buttery water dotted here and there with bits of red and green mystery vegetables.

"Thank the goddess we showed up when we did," she says. "Someone has to keep the masses from getting too comfortable."

"No one better get comfortable with this," I say, holding the can up again. "Mexicorn, my ass."

Her laughter rolls down the aisle. Stella has a very distinctive laugh. It's unmistakable, even from the other side of Fool City, which is where maybe-Naomi must have been hanging out, because within seconds, she comes spinning around the corner toward us. And yes, I know that's not her name. And I know I just gave Stella crap for not remembering the name of the girl she said hi to when we got here. But this is different. For one, I didn't sleep with her at a party a couple of weeks ago.

"I *knew* that was you!" she squeals, hooking Stella into a hug.

When they pull apart, maybe-Naomi flicks me a chin greeting.

"Hey, Daya," she says.

"Hey." I nod, sort of. Smile, sort of. But all I really want is to get out from under the uncomfortable scorch of her gaze.

She goes, "I like how you're doing your hair now."

My hand shoots up, tries to smooth my bangs over my face. "It's the same as always."

She smiles. "So, who you going to prom with?"

I look at Stella, but she's no help.

"Uh . . . no one," I tell her.

Her smile stretches even wider. "Cool."

No. Not cool. The day just keeps sinking farther into an abyss of weirdness. I need to find a way out of this hellscape. But it seems maybe-Naomi has a different agenda.

"I hope that means you're going to Vanessa's party, then?" she asks, trying hard to hook me. So far, maybe-Naomi doesn't seem like the catch-and-release type.

"I don't . . . I'm not . . ."

Stella finally intervenes. "Go buy your food, Daya. I'll meet you outside."

I wasn't planning on buying anything until she lobbed me that save.

Maybe-Naomi throws me a peace-out as she follows Stella up front to pay for the bag of Fuego-Extra tortilla chips and a bottle of pineapple Jarritos I know she's going to get. I go to the back where they make sandwiches and Mexican food so I can breathe some air back into my lungs.

Stella's waiting out front when I come out, and maybe-Naomi is nowhere to be seen, goddess bless.

As we head back to school, Stella takes a swig of Jarritos, burps, and goes: "My mom's seeing someone new."

She squints against the reflection of sunlight blazing off the sidewalk and chomps those tortilla chips like a fucking T. rex.

"Is this a *new* new guy?" I ask, peeling the foil wrap off the burrito I bought. "Or the same new guy she had from a couple weeks ago."

"Oh, a *new* new guy. And you wanna know the best part?"

Her sarcasm meter is off the scale as she shakes her chip bag in my direction. I slide out one tortilla chip and eat it, licking the red Fuego-Extra dust off my fingers before it can stain. But I'm also watching close as her face twists like she's fighting something, and I don't know if she's about to break into a million pieces of sadness or rage-vent at the next person she sees.

"It's *Mr. Zapata*," she says. "Can you believe that shit?"

I stop walking for a second. Stella leans over and holds my hand steady as she takes a bite of my burrito. Meanwhile, my brain scrambles to catch up.

I say, "Wait, you mean—"

"Yes, Daya," she says around a chunk of deep-fried burrito. "I do mean. Mr. Zapata of second-period math. He touches my mom with the same fingers he does proofs with in class, and I now have to sit there and look at him every fucking day and think about him and her instead of derivatives and integrals."

Well, that explains some things about how Stella's been acting. I can't even laugh about it, because this obviously isn't a joke to her.

"Can't you switch out?" I ask.

She looks at me like I'm deranged. "It's *May*. The year's almost over, and besides, what am I supposed to tell them? *I want to switch out because my teacher's boning my puta mom?*"

She goes from eating chips to chewing on what's left of her thumbnail.

"I wouldn't exactly call your mom a—"

"I can't wait for this fucking year to be over," she cuts in. "I just want to go to prom, take my finals, and get the fuck out of this drama pit, at least for the summer."

I look over at her as we walk. "You never said anything about going to prom."

"Because *who goes to prom?* But then Valentina hinted that she wants to, and the more I thought about it, the more I got into it. I've already picked out my tux and everything. I just . . ."

She spits out a little chunk of fingernail. I'm surprised there's enough left for her to bite off.

"It's not like I have cash to burn, Daya," she adds. "You can't pay for something like prom with charm and good looks, or I woulda been going for free every year."

My head tips heavy in her direction. "It's not just about the money, Stells. You have to tell them who you're going with. And they won't sell you tickets if they know who your date is."

She goes, "You understand that not everyone goes to prom in couples, right? You can buy a single ticket. So, I buy a single ticket, and she buys a single ticket, and voilà! Now we're at prom together and no one has to get wrecked about it."

"They will once you start doing the tongue-tango out on the dance floor."

She goes back to chewing her nonexistent thumbnail.

"Yeah, well, it doesn't really matter at this point, does it? Either way, I can't hit prom without some cash flow."

Stella goes real quiet as we make it back to campus. Meanwhile,

I'm visually drifting between couples and cliques and food fights and Frisbee on the lawn, and posters with a million end-of-year reminders for students, like about finals and yearbook distribution and graduation and prom.

And Pure Prom.

"Hey, Stells?" I fish the flyer Beckett gave me this morning out of my bag.

She goes, "Mm?"

"Have you heard about this?"

"Maybe. What is it?"

I hand the flyer to her, watch her eyes scroll down the paper.

"Is this for real?" she asks.

"Yeah."

She busts out laughing. "This has to be a joke," she says. *"Pure Prom?"*

"Okay, so it's a bad name—"

"Daya, I wouldn't stick one toe in something called Pure Prom even if they *paid me* to take a girl as my date."

"Why not?"

"God gets all the GLORY?" she quotes off the flyer.

"I know, but it's *free*. And you can pretend you're not a couple there just as easy as you can at the other prom. Lots of people—"

"Oh, come on." She hands the flyer back to me. "It's probably just conversion therapy disguised as giddy frolic."

She's right. Of course she's right.

I take a breath. That was the reality check I needed. There is no "safe prom alternative" for people like us.

Not at Escondido High.

Not in the town of Escondido.

And especially not somewhere like Grace Redeemer.

I crumple the flyer into a tight ball and toss it in the next trash can I pass. I need to pull myself together. Even if I did go to Pure Prom, Beckett would still be there with Cason. I won't be able to dance with her. I won't be able to talk to her the way I did at Justin Tadeo's party. Or in my room yesterday. I'll be sitting there like someone's kid sister, watching her have all the hetero fun in the universe and feeling miserable about it. Whatever fantasy I have that going to Beckett's prom is the same as going to prom with Beckett is just that.

A fantasy.

Ten

CHULA'S

Oscar Díaz tosses a folded piece of paper onto my desk as soon as Señora Muñoz turns her back.

"Yo, why don't you two get a room or something?" he whispers to me, loud enough for a handful of people to hear. I tune out their giggles and open the note.

meet out front after school?

I look up at Beckett. She's twisted around in her seat, smiling. Blush and heat flash off my face as I nod my answer.

After school, I rush out front and spot Beckett straddling her scooter at the curb in front of the flagpoles.

"Want to go for a ride?" she asks as I move closer. She's holding two helmets.

I run the tip of my finger along the fender of her hand-painted Vespa. Paisleys. Polka dots. Mountains. Flamingos. Palm trees. I'd drink in all that color, if I thought it would radiate out of me the way it does with Beckett.

"Did *you* paint this?"

"Yeah."

"It's really cool," I tell her as I walk around it.

"Thanks." She says it with a shrug, like it's no big deal, like she hand-paints a vintage scooter every other Tuesday.

"How do you even have this?" I ask.

"I worked my ass off at the shop since I was, like, twelve so I could buy it."

I glitch on the word *ass* coming from her.

"Here," she says, handing me a helmet.

I stare at it before taking it from her, watch as she buckles her strap. She turns to smile at me.

"You coming?" she says, and my mouth goes so lust-dry, all I can do is lick my lips and nod.

I keep my arms loose around her so I don't come off pervy as she reaches low between her legs to switch something on. Then, with one foot still on the ground, she tips the scooter to the side a degree or two, and I have no choice but to tighten my grip so I don't fall off as she starts the engine. With barely enough room for a passenger, there's nowhere for Beckett to be but pressed all the way against me. The scooter is vibrating. *I'm* vibrating. My whole body. Every cell of it. This girl . . . this daydream of a human, this cloud floating silently by me every day for three years . . . somehow, I'm sitting on the back of her Vespa, and she's pressed into me, and I'm the one who's floating.

I don't ask where we're going—honestly it doesn't matter. I'd ride across the face of the earth as long as it means leaning up against her like this. Her hair teases me through the opening of the helmet. Not much more than a warm breeze separates me from the curve and softness of her skin.

We pull up in front of a card table restaurant called Chula's.

Escondido has lots of these little hole-in-the-wall restaurants, but there's only one Chula's.

"Excellent choice," I say, sliding off the back of the scooter.

"They have the best coffee," she tells me. "Better than any chain."

"And killer tortillas."

Her face lights up. "I know, right? *So* good. And they're *huge*."

Inside, we order two coffees and a basket of homemade tortillas and sit down at a rickety table near the back. Waves of music, strings and horns, dance around us.

Si la Adelita se fuera con otro,
La seguiría por tierra y por mar. . . .

"I saw you today," she says. "At lunch."

"You did? Where?"

"Down at Food City, with your wife."

My face flames out for a second.

A woman in a Chula's shirt comes by and sets our coffees and the basket of tortillas on the table. Beckett reaches over, tears a strip off one of the tortillas, and inhales deeply.

"Holy *crap*, these are so good," she says on the exhale.

I watch her fold the strip she peeled off and pop it into her mouth, and when she's fully loaded and unable to talk, I say, "Fool."

She stops chewing.

"What?"

"Where you saw me today? It's . . . it's Fool City."

"*Fool* City?"

"The curve of the *D* is burned out on the sign out front."

"Huh." The tiniest smile tugs at one corner of her mouth. "I never noticed that."

"Yeah, so. Now it's just Fool City. And Stella's not my wife. She's my best friend."

I notice how her neck tenses up as she finishes chewing and swallows.

"Okay."

Now that things are awkward, I tear off a piece of tortilla as well, roll it up, take a bite.

"I'm a little disappointed in myself," she says. "I'm usually better about noticing those kinds of details. About the sign?"

She squints like she's conjuring an image of it, trying to visualize the burned-out part of the letter.

"Details matter," I say, reaching for a sugar packet.

I'm just about to rip it open when Beckett says, "Wait," and wraps her hand around mine, sugar packet and all.

"Watch this." She lets me go, then pulls her coffee cup directly in front of her.

I pry my attention away from the invisible imprint of her hand on mine and watch as she picks up a small metal pitcher. From several inches above, she pours a thin, slow stream of cream into the cup, and we lean in close so we can see what happens through the clear glass.

The reaction is immediate.

"I love how it spins into itself," she says. "Like it's forming a tiny galaxy inside a miniature universe."

I look up at her, but she's still lost inside her tiny coffee galaxy.

"You should try it," she says.

I slow-spill the cream into my cup exactly the way Beckett did and watch as it swirls.

I go, "I have to admit, that's pretty cool."

"That's one of the reasons I love coming here," she says. "You can see everything inside these clear mugs. Any little thing you do sets off a whole new chain reaction. So, then, if you do this . . ."

She flicks a sugar packet, meticulously peels it open, and pours it into her coffee so slow and deliberate, I can almost count the individual granules of sugar going in. Unlike with the cream, this reaction is frantic, almost violent—like a mini–Big Bang. Before long, it settles into a kind of nebula, where the sugar crystals fall away like shooting stars.

"You like being the deity of a teeny-tiny universe, don't you?" I say.

We both laugh a little, but our laughter fizzles back into silence pretty fast.

I decide to add sugar to my cup to see what happens.

"I can't say fool," she says out of the blue.

I look up.

"What do you mean?"

"My dad . . . I'm not allowed to use the word *fool*."

"Why not?"

"It's in the Bible."

A gut-punch reminder of how pointless it is to ache for someone who could never ache for me back.

"He says the Bible uses the word *fool* for anyone who isn't a believer," she tells me. But then she shakes her head a little, that smile still tugging at her. "Fool City, though. That's kind of perfect."

She picks up her spoon, stirs the cream and sugar around in her cup. Her lips just barely brush the rim as she takes a sip.

"Seriously," she says. "I don't know what they do here, but it's just . . . the best."

I'd give anything to be that coffee mug she keeps pressing her lips against.

The awkwardness is so dense now, I can't tunnel to the end of it.

Beckett seems to feel it too.

She goes, "Okay, rando question."

"Do it." I take a sip of coffee to help clear all that soft-focus out of my head.

She goes, "What's the last picture you took with your phone?"

Easy. "I snapped some graffiti on the side of the parking garage at the old mall the other day."

"Graffiti?" She makes a strange face. "Why graffiti?"

I think back to when Joanna taught me about counting train cars when I was little. How, when I'd hang out with my grandpa, he taught me to look even closer, at how they were painted instead.

"It's all about the lines of it," I tell her. "And the saturation of color. It's pretty spontaneous too."

She couldn't be more confused if I told her I'd taken a picture of a UFO that landed nearby.

"Why the face?" I ask.

"No, I . . . I guess I just never thought about graffiti that way."

"What way?"

Her gaze floats around the room.

"Like . . . art," she finally says.

Now I'm surprised. "What else would it be?"

"I don't know, I guess I always just thought of it as, like . . . visual noise," she says. "Like something that's not supposed to be there."

Wow.

"Why the face?" She echoes my question from earlier, but there's no smile behind the poke.

"No, I'm just . . . I'm confused, because . . . I mean, you're an artist."

"Yeah, I know, but . . ."

She sounds defensive, like she thinks I'm judging her. I'm not, though. I don't think I am. I'm just curious. And she's a curiosity.

I spin my cup a few times, waiting for her to finish her thought. When I change directions, the current inside the cup shifts with it.

But she doesn't say anything else, so I go, "My grandpa had this thing he used to say. Something like, when we can't see an object as art, it's only because someone has convinced us it isn't."

She picks up her cup, holds it in both hands, lets her gaze drift out the window. I can't tell if she's mad, or just thinking, or if it's something else. I scramble to come up with another kind of question to get the conversation going again.

"Okay, I've got one for you," I say. "What's the most repeated song on your playlist?"

She swings her gaze back to me.

"'Nowhere, Girl,'" she says without even blinking.

I'm the one who's blinking.

"By Cassie Ryan?" I ask.

She nods. "I love that song."

"Cassie Ryan, the—?" I stop short before saying the words *queer icon*, simply adding, "Your parents are okay with you listening to her?"

A wash of pink crawls up her neck into her face.

"My parents think I only listen to the music they've bought me. Plus, they don't actually know what I listen to since I always use head-phones, and . . . yeah. I bought the CD so I wouldn't have to download the album on their account." She cuts a look in my direction. "They definitely have no idea she was the first secular concert I ever went to."

My brain is reeling with questions. So many questions. Beckett likes C.Ry? How does she even know C.Ry? Maybe it's because her music feels rebellious, and someone like Beckett would need safe ways to be rebellious. But I mean, "Nowhere, Girl" is literally an under-ground lesbian anthem, and it's also the most played song in Beckett's playlist, and I can't figure out how those two things can both be true. I bet her parents would freak if they knew what that song was about. I bet Beckett would get excommunicated from church if they knew she listened to "Nowhere, Girl."

Why don't we head out to nowhere, girl?
Just hitch a ride to you-know-where, girl?

The sound of ice dropping into a cup at the fountain hits the air hard. Even the rush of bubbles pouring over the top of the ice sounds magnified, the shuffle of a customer's shoes against the floor as they move from the soda fountain to a nearby table.

"So, did you sneak out for that concert?" I ask. "Or . . . ?"

"They knew I was going to a concert, I just never said which one. Rays of Son was playing at church that night, so I guess they assumed that's where I went." She shakes her head as if that will erase the memory. Or the sin. "I felt bad about lying to them, especially because they never found out."

I felt bad about lying to them. Not: *I felt bad about going to an underground lesbian concert instead of the Christian rock concert my parents thought I went to.*

She takes another sip of her coffee.

"I see how you're looking at me," she says. "I'm not a bad person."

I'm not looking at her like she's a bad person. Am I? Because I don't think that liking C.Ry makes Beckett a bad person. But I do feel like it makes her a confusing person.

"They don't understand that secular stuff doesn't have to be sinful," she says, even though "Nowhere, Girl" would definitely qualify as more than just "secular." "And there's no point trying to argue with them about that. There's no point trying to argue with them about anything when the only answer to every question is *because* . . . y'know? *Because I said so. Because it's God's will. Because* is the thing parents say when they don't want anyone to prove they're wrong about anything. Besides . . . my parents don't believe in explaining their logic, or even just . . . giving reasons."

"Is that why you sneak around sometimes?" I ask.

She looks at me like she's hurt or offended.

"I mean, like Justin's party. I'm just trying to understand," I say.

Her forehead wrinkles. "You can't. No one could ever understand what it's like."

"What what's like?"

I hold my breath so I don't scare her answer away.

She looks into her cup.

"It's weird, because . . . my parents tried for ten years to have me. My mom . . . like, every time she got pregnant, it ended in a miscarriage. She did have one baby, but it was too premature to survive. Then she got pregnant with me, and . . . I think she kept waiting for things to go bad. For nine months they prayed that I'd be the healthy, normal baby they'd always wanted. And I was. They believed I came into the world perfect, sent to them as an answered prayer and a gift from God."

Her words drip down around us.

"You have no idea how hard that is, Daya. Seventeen years of holding myself to their standard of perfection."

"Then stop," I say. "No one's perfect. It's impossible and unfair."

She shakes her head, starts to fidget, her fingers twisting around each other on top of the table. She spins that thin gold ring she always wears, slips it halfway up her finger, then down again.

"They don't know who I really am," she whispers.

I wonder if Beckett knows who she really is. Or if she'd be able to accept who she was once she did know. Is she doing things that go against her own nature just to keep up her parents' dream of a perfect daughter? The same way I try to keep Joanna's fantasy of a "normal" daughter afloat.

"Why do you keep looking at me like that?" she says.

"Like *what*?"

"Like that," she says. "That face you're making."

127

But I never get a chance to answer.

Beckett's phone goes off. She looks at the screen and says, "Oh, *shit.*"

"Everything okay?" I ask. Stupid question. Obviously, everything isn't okay.

She shoves her phone and wallet back into her bag as fast as she can. "I can't take you home, Daya, I'm *so* sorry."

"That's cool. Um. Maybe we can get together tomorrow, for our project?"

"I'll try," she says, rushing to the door. "I promise."

I'm still staring through the window a few seconds later, at the empty spot where her Vespa had been parked. At the invisible shape of her, just before she sped off. My brain works double time to fill all the negative space Beckett leaves behind. . . .

She loves C.Ry.

She loves making mini-universes inside cups of coffee.

She sneaks out of the house sometimes to peel off some of the constant pressure she's under to be perfect.

Only she's not perfect.

There are all these layers to her that I never saw before now, all cracked or flawed in some way.

I wish I could tell her how amazing all that imperfection actually makes her.

If I'm lucky, I'll get the chance to.

Tomorrow.

Eleven

THE KITCHEN

Going home after school can feel like a walk-on in one of my mother's murder shows. There's a fifty-fifty chance the house is either empty or someone is lurking behind the drapes with a machete.

Today feels like a machete day.

It's a couple-mile walk from where Beckett left me at Chula's with a basket of tortillas and two mostly full cups of coffee. The half-vacant strip mall is midway between where the streets turn into boutiques and gastropubs toward Beckett's end of town and the mostly boarded-up shops and dilapidated buildings on the way to mine.

I head out a few minutes after she does and start walking—past the abandoned gas station where they filmed a Christmas movie a few years ago called *Saguaros and Santas*. Between the Mercado El Toro and Escondido Methodist, where a gigantic mural of happy, smiling white people on one side of an open Bible and Mexicans toiling the fields on the other side has mostly faded into a memory. I wonder if Beckett thinks this mural is visual noise too. In my eye, there's more visual noise in this piece of whitewashed historical fiction than in a thousand pieces of graffiti art.

When I get home from Chula's, Joanna's car isn't in front of the house, and I breathe a little sigh of relief about it. But it's only a temporary relief. There's nowhere to hide in this house. There's nowhere to hide in this whole town.

Even though the walk home isn't horrible, I still collapse on my bed as soon as I get there, and instantly fall into a deep sleep.

The sound of the front door slamming shut jolts me out of a dream tunnel. I check the time on my phone.

Six fifteen.

Joanna's home and I haven't even started dinner yet.

She's in the bathroom, showering away the day's makeup and formaldehyde, when I scramble out of my room. I sneak into the kitchen, hoping to get something started before she comes out.

I'm still looking through the cupboards when she shuffles in wearing her standard yoga pants and an oversized T-shirt.

"Is grilled cheese okay?" I ask.

"That's fine." She sits at the table with her mineral water, twists her legs up lotus style, closes her eyes, and begins to breathe deep. She sometimes pretends to do the relaxation exercises her therapist taught her back in the day, but I feel like it's mostly for show. Maybe I wouldn't feel that way if there had ever been some kind of tangible change in her mood as a result.

I move slow and careful as I get out a loaf of bread, a block of cheese, a stick of butter, trying my best not to make too much noise. The air in the kitchen is so thick and still that the sounds of the stove clicking on and the butter sizzling in the pan hang suspended deep inside it.

She doesn't unfold herself or open her eyes until she hears me set a plate down in front of her. Then she tracks my movements to the counter and back to bring napkins. Her gaze lowers in sync with me as I take my seat.

"What?" I finally say.

"Where is it?"

My mind buzzsaws through everything she could possibly mean.

"Where is what?"

"Suzanne told me she's seen you take things. I just didn't want to believe it until now."

My aunt has seen me *take things?* I lay the triangle of grilled cheese back on my plate. Like what, my grandpa's Adelita statue no one else wanted? I literally took that out of a box of his stuff she was donating to Goodwill.

"Are you selling them, is that it?"

. . . there's so much shit in this yard . . . occasionally when he goes out of town, I sell some of it off.

B'Rad . . . the estate sale . . .

"Are you talking about the urn?" I say.

"Yes, Daya, where is it?"

"I hid it."

She wasn't expecting me to say that—I can see it on her face.

She goes, "You *hid* it?"

"Yes."

"Why?"

But I can't tell her why. I can't say it's because I had company over. That's one of Joanna's house rules. *I don't want you having people over when I'm not home.* She never says boys. She always says *people.*

"Why would you hide it?" she asks again.

"It was upsetting."

She puts her finger to her lips and frowns into it. "Upsetting, how?"

"Thinking about Grandpa being inside there," I say.

It's not untrue. It's just not the truth about why I moved it yesterday.

She drops her finger, leans forward.

"He's not in there," she tells me. "I haven't been able to bring myself to put him there. Suzanne keeps telling me he needs a permanent home, but—"

"He had a permanent home."

My mother tips her head.

"He was sick, Daya. Grandma couldn't take care of him anymore, you know that."

"I think it's wrong to stick him in a little box and call it a *home*," I tell her. "I think it's wrong to leave him on the bookcase like he's a souvenir."

She nods like she gets it, but I doubt if she really does.

She says, "That's because you're still grieving him."

"Aren't *you* still grieving him?"

She swallows, takes a breath.

"Your grandpa isn't in that box, Daya. Even if his ashes were in there, that's not him."

"He still deserves better."

The thick veil of her lashes absorbs her tears before they can fully surface.

"Sometimes, what we think we deserve isn't always God's plan for us," she says.

I count twelve clicks of the second hand on the wall clock before quietly saying, "I think that's BS."

It's obvious by the look on her face that I've hurt her, but I'm not sure what to do about it. I can't force myself to accept her theory of a God whose "plan" for us means less humanity than we deserve. Even after we're gone.

"After dinner," she says, "I want you to go get the urn and put it back."

"I'll do it now. I'm not hungry."

"No, sit down," she tells me. "I have more to say."

I slowly lower myself back onto the chair.

She pushes her plate away by an inch or so.

"Last night was a real wake-up call for me, Daya." She nods like she's encouraging herself to go on. "I think Stella is a bad influence on you—"

"Don't you mean *Suzanne* thinks Stella's a bad influence on me?" I ask.

I can't stop myself, even when I see the basket-weave of anger and hurt all over her face. Suzanne is doing a real head-job on my mom. I'm watching in real time as my aunt turns her into Suzanne 2.0. Joanna needs to hear the truth.

She leans back.

"Why don't you like Suzanne?" she asks.

"*You* don't like Suzanne," I tell her. "You've said it yourself."

"No. I never said that. I idolized her, Daya. I did everything she did."

"You said she bullied you into doing what she did so you would be just like her."

Joanna's not convinced. She likes her version of the story better than mine.

"Honestly?" I say. "I don't blame you. I'd probably do . . . literally *whatever* to get Suzanne off my back too."

"So, you think taking my life in a positive direction is just me trying to appease my sister?"

"I don't know. Maybe."

She crosses her arms, drums a single finger against her shoulder, and suddenly I'm ten again, telling my mom, "I know you gave all our old stuff to charity, but I think it's time to get some new furniture. You shouldn't be sleeping on the floor. Neither of us should." I remember feeling so grown-up that day—with zero understanding of how unhealthy that role reversal actually was. How, in some ways, it hasn't completely shifted out of that, even now.

"You know, it's really okay to do things Suzanne wouldn't approve of," I tell her.

If I had to guess by her expression, this thought has never once crossed her mind.

"What do you mean?" She sounds both defensive and curious. "Like what?"

"Like . . . not keep Grandpa in a claustrophobic urn, when you and I both know he would have hated that."

Joanna shakes her head. "What would you rather—"

"Take him to the Grand Canyon. Or Joshua Tree. Let him be somewhere he loved."

She looks like she might possibly consider this, but all she says is, "Suzanne would kill me."

I want to tell her Suzanne's already killing her. That she's slowly suffocating her with her need to be right. To be right*eous*.

But I don't.

I don't think my mother could handle that right now. She thinks she's taken her life in a positive direction, and maybe that's true. Except I know how she operates. In a way, it's like an addictive person trading in cigarettes for sweets. She's still meeting a need without understanding what's driving her to it. And I know that Joanna is fragile, always one small life-quake away from absolute shatter.

Again.

I lie on my bed with only the string lights on overhead. Not so much doom-scrolling as dread-scrolling. Because my feed is full of either prom-related posts or church-related posts, and I'm not interested in either one right now.

Tell me something good, I text Stella.

Good is for angels and chumps, she writes back.

Then tell me something spicy.

Valentina Orozco is a bomb-ass kisser.

She's no help.

I go to Beckett's feed. She hasn't posted anything new today.

I go to Lucy's feed, out of simple curiosity. It's mostly all group pictures.

Her and Javi Benitez.

Her and Javi and Cason.

Her and Cason.

Her and Beckett.

Her and Beckett.

Her and Beckett.

Her at youth group, it looks like.

Her up on the stage at Grace Redeemer, getting dunked in a tub of water. The sign in the background says: THE REDEMPTION BAPTISM EXPERIENCE. It's from last July.

Is that what Joanna not-so-secretly wants me to do? Is that what a connection to God looks like, Grace Redeemer–style? Getting baptized onstage in front of everyone, with a live internet feed so anyone who wants to can watch? It's performative Christianity, that's all. It doesn't feed people. It doesn't clothe people. It doesn't put a roof over anyone's head.

I swipe one more time, land on a group photo where everyone's dressed in formal wear. It's from a year ago, so . . . prom? I pop in to get a closer look at Beckett, standing between Lucy and Cason. Lucy is turned, smiling at her bestie. Cason looks like he's trying to use X-ray vision to get a peek at his girlfriend's chest.

And Beckett? Beckett looks . . . radiant. I don't know how else to put it. Even surrounded by their weird, murky energy, she's luminous.

I wish I could have been there with her, instead of Cason. I wish there was some configuration of the universe where Beckett and I could go to prom, dance, kiss. Maybe lie out under the stars after and reflect ourselves back to them. Our flawed, imperfect selves, so open and willing that we don't need to be perfect to shine back into the universe.

I let out a breath I must have been holding, close out of IG, and shoot a text to B'Rad.

What ru doing right now?

He sends me a hot dog emoji.

Can we meet at lunch tomorrow? I want to ask you something.

I get a thumbs-up in return.

If he wasn't working, I would've just asked him.

But he's too busy to talk, which gives me time to change my mind, if I want to.

As C.Ry sings track 8, "What's It Gonna Be?," in my ear, I ask myself:

What's it gonna be, Daya? Are you bold enough to follow through with this?

Or are you gonna chicken out by tomorrow?

Twelve

THE GREAT WAIT

"Thanks for walking early with me," I say as we pass between the stone columns in front of school.

"It's no sweat," Stella says. "Besides, I was gonna go retake Zapata's calc test anyway. Gotta keep my A up in that class."

"You mean, having your mom be his booty call isn't enough?" I say, nudging against her, relieved that she finally told me about this. Once Stella speaks a thing into existence, it usually takes all the power out of it.

"Right, okay, well . . . you're going into a Conversion Club meeting, so. Looks like you may already be brainwashed," she says back, waving her middle finger at me as we split off in different directions.

There's a sting in her tease. I know she's quasi-joking. I know she doesn't get how the whole Grace Redeemer experience hit me, because I've been blowing it off every time the conversation swerves in that direction. And she's not stupid—she knows the vague shape of my feelings for Beckett. I mean . . . I've had a proximity crush on her for three years. But I've never felt the need to share the finer details of it even with Stella. Some things have to belong just to ourselves.

As usual, the only people around school this time of morning are a handful of teachers and custodians, and of course, a steady trickle of Great Wait members.

The door to room 333 is closed when I get there. I don't know if Beckett's inside yet. All I know is, I definitely don't want to be the first to go in.

I jump at the sudden *"Boo!"* next to my ear. At least she doesn't cover my eyes from behind. I hate that.

"You're back," Beckett says when I spin around.

I feel like I just got caught peeking through her bedroom window or something.

"Yeah, I . . . uh . . ."

She hijacks my awkward attempt at an explanation by asking, "Does this mean you're coming on Saturday?"

"I don't know," I say, my heart stammering just a little because of the deal I made with myself last night. After a couple hours of back and forth about whether to ask B'Rad to do Pure Prom with me, I decided to go to one more Great Wait meeting. The answer, I felt sure, would be here. "I mean, maybe."

"You're such a tease, Daya!"

The word pulses in the air between us.

So far, Nestor and Alexa are the only other people here. They're wearing the same blue *True Love Waits* T-shirts I saw on Sunday, only these say *Ask Me About Pure Prom* on the front, in big yellow letters.

"Wow," I whisper as we head to the back of the room. "That's next-level commitment."

"They're handing them out again today," Beckett tells me.

"Handing what out?"

"The shirts." She nods in Nestor's direction.

I blink a few times before asking, "To who?"

"Everyone. They've been going around since spring break, from campus to campus, every school from here to Oviedo, handing them out." She catches the look on my face and adds, "It's to boost attendance."

"Wait, so . . . they're handing all those T-shirts out for *free?*"

"Yep."

I think back to Sunday, to the "giving" portion of the service. All the options for ways to donate. How everyone in the jam-packed building took out their phones or their wallets, credit cards, phones, cash, and paid *something*. I can't even begin to calculate how much money that must bring in every week. No wonder they can afford to give out free T-shirts by the truckload.

Beckett tilts toward me and drops her voice even lower.

She goes, "Sorry about ditching you yesterday."

The touch of her arm pressed against mine stitches itself into my skin.

I back away without being too obvious about it. It's hard enough just to sit in the same room with her, knowing what's real and what isn't. And I never want to be one of those people who confuses niceness with flirtation, but damn if this doesn't feel like something a few notches above merely *nice*.

Beckett instantly notices the shift.

"Everything okay?" she asks.

I nod. "Everything okay with you? I mean, you bolted out of Chula's pretty fast yesterday."

She starts fidgeting with her gold ring again.

"I promised my dad I'd do something for him after school, and—"

I wait for her to finish, but she stops there.

"And . . . ?"

Her gaze drops completely away, but all she says is, "He has this thing about being trustworthy."

The door to room 333 swings open and Cason rolls in, followed as always by Lucy and a few others.

Cason scuds right for us.

"Hey, babe!" he says, dive-bombing Beckett with a kiss.

Nestor lobs a swift look in their direction, smoothing down the front of his True Love Waits shirt.

I swallow hard as I watch them in my peripheral vision. His technique could use some work. Like he's channeling the proverbial bull in a china shop. I would kiss her slow. And soft. Like tasting the first peach of summer—not like diving into a bucket of hot wings from the QT gas station on route 9.

Lucy throws me eyes like she can tell what I'm thinking.

After Cason plants one last chicken-peck on Beckett, he straddles the chair on the other side of her, and Lucy sits directly behind us, weapons-grade shade pouring out of her in my direction. I look away as the room begins to fill with people and the band starts playing a fresh acoustic jam.

Nestor finally comes to the front and calls on us to bow our heads in prayer.

"Lord, we ask for Your blessing in every endeavor. We choose to glorify You in word and deed, Lord, to commit ourselves to purity in our hearts and purity in our bodies, because all our thoughts and actions sanctify You."

His *amen* is echoed by everyone in the room except me.

Alexa comes forward next and reads off the day's action plan.

"If your team still needs to buy stuff, purchase orders are now in your packets, so you can go after school and get whatever you need. Food committee, you can buy things that don't have to be refrigerated, like candy, but the parent team will get everything else. Oh, and save your receipts. Team leaders, come get your manila envelopes with your group's budget, purchase orders, and task list inside."

Beckett bumps me with her elbow and motions me to follow.

Cason is too busy talking to Javi Benitez to notice what his girl-friend is doing. Lucy, on the other hand, tracks every movement Beckett makes, like she's her personal Secret Service detail.

I stare at her for a beat or two as I follow Beckett down the steps. She's not shy about staring back.

I don't care. Whatever Lucy's jealousy is made of, I kind of hope she chokes on it.

As we wait in line for the officers to hand out committee packets, Beckett tells me, "We're signed up for Ticketing. It seemed like the easiest one."

We? She must mean her and Cason and Lucy, because I never said—

"How many on your team?" Nestor asks as Beckett steps forward to get her packet. She takes the envelope from him and says, "Four." She looks at me and smiles. "Five."

I toggle from Beckett to Nestor, then back again. "Wait, no, I never said I was—"

Before I can even finish, he hands her five T-shirts and pushes us off to one side, where Beckett slides the paperwork out and gives it a quick once-over.

I'm one part elation and one part terror at the possibility that my indecision may have just answered itself. She said *we*.

She wants me there.

She wants . . . me.

"Yeah, so, all we need is those vinyl wristbands that are impossible to tear off, which I think we already have. And we should each download the QR scanner too. Then on prom night, we just scan tickets and make sure everyone gets a wristband. As soon as they close the doors, the rest of the night is ours."

Sometimes, Beckett Wild walks around like she's permanently wearing one of those sparkle filters that she and her friends seem to love. *The rest of the night is ours.* Man. If only that could be remotely true. *Ours.* As in *mine and hers.*

She looks up at me, smiles.

"What?" she asks, and I shake myself out of it.

"Aren't we supposed to monitor who comes and goes or something?" I ask.

"We?"

Whoosh. Ignition.

"If I go, I mean."

"You do realize that's your first *we*." Her gaze eases into mine. "I guess that makes it official."

It does. I'm officially a flame that can no longer be extinguished.

"Don't worry," she says. "No one can come or go. It's a lock-in."

"It's a . . . what?"

"A lock-in?" she says.

"Okay . . . what does that mean, exactly?"

I can't tell if she's confused or amused.

"It literally means they lock us in overnight. Which is great for us."

The phrase *lock us in* knocks the wind out of me. But the *great for us* part finishes me off.

"Great, *how?*" I ask.

She slips the papers back inside the envelope. "No exit privileges means we're off the hook as bouncers. We can just go have fun."

That word rings in my ears like someone shot off a rifle next to my head. And it keeps ringing as we meet back up with Cason and Lucy to dot the *i*'s on the to-do list in our instruction packet.

In fact, the whole phrase *we can just go have fun* screech-echoes on reverb.

People like Beckett can *just go have fun* at something called Pure Prom. People like Beckett and Cason can dry hump in the front seat of the car and tell themselves they're still chaste and pure and virtuous or whatever, and everyone is okay with that. People like Lucy can judge me for being the token lesbian at a Great Wait meeting without worrying about sounding less like a protective friend and more like a jealous girlfriend.

But people like me have to peek through the fence slats on a daily basis. Lift the bottom hem of the curtain, wondering who's coming for us. We don't just listen to a person's words—we study the spaces between the words. The exhale of a person's breath. The shape of the letters as they talk to us, or about us. We would never *not* know if the curve of the *D* is burned out on the Fool City sign. Someone like me doesn't get to go to Pure Prom and *just have fun*. We have to look over our shoulder, hold our breath until we make it home safe—if home even *is* safe. We don't get to *just have fun*. It's not fun. It's fucking exhausting.

B'Rad shoves a pink pastry box across the lunch table at me. "So what did you want to ask me about last night?"

Damn. I was kind of hoping he'd forgotten about that.

"Nothing," I say. "Just a rando late-night idea."

A rando late-night idea that I'm ridiculously fixated on. Even though the possibility of going to Pure Prom to spend time with a girl who's probably-straight-but-giving-off-Care-Bear-energy is so far out there, it has no place to land. I mean, really? Go to a dance where I can't technically be with the person I want, surrounded by people who hate who I am? On what planet?

"I love rando late-night ideas," B'Rad says.

I shake my head. "It's so cringe!" I say with a pained laugh.

But B'Rad just sits there, waiting to hear it.

"Okay. I know it's not your original invitation, but . . . did you know that there's a prom alternative . . . and it's free?"

B'Rad's nod is not unlike the nod he uses when negotiating a deal on shit from his granddad's lot. "Go on," he says.

"It's . . . it's Pure Prom." I hope my face adequately reflects the pain of this agonizingly embarrassing suggestion.

But B'Rad seems unfazed.

"Honestly, Daya, it doesn't matter which prom we go to," he says, reaching into the pastry box. "Prom, Pure Prom . . . Alien Prom, it's all the same to me."

"Really?" I slide out a donut, courtesy of Mrs. Morales, who saves B'Rad the leftovers from the Great Wait meetings whenever she can. She knows he doesn't always get breakfast.

He says, "I just want to hang out and have fun with you. Look. I already offered to be your date. So, what you're really begging me to be is your—"

"I swear to God, B'Rad, if you say *beard* . . ." I tell him. "This whole thing is already confusing. Don't make it weird, too."

"Fine, I won't. But . . . maybe someone whose super-clandestine crush will also be at said event might *need* a beard."

The whoosh of my heart is literally the only thing I can hear for a few seconds.

"Shit . . . really?" I say when I finally exhale again.

"Don't worry," he whispers. "Your secret's safe with me."

"Is it that obvious?"

B'Rad pushes his glasses up.

He goes, "It's more of an energy thing."

This is bad. If my feelings for Beckett are obvious to B'Rad, who else are they obvious to?

"What up, bitches!"

Stella appears out of nowhere and plunks herself next to me on the concrete bench. I give B'Rad a desperate look and a minuscule shake of my head, praying he gets the message. He volleys a subtle nod that he understands: My secret stays on lockdown, even from Stella. She's like a sister to me, yes. But sometimes my sister has a mouth big enough to remind me that things like this aren't always safe in her hands.

"*Donuts!*" she blurts.

He slides the box toward her, and she spends way too long deciding which one is worthy of her consumption. I've seen her land a girl at a party faster than this.

"So, what are we talking about?" she asks, shoving a chocolate bar with sprinkles into her mouth.

"Just so you know?" he tells her. "That's a Jesus donut. You're eating the body of Christ."

"As long as it doesn't make me straight, it's all good."

B'Rad snickers, and I go, "You *both* need Jesus."

"Since you asked," he says, "we were debating the pros and cons of zoos."

He launches into a recap of a conversation we never actually had, and I'm fascinated by how easy this bogus narrative just spills out of him. Same as he did with Joanna at his "estate sale," with that story about his parents dying some horrible death.

By the time Stella finishes her donut, B'Rad has successfully pulled her into a debate about the cruelty of keeping animals in captivity simply for the gaze of the curious human.

While they go on, I quietly roll thoughts of Beckett around in my head. Her arm heat-fused to mine at the meeting this morning. The way she says *the best* about anything from coffee to my line doodles. How beautiful she's going to look at prom. How at some point, Cason

Price will drape his arm around her without even thinking about what it really means to be able to touch her, and I'd die a hundred kinds of death wishing it was me, not him.

She's coming over after school today. All I should be thinking about right now is making sure we crush our presentation. Not the endless ways in which I pathetically crush on her.

Valentina Orozco strolls by, head-to-toe the fly vibe Stella always falls for, and Stella's whole chest and neck goes red when she sees her.

"Have fun, kids," she says, swiping another donut out of the box before she runs to catch up with her. I watch her give the donut to Valentina, watch Valentina peck her on the cheek as a thanks, watch a kid nearby call out, "God hates fags!"

Stella goes, "She hates hypocrites and liars too, so you can fuck right off."

B'Rad snort-nods.

"I wish I knew how to do that," I say, watching them walk away.

"Do what?"

"I wish I could be part of Stella's zero fucks club, you know? That *God hates fags* bullshit freaks me all the way out. You can't get away from it. Not at this school, not in this town. It's like . . . there are some things even adults have no trouble looking away from. I wish I could challenge it the way Stella does."

He rubs his ear and goes, "Why can't you?"

I think about Joanna. How even early on, there were subtle messages, about how we were not to draw attention to ourselves in general, or let people see our flaws specifically. I get how her fear of being humiliated probably came from the way people at St. John's turned on her, how my dad's sins were rewritten and projected on to her in a lot of ways. But the remnants of those days still exist, and they still hold me back from defending myself or anyone else in those *God hates fags* moments. The stakes are too damn high, especially in this town. And they rise higher every single day.

But all I can say is, "It's complicated."

The bell rings, and as we pack up our stuff to walk to class, he goes, "So it's set, then. I'll be your date on Saturday." He uses air quotes around the word *date*, adding, "And, uh . . . I'll make sure Cason is impaired enough to give you some time alone with her."

Oh God . . . this whole Pure Prom idea just went from impossible to ridiculous. Me, going to Pure Prom with B'Rad. B'Rad, making sure Cason Price is super-stoned so I can low-key pretend I'm there with his girlfriend. It's too messy. It'll never get off the ground. . . .

My eye catches Beckett across the commons, walking with a group of girls I recognize from the Great Wait meeting this morning. I went to that meeting hoping the universe would give me a sign about going to Pure Prom. And I thought the message was a loud and clear NO.

But now, watching Beckett ripple past with B'Rad's still-fresh offer lying like drops of nervous sweat on the surface of my skin, I feel pulled in a very specific direction.

It makes no logical sense to say yes.

But when I look at Beckett . . . *yes* is all I know.

Thirteen

MY ROOM

I wish we could have gone to Beckett's house this time, but she doesn't seem interested in inviting me there. Maybe she's afraid of what her parents might think if she rolled in with someone like me. It's obvious how they feel about queer people, especially after what I heard at Grace Redeemer on Sunday. Maybe they think being gay is like being a vampire, and once you invite it into your home, it will never leave.

I forage for snacks before she gets here, but all I find is a half-empty bag of pretzel sticks and four cans of off-brand diet cola that have been rolling around the vegetable bin of our fridge forever. There's also a bunch of Joanna's mineral waters, but I don't know anyone besides her who likes mineral water, so I'll just have to make this work. For a split second, I think about running down to the QT at the end of the street to buy some microwave popcorn or something, but just as I reach for my bag, the doorbell rings and I'm an adrenaline bomb all over again.

I smooth down my hair and try to French tuck the front of my shirt, still messing with it as I open the door. Beckett's standing on the other side, smiling in living color.

I step aside so she can come in.

"Okay, so I brought provisions this time," she says, holding up the bag. "Two kinds of licorice, because I wasn't sure if you liked red or black. And some Cokes—sorry, but if you're Team Pepsi, we probably can't be friends."

"No, that's perfect," I say, spinning a little. "All I could find were some grossly stale pretzels and a few diet colas that may or may not be left over from my middle school graduation party. If you could call that pathetic gathering we had a *party*."

She makes face and we laugh, and she goes, "That's just sad."

"I know, right? Anyway. Joanna only drinks mineral water, and I don't do diet-anything, so."

"Yeah."

When we get to my room, I close the door and take the grocery bag from her.

She went to Fool City.

"You're not wearing your Ask Me About Pure Prom shirt," I say, sneaking a peek at her as I set the licorice and Cokes out on my desk.

"Neither are you," she says.

I smile again. "Touché."

"I went home and changed first." Her face skews pink as she says this.

I nod casually, like it doesn't mean anything that she came to my house looking fly as hell instead of like a walking billboard for purity.

I pick up a Sharpie from my desk and spin it between my fingers so I have something to do with my nervous hands.

She settles onto my bed, up near my pillow, and pulls her backpack onto her lap.

"So, Joanna," she says, digging out her notebook. "Is that your sister?"

She doesn't know—how could she?

I go, "No, actually. Joanna's my mother."

"She lets you call her by her first name?"

"She doesn't know I call her by her first name."

"Oh."

"That's a not-in-her-presence situation."

She slow-nods, makes a *gotcha* sound.

"She must've done something pretty bad to get stripped of her mom status," Beckett says.

My hand goes to the scar on my cheek, but then I push it the rest of the way into my hair so she doesn't notice. It's not about the haircut—it was never just about the haircut, or even the scar. It's about the lie she told my dad about what happened. It's about something between us that got lost that day.

Beckett tracks the movement of my hand, so I pick up the Sharpie and start spinning it again.

She goes, "Did I say something wrong?"

"No, it's just . . . after my dad left, she really struggled. She's fine. I mean, she's been working on herself, it's just . . ."

I fumble the Sharpie, bend down to pick it up. It's weird to talk about this. I've never told anyone but Stella about what happened with my mom, or about which of my dad's sins hit her the hardest: rejecting God or rejecting her.

"I don't usually talk about any of this because . . . it was all *she* talked about for a really long time. And then one day she just . . . stopped."

I lock the Sharpie between my laced fingers and glance up at

Beckett. I'd swear there's a bubble of safety and protection around us. We're untouchable in here. I feel like I can say anything.

"I always wondered where all her hurt and anger went—there's no on/off switch for that, y'know? Hurt feelings don't just go away. Anger doesn't just go away."

"When did they split up?" Beckett asks.

"When I was seven." My throat tightens around the words.

She goes, "I can't imagine what that would be like," and I don't have a response to that, because she's right. She can't imagine, not from the filter of her perfect life.

"I think she thinks those bad feelings have been healed, especially now that she—" I stop myself before saying *now that she goes to Grace Redeemer.* For a nanosecond, I'd let myself forget about Beckett's connection to that church. I don't want to shit on her experience, but I'm pretty sure Grace Redeemer hasn't taken any of that away from Joanna. Not when it drips into the space between us nearly every day.

I use the capped Sharpie to trace the overlapping circles I drew on my shoes during third period. She reaches out, slips it from me, uncaps it, and adds a couple more to the chain. When she gives it back to me, I continue the trajectory of circles up the leg of my jeans.

Beckett sticks her arm out, pushes up her sleeve, exposes the freckled skin of her forearm. I'm not sure why, until she takes the Sharpie again and draws a circle just below the bend in her elbow, then hands it back to me.

"You can't repeat a shape," she says. "And they have to have at least one point of contact."

I stare at her for a second before breaking into a slow smile.

"Okay," I say.

The triangle I draw pushes just inside her circle.

"You'd probably never have a reason to secretly call your mom by her first name," I say, handing her the pen.

She goes, "Yeah, I don't know," but then she drifts away again, like she did at the meeting this morning, and at the coffee shop yesterday afternoon. I want to say something else, something to fill the silence, but sometimes you need to give a thought room to breathe.

She adds a square that touches corner to corner with my triangle before finally, quietly adding, "It's complicated."

Our fingers touch when she hands the pen back, and the sensation fires off bottle rockets inside me.

I wait for her to explain, but she doesn't, so I ask, "What's complicated?"

"My mom. Me and my mom."

"In what way?"

I fill her square with an infinity symbol made up of tiny dots.

"Well, for starters, she's *obsessed* with my virginity."

The answer comes out quick and sharp. I look up at her, still loosely holding her wrist to keep it steady.

"Your . . . *what*?"

She pushes her hair behind her ear. "You know how, in the old days, a family would trade their daughter for cows or goats in exchange for her hand in marriage? That's what it feels like. Even just the word *purity* . . . It's like my virginity is some kind of . . . I don't know, like . . . commodity to them. *Beckett's purity—now trading on the New York Stock Exchange.*"

Since my mouth is already hanging open, I ask, "Why would your virginity be the topic of conversation in *any* context?"

"That's all we ever talk about, especially at Great Wait. We even had to make a purity promise." She holds up her hand. "I have the ring to prove it."

"Wow," I say, shaking my head in disbelief, the Sharpie hovering over my unfinished infinity symbol on her arm. "So, is it cool that I'm, like . . . holding your hand right now, or . . . ?"

We laugh uncomfortably because we both know I'm not really holding her hand. Except that I know I totally am.

She goes, "My turn."

The way she slides the Sharpie from my grasp this time . . . there's a linger to it.

She draws a circle with a line through it around my infinity symbol.

"What's that?" I ask.

"The universal no," she tells me.

"I thought you said no repeats."

"It's a different symbol."

"But it's the same shape."

We lock eyes. No one blinks or looks away. It's a game of chicken that feels like a lit match—too close to being a flame.

I'm going to have to take one for the team.

I disconnect my gaze from hers, let my fingers slip from around her wrist.

"We'll have to agree to disagree," I tell her, hoping she can't hear the pulse and shake in my voice.

Her smile still has heat behind it, like she's still in the game.

"Okay," she says.

I go, "I just need to know one thing."

"Yes?"

"Are you team red? Or team black?" I ask as I reach over and pull the two boxes of licorice off my desk and wiggle them at her.

She leans back and studies me.

"I guess that depends," she finally says.

I open the packs, take out one of each, and offer them to Beckett. She slips the black one from between my fingers and bites into it.

I tell her, "You know, most people are rabidly pro one or the other."

"Is that right?" she says.

"That's right," I say. "Black licorice is a polarizing taste. It's highly unusual for someone to like both."

Beckett chews slowly. She watches me like she knows I'm making shit up, finishes chewing and swallows, but she doesn't stop staring.

"What?" I ask.

"It's not that unusual," she says. "To like both."

Beckett Wild speaks in puzzles. She is a puzzle. A million-piece puzzle with no clear picture on it—just a landscape of disorienting and beautiful colors.

She holds the black licorice in front of my mouth and goes, "See for yourself."

I lean in. Take a bite. I don't tell her I've only ever liked the black kind.

"God, Daya," she says, and her smile evaporates into the thick air of my room. "Is it wrong that I really want to kiss you?"

My thoughts fly apart in a tornado-spin of sounds and letters with no sense or meaning to them.

"Can I?" she whispers.

I can't speak. I can barely breathe. All I can do is nod as Beckett leans in and her lips open just a bit, and right as they touch mine, I feel her smile into our kiss. And then I smile too, and since we're both smiling and kissing, our teeth click together, and I pull back thinking that's probably not supposed to happen.

We giggle, and then we stop giggling, and she eases back in. I lift my hands, stroke her hair, brush her cheeks. Of all the girls she could have picked to kiss for the first time, she chose me, and I'm too crush-drunk to process it. I open my eyes to make sure any of this is real.

Beckett is doing the same.

We laugh again softly, and I pull away shy and slow. And then we're in a free fall, like a shooting star full of galaxy dust and black licorice tongues and graffiti murals and rebellion.

"Is this okay?" she asks, pulling back to look at me.

I nod. It is. It's more than okay. It's a kaleidoscope of strange and confusing and, like, pure bliss. She presses in again, but just barely, traces my lips with her tongue. We're weaving a cocoon around us, and all I can hope for is that when we emerge, we'll be something different. Something fully formed, and beautiful.

My lips are humming by the time we finally come up for air. My whole body feels like it's found its own frequency.

She picks up my hand, studies my fingers, strokes them lightly between hers. Then she slips the promise ring off her finger and pushes it onto mine.

"It doesn't fit," she says.

"I have big knuckles."

"No, I mean . . ." She traces the outside of the gold band. "That whole idea of purity. It just . . . it doesn't fit—"

". . . Daya?"

Beckett and I snap away from each other as Joanna's slender frame fills the doorway.

I shove the ring back into Beckett's hand and inch off the bed. "Mom. This is—"

"What's going on?" she says.

"This is Beckett," I say. "From church. I . . . we're working on a Spanish project."

I pray she can't see the trail of Beckett's lips all over my face and neck as she scans the room like a forensic detective in one of her murder shows, looking for evidence of a crime.

She finally lands on Beckett.

"I think it's time for you to leave."

Beckett slides off the bed, throwing her backpack over her shoulder.

"See you tomorrow, Daya," she tells me.

I'm floored by her boldness, by the way she walks by my mom with her head all the way up on her way out.

Joanna doesn't move, not even as she tracks Beckett squeezing past her. The front door closes, and my pulse is frantic as she turns her confused eyes to me.

"What were you doing?"

"She's from church—"

Her face shifts from confusion to anger.

"What have I told you, Daya?"

"You've told me a million things—"

"I don't want you having people over when I'm not home."

Her words ring through my room with a note of panic.

"We have this huge project that we have to work on outside of class," I tell her. "What was I supposed to do?"

"Study at the library," she bites back. "Somewhere with other people around."

"What difference does it make?"

"People will *talk*."

The truth reverberates, coming back to me again and again in crushing waves. She can't let it go. She can't walk away from what happened at St. John's, no matter what other church she goes to.

"They already talk about me," I say. "All the time. That's what people do here."

I don't say it because I think she doesn't know. She knows—I see the memory of it in her flinch. The things they said. The ugly rumors. About my father. About her. And now . . . about me.

"*This* . . . is not about what happened back then," she says, pointing to my bed. "It's not about *me*."

"No, you're right. It's about *me*. It's about what people say about me. It's about what *you* hear them say. About *me*."

"They call you a *dyke*."

"I *am* a dyke."

My words shock her into silence. It's the first time she's heard them from me. It's the first time I've said them to her. Dust particles float in the air between us, backlit by the late day sun coming through my window. Hard, shallow breath labors in and out through her nose, full of something that can't be trusted.

"Why would you say that to me?" she whispers.

"Because it's true."

"It's not—"

"You and Dad used to talk about it—you even fought about it sometimes. I heard you. You've always known."

"I don't accept you that way. You need to find your way back to God—"

"No, I need you to hear me—"

"God won't accept a lesbian into His arms, Daya!"

There it is. The unspoken line we've never crossed with each other.

God won't accept an adulterer into His kingdom, she screamed at him. On her knees. *Please come back*. Tears streaming down her face. *Come back to church*. Seven-year-old Daya crouched behind the door, watching, praying to the God she always knew would love her exactly as she was, confused about why her mom couldn't seem to do the same. *Find your way back to Him, Jon, I'm begging you.*

"*You* won't accept a lesbian into your arms," I say. "It has nothing to do with God."

I grab my bag off the floor and push past her the same way Beckett did.

I have no idea where I'm going.

Only that I can't be here.

Fourteen

A PONTOON BOAT

I text Stella from a booth in the far corner of El Wok-A-Molé.

meet @ EWok?

She shoots back: **brt**

I need to talk to my best friend right now. I'm just not sure how to tell her about my fight with Joanna without telling her about Beckett, and I can't tell her about Beckett, period. When someone like her kisses someone like me, it's a secret that can never be shared, not even with a best friend. Things could get really bad for her if literally anyone found out.

Stella cruises through the door not long after I text her.

"What's wrong with your face?" she says.

I know it's meant to be a joke, but if I try to say something, I'll just start crying again.

She recoils in mock horror. "Girl, you know I love you, but damn, you do *not* cry cute."

I'm not ready to go there yet. I'm not ready to let Stella fix things by being funny.

I look out the window.

"Gotcha. Okay," she says. "Did you order anything?"

I shake my head, and she slides out of the booth. I reach into my pocket for my debit card, but she goes, "Don't sweat it," and a minute later she comes back with a table number and two Cokes. She doesn't comment on the half dozen balled-up, snot-filled napkins on the table.

"I got some egg rolls," she says.

"I'll pay you back," I sniff.

"Seriously, don't worry about it. Mr. Zapata handed me a twenty as I was leaving. He was like, *Have a good time with your friends, Stells,* but I think he just gave me money because he's excited to have my mom to himself for a change." She lifts the straw to her lips and goes, "Perv," before taking a sip.

I make face. "Has he moved in already? Cuz that would be a landspeed record."

"No, but he will. It's inevitable. I mean, it's disgusting how much they genuinely like each other. I've never seen her this way before. I don't know how to process it."

The plate of egg rolls lands unceremoniously on our table.

"Can we get more hot mustard, Ashlyn?" Stella asks, reading the woman's name off her badge. Ashlyn swipes our number off the table and heads back to the kitchen without answering.

We each take an egg roll. I dip mine in the cup of sweet chili sauce and blow on it. Stella drags hers through the minuscule dot of spicy mustard huddled against the side of the cup and bites right in.

"Wanna talk about it?" she asks, bouncing the egg roll around on her tongue to keep from scorching the inside of her mouth.

"Not really," I say.

"Do you think maybe you should?"

I open-mouth chew the bite I just took, because apparently I learned nothing by watching Stella incinerate *her* mouth literally five seconds ago.

"It won't matter," I tell her.

Ashlyn comes back, plunks Stella's hot mustard on the table, and walks away.

"Is it about Joanna?" Stella says. "I mean, most things are."

"Yeah, mostly." I drip sweet chili sauce onto my egg roll from the spoon and take another bite. This time I fully chew and swallow before adding, "Can I stay over? I don't want to be home tonight."

"Sorry, dude, I don't want to be home tonight either. You know how small our place is. The last thing I want to know about Mr. Zapata is whether he shouts out calculus functions when he comes."

"Ew!" I shriek. "Why would you say that? Now I have this image I can never unsee!"

Stella goes, "You think *I* want to be alone with that image?"

I can't help it—I start laughing, and Stella laughs with me, and her laugh is so pure and unfiltered, it makes things feel a little easier in my body.

"So, what are we gonna do until your mom and Mr. Zapata are done—*ew*. I can't even finish."

"That's what *he* said." She laughs at her own joke, and I can't help laughing, too.

I go, "Jeez, how old are you?"

She uses her egg roll to scoop up a huge blob of hot mustard.

"That's gonna hurt," I tell her.

But Stella shoves it in her mouth anyway because she's Stella, and I shake my head as her face turns red and her eyes water.

"So good!" she says through a cough, ignoring the tears streaming down her face.

I lick the grease off my fingers, then wipe them on a napkin. For a few seconds, I stare into the bowl of spicy mustard, thinking how it reminds me of something, and when I realize what that something is, I tell Stella: "I have an idea about tonight."

I pull out my phone, fire off a quick text, and wait for the reply.

It isn't long before B'Rad's rusty yellow VW wagon pulls up in front of where we're standing outside El Wok-A-Molé.

"You gotta be shitting me," Stella mumbles.

"Thanks for picking up the bat signal tonight," I tell him as we climb in.

He goes, "I know a distress call when I hear one."

"You're not as all-knowing as you think, Be Weird," Stella tells him.

"Is that right?" he says, pulling out of the parking lot toward route 9. "Do tell."

I tune them out as we cruise toward the outskirts of the Flats where the electric fields are. There's an edge to their banter that I don't want any part of. No more edge tonight. I want ease. I want to sneak back into the bubble that existed for a sliver of a moment this afternoon, when Beckett kissed me like kissing me was as natural for her as breathing. The muscle memory of that kiss is still flexing in every part of my body.

The car ride goes silent just before we get to B'Rad's, and no one speaks even as we climb up onto his boat. He scrambles around for the sleeping bags from the other night, and I help him spread them out while Stella stares across the heap of junk in his granddad's yard.

After a few minutes, she pushes away from the railing.

"Damn, it's creepy out here. Seriously, Be Weird, how do you keep from losing your fucking mind?"

"I have my ways."

"I believe you," I say. "You're like freaking MacGyver."

"Well, spill your survival secrets, MacGyver. It's starting to feel like the pontoon boat version of *The Cabin in the Woods*."

A message pings from the phone in B'Rad's back pocket. He checks it, tells us, "I'll be right back," and jumps off the platform. Within seconds, a pair of yellow running lights squints down the dirt driveway toward us as B'Rad shuffles over to his car. He unlocks the passenger-side door, clicking the glove box open as a small sedan rolls up next to him on the driver's side. He locks everything back up while this dude in a snapback gets out and meets B'Rad in the dusty golden beams of the other car's running lights. Their exchange is so muffled and backlit, it's hard to see what's actually going on. Less than a minute later, the dude in the little black car slips back down the driveway, just as stealth as he drove in.

"Was that Tanner Scott?" Stella asks, but I'm like, "Man, are you *shitting* me right now?"

B'Rad ignores us both. He comes back around to the passenger side, unlocks the door, pulls something out of the glove box, then locks it all up tight again before coming back to the boat just as quietly and carefully as he hopped off. This time, he's carrying a rolled-up T-shirt, which he gently unfurls and hands to me. In the moonlight,

I see the red, white, and blue letters spelling out Pray for America across the front of the shirt, and the beam of light bouncing off the metal bowl inside the pipe.

I go, "Dude . . . you're dealing *drugs* out here?"

But Stella's voice cuts right between that shirt and me.

"*Now* we're talking!" she says with a huge smile.

B'Rad kicks a quick look in my direction as he sets out the pipe and a couple of nugs he apparently keeps hidden in his car.

"Not really," he tells me. "I just help a few select friends stay stocked up on some basic needs."

"Fire that shit up, Be Weird," Stella says. "Let's see what you're made of."

Great. Nothing says bonding like Stella and B'Rad burning one together on a pontoon boat in the middle of the electrical fields.

"Daya doesn't smoke," she tells him as we cluster together on the sleeping bags like some kind of weed-worshipping coven. "So. I'll have hers."

"You're fired from being my spokesperson," I say. If ever there was a time when I'd want to try a little, this would be the night.

B'Rad tips his head, adorable-puppy-style, while he packs the bowl, then manifests a box of about three thousand matches and strikes one.

"What do you do to get loose, then?" he asks me, puffing on the mouthpiece to get it sparked. "I mean, when the world gets too heavy."

He takes a hit, hands it to Stella.

I intercept it, push the end against my lips, inhale. When the smoke hits my lungs, I can actually feel the membranes shrivel up and die. I visualize them morphing brown-to-black like a marshmallow over a campfire.

For some reason, these two think my coughing fit is hilarious.

"Don't give up," B'Rad giggles. "It gets better."

"Where have I heard that before," Stella says dryly, snagging the pipe from me so she can take her hit.

They snicker together. Stella passes the pipe to B'Rad when she's done, and he takes another long inhale, an equally long pause, then exhales slow and smooth.

He holds it back out to me. "Go again?"

"That's my limit," I say.

B'Rad nods and takes the hit that would have been mine. On the exhale, he goes, "That shit'll cure whatever's ailing you tonight, even if you *don't* want to talk about it."

"Well, my mom's at home fucking my math teacher right now," Stella says. "So, light it up again, Be Weird. I got issues I'm not afraid to discuss."

I shiver at the thought of Stella Avila buzz-sharing her issues with B'Rad Anderson in the middle of what has already been the most intense day in recent memory.

The three of us sprawl out on the sleeping bags, B'Rad in the middle, the box of matches on his stomach. The moon is on the rise, and now and then a coyote howls off in the distance, but at least for now, it's quiet out here. I close my eyes, hear the soft drag-and-pull of their lips against the pipe, and the now-and-then scratch of B'Rad flicking two match heads together to see if one of them will light. Only the crickets are talking at this point, their chirps echoing toward us from a distance. When I open my eyes again, the moon is so electric, you can almost hear a hum coming off it, like those old-style TVs that throb blue light into a room. I feel lit up inside in kind of the same way. Blue, mysterious, throbbing light, running currents of electricity into places it has no business going.

And I can't even tell anyone about it.

I look up. The moon is hanging right there above us now, so close you could almost reach up and run your fingertips along the veins of gray cracking through its white-marble dome. For a moment, I do reach up. Hold out one finger. Follow the cracked lines of the moon's surface. Only the lines keep shifting. I move my finger, try to follow a single, steady vein, but I can't. Everything's changing and it's disorienting as hell. This whole day has been disorienting as hell.

B'Rad flicks the match heads again.

"Why matches?" Stella says. "Why not a lighter?"

"I have a lighter," he says. "I just like matches better. Makes lighting something more of a decision."

B'Rad's granddad starts his nightly rant inside the house, but this time we all pretend not to hear it.

"If you can light one that way," Stella says, "I'll tell you a secret."

B'Rad drops his head to the side so he can see if she's bullshitting him.

"For real?" he says.

"Sure, why not. I'm an open book."

Oh man . . .

"What about this," he says. "What if we pass the box, and every time you flick two matches together and one of them lights, you have to reveal something about yourself?"

"Matchbox truth or dare?" she says.

"Only without the dare," I cut in, suddenly glad I stopped at one hit. "And you can only reveal something about yourself, *not* anyone else."

Stella goes, "Okay. Sure."

B'Rad flicks his matches together, but nothing happens.

He passes the box to Stella, who also strikes out.

Mine lights on the first try. I don't even want to play this stupid game, but now I'm supposed to tell these two a secret about myself, and the fucked-up part is, I actually have one, and it's burning a hole inside me.

I shudder, knowing that B'Rad has a sense of it. He guessed it the other night at the Hound's Tooth. I just hope that bowl he's smoking doesn't loosen his grip on my story.

The two of them are watching me like a couple of strung-out turkey vultures.

"Um . . . I threw up in the middle of Pinkie's on my twelfth birthday," I say.

"Pinkie's near the highway?" Stella asks. "Or Pinkie's across from Dickie's?"

"Pinkie's across from Dickie's."

B'Rad snort-laughs. "Was it crowded?"

"It was a Wednesday night," I say, and they both groan because Wednesday night is Bible study night in Escondido. Families, sometimes entire congregations from smaller churches, meet up for dinner afterward. As was the case that night at Pinkie's Mexican Cantina near Dickie's BBQ, not the one by the highway but the other one. With Joanna. And my grandparents.

"How come you never told me that?" Stella asks as I flick my burned-out match between two fingers and aim for the moon.

"Would *you*?" I ask back, adding, "Skip it. Of course, you would. No such thing as a humiliation filter in the Stella-verse."

B'Rad snorts as he takes out two new matches and strikes them. One of them lights this time.

"In seventh grade," he says, "I definitely played the entire first half of a basketball game with my shorts on inside out and backward. The tag looked like a sad little white flag of surrender."

"Wait—in gym class?" I ask through a snicker.

"Nope. Actual game."

Stella giggle-asks, "Who was it against?"

"Santos."

This time, Stella and I are the ones who groan in empathy. Santos Junior Academy is our crosstown rival for middle school.

"Sports never really was my thing," B'Rad says after relighting the pipe. He gives the match a sharp flick to snuff it and tosses it at the moon.

"Did you hit it?" I ask.

"Shot short. Did a lot of *that* in basketball too."

The three of us giggle at that, then Stella gives her matches another go, and this time one of them flares.

"If I had a porn name," she says, "it would be Harry Caucus."

B'Rad explodes with stoned laughter, but I just say, "That's not a secret. Everyone knows that about you."

"I didn't," B'Rad says.

I shake my head. "Still calling an audible."

"Fine," she says.

B'Rad takes another hit while she goes again.

"I hate exercise—"

"Also not a secret," I say.

"Shut up, I'm not finished." Stella sits up. "Sometimes when I'm home alone, I find old jazz stations on TunaMelt Radio and pretend I'm tap dancing."

I shift my whole body to face her, and B'Rad pulls his glasses down to stare at her over the top of them, and for a few weirdly long seconds no one says anything.

Stella finally breaks the silence.

She goes, *"What?"*

"Wow," I say. "You think you know a person, and then in the span of five seconds—"

"—they not only confess to fake tap dancing for cardio," B'Rad joins in, "but also that they listen to—"

"TunaMelt Radio!" we both shout at the same time.

"Not Your Grandparents' Music Station," I say, quoting from the music platform's current ad. "Except that it totally is."

"Also?" Stella turns to B'Rad and sticks her finger right in his face. "Duke was the best thing that ever happened to either one of us, Be Weird. Just so you know."

Uh-oh.

"Who's Duke?" he asks.

"Daisy?" she says. *"Webster?"*

B'Rad scratches that patch of hair on top of his head. "I . . . yeah. That was in, like, eighth grade. And we didn't really date, I just—"

"Well, *we* did," Stella cuts in. "*Really date*. And then we really didn't. And then there was you."

I hold my breath. Maybe the one pipe hit I took was enough to make me nervous and paranoid, or maybe Stella just turned into a loose cannon, but I've spent the last few days hoping this wouldn't come out between them, and now it has.

This night is going from sideways to downhill fast.

"I don't actually know anything about that," he says. "I just know she was really sad, and I tried to make her laugh and feel better, and then one day she declared we were dating, and a few weeks later, I heard we broke up."

Stella goes, "It wasn't that simple for some of us."

It really wasn't, I think to myself. Duke was Stella's first relationship, and she was pretty busted up about how it ended. It kind of set the tone for all her future relationships, where she just wanted to keep things light and move on before it stopped being fun.

"Look, man," he says to her. "I'm not blind. I see you around school. You're always with someone different, so . . . I'm pretty sure you would have dumped her eventually."

"Yeah, well, maybe if *you* hadn't come along, I wouldn't have had to." Her gaze drifts up into the cosmos. "Don't you ever think about how different everything would be if just one single thing in our lives had happened another way?"

"All the time," he mumbles.

"Preach," she says. "Anyway. Daya's our only hope for a happy love story now."

"Leave me out of this," I tell her as B'Rad passes the pipe to her.

"I mean it." She looks down like he's handing her his own turd, but takes it anyway, and waits for him to drop a lit match into the bowl until it sparks. She leans in, takes a drag, holds the smoke deep in her lungs. Lets it out long and slow, then flops back down.

"Daya's not out there just hooking up with random people," she says. "She can't even get with someone unless she's all in her feelings about it."

"Flag on the play," I say. "You're not supposed to talk for someone else in this stupid game."

"Nothing wrong with being demi," B'Rad says.

Stella busts a laugh. "What do *you* know about that, Be Weird?"

"Demisexuality isn't just for queer people," he tells her. "Straight people can be demi too."

"Why are you labeling me?" I ask, but they both jump on me at the same time, defending their shared perceptions of my demisexuality. "Maybe I just have trust issues. Ever consider that?"

Stella snorts and goes, "No," but B'Rad turns toward me a degree or two.

"What kinds of trust issues?"

I take the box of matches, pull two of them out, strike them. This time, they both light.

"Y'know, the usual. My dad jumped ship to *follow his heart*." I add air quotes to this. "And it just about killed my mom. And it sucks watching your parent get thrown an emotional curveball like that, because she's still not over it."

I rub my two burned-out matchsticks together like I'm trying to start another fire.

"But I guess my aunt talked her into going back to church, so . . . she's fine now."

"Yeah, right," Stella says. "I think you mispronounced *fanatic*."

The burnt match heads break off and fall into my lap. I brush them away.

"Joanna's got this . . . anchor around her," I say. "Like this emotional anchor that just weighs everything down."

B'Rad clears his throat. He squints up at the sky, adjusts his glasses.

"An anchor has *two* functions," he says. "One weighs things down. The other holds things steady."

I roll my gaze across the platform and back over to him. He's right. Even though Joanna had some kind of breakdown when my dad left, we never went hungry. We never lost our house. Maybe she was stuck in place, but we never went under either.

"I'm saying this as someone who lives on a boat," he adds.

Stella goes, "Yeah, but Joanna just traded in one anchor for another. Now church is her anchor."

"Which is funny," I say. "Because she honestly thinks Grace Redeemer has cut the chains that held her captive all this time, and now she's free."

"Right," Stella says. "Free to shame. Free to judge. Etcetera . . ."

"So you think the reason you don't just hook up with people is because of what happened with your parents?" B'Rad asks.

I feel momentarily tased by the question.

Stella tries to answer for me by saying, "Well, duh," but I go, "Um, *no*. The reason I don't just hook up with people is because I'm queer and I live *here*."

I lean against the railing that's stuck at a slight tilt toward the house, where B'Rad's granddad is barking back at the TV.

Stella goes, "That's true. You can't even scratch your tits in this town without someone calling it *perversion* and wanting to make a city ordinance about it."

"The thing is," I say to B'Rad, "everyone's childhood got messed up in some way. I mean, if that's the bar, we should *all* have trust issues. And if we all have trust issues, what's the point of putting labels on ourselves?"

"Thank you for coming to my TED Talk," Stella mumbles into the fizzling silence. And because Stella hates silence, she adds, "You know what? This is bullshit. I'm starving. Is anyone else starving?"

I know this move. This is Stella Avila doing what she does best. Deflection is high on her list of coping skills, but for once I don't mind. I hate this truth or dare game.

"I brought home some mistake dogs," B'Rad says. "If you promise not to narc, I'll share."

His eyes cut to me for a split second.

"I'm always down for a secret," I tell him, hoping he takes my hint. His minuscule wink tells me he does.

Stella perks up. "A fucking pontoon picnic—cool! Bust out the munchies before I kill someone."

We lay the hot dogs out on the foil blanket, and B'Rad manages to find a few plastic-wrapped forks and napkins that he may or may not have also brought home from work, not that I'd ever tell. I pull those condiment packets I stashed at the kiosk last night out of my pocket and lay them down by the hot dogs, in case anyone wants it.

"Those better not be from the Hound's Tooth," he says.

"Only the relish," I tell him. "The ketchup was from Sonic."

For some reason, they both find this hilariously funny. They giggle so hard they can barely keep from spitting out their food.

"Daya likes to take things," Stella says.

I drop my foot sideways and kick her in the ankle.

"Ow!" she yelps.

"Quit telling my business."

"This is just like in that movie *OutBound*," B'Rad says around a bite of hot dog.

"Which one is that?" Stella asks.

"Dude volunteers to spend the rest of his life doing scientific research on some remote planet, and all they can send up to him is junk food because it's the only thing that can survive the trip. You know that shit's preserved forever."

"I'm pretty sure that's based on a true story," Stella says.

We both look at her like *she's* the one on the remote planet.

"Are you kidding me?" B'Rad snorts.

She goes, "What?"

"Totally not real," I say.

She seems so stun-gunned, it's almost funny.

She says, "But didn't we—"

"No," he tells her.

176

"—send people to—?"

"No." He shakes his head with absolute conviction. "The moon. We sent people to the moon and then we gave up. We've never sent humans to live on another planet."

"That we know of," I add.

Stella's lips twist into a skeptical pout. "Okay, you know what? Ya pa'que. The aliens would probably just kill us when we got there anyway."

"Nah," B'Rad says. "That's what *we* would do. Humans are the real assholes in this scenario. We'd probably bring space Glocks with us and cap the aliens as soon as we landed. Manifest destiny motherfuckers."

Space Glocks. Now that shit's funny and I'm barely even stoned.

"Or nukes," Stella adds.

She's baked. They're both baked. Maybe we dodged Stella's angst bullet tonight after all.

But not B'Rad's. He makes a gun with his fingers, points it toward the house where his granddad is diatribing about who-knows-what inside. Closes one eye like he's aiming and mumbles, "Hey. If you can't shoot a thing, blow it up, right? If you can't blow it up, light it on fire."

Stella and I go silent as B'Rad stares down his imaginary barrel at the house. The crickets are chirping on speed. Even the stars seem to be rolling through the sky at a sudden, frantic clip.

"B'Rad . . . ?" I say.

Stella goes, "Dude, should we be worried about you?"

"What's it look like?" he asks back.

Stella says, "It looks like you smoked a bowl and now you're all morbid and shit."

His gun arm falls to his side and, after a moment or two, he flops onto his back again, takes a single match out, and strikes it against the side of the box. It flares yellow-orange light against the metal siding of the pontoon boat.

"He didn't want me," B'Rad says.

Neither of us breathes a word as we watch that match burn down the wooden stick toward his fingertips. He doesn't even flinch as the flame snuffs itself out against his bare skin.

The smoke that rises from the match head seems to snap Stella out of her daze. She goes, "Who didn't want you?"

"The old bastard in there," B'Rad says, launching the match carcass at his granddad's house. "Missed again," he whispers.

"What do you mean?" I ask. "Didn't want you, how?"

He lights another one.

"After my parents died," he says, letting this one burn toward his fingertips too.

Wait a minute . . .

"How'd they die?" Stella asks.

I watch how his glasses fog up, how his eyebrows creep toward each other. He shakes the flame out and throws this match even harder than the last one.

"Murder-suicide."

I sit all the way up.

I thought that was just a bullshit story.

Stella says, "Holy shit." An unfinished bite of hot dog puffs her cheek out from the inside.

He pulls out another match. Lights it. Lets it burn down some before blowing it out. Throws it at the moon. Lights another. Then another. The next match is still lit as it sails—luckily that one whiffs out in midair. The surface of the moon is shifting by the second. The ground feels like it's shifting too. Nothing feels stable. Nothing feels anchored. Maybe it's because we're on a boat, but it feels like any minute we could all just drift up into the stratosphere and float away like that guy in *OutBound*, not to give away the ending.

B'Rad looks like he's getting ready to throw another match. I put my hand on his arm, and he hugs the box of matches to his chest. No one says anything else for a long time, until B'Rad goes, "I was nine. They took me into protective custody and made me a ward of the state. . . . There's some vocabulary not every kid has to learn. Anyway. When they figured out I had a living relative, they asked him to take me. He refused."

Stella points toward the house. "But now you're—"

"They made him."

"*Damn,*" she says, blowing the word into the air like she's exhaling a bong hit.

"I can't believe it," I whisper. "I thought that was just a story you made up to get my mom to buy your . . . you know."

The way he looks over his shoulder at me . . . it's pure haunt.

"I'm pretty good at telling a real story like it's part of someone's fictional life," he says.

In the swirl of cricket chirp and breeze and moonlight, I start to shiver. I toss our empty food wrappers off the foil blanket and fold myself up inside it, but the shiver won't stop. The words *murder* and *suicide* won't stop either—they just crash together inside my head. I can't process those words in relation to B'Rad Anderson, much less nine-year-old Brad, as he would have been known back then. I mean . . . shit.

Stella eases back down on the sleeping bag. "So how did he do it?"

"*Stella.*"

"It's fine," B'Rad says, staring off into space. "Everything's fine."

He pushes the box of matches open, then changes his mind and closes it. When he starts talking again, I slip it away from him.

"You don't need to tell us," I say.

"They're just details. Puzzle pieces."

He lifts his hands toward the sky, pantomimes moving a puzzle piece as he says, "I found out my dad left a note."

He slides another piece into imaginary place. "*Love makes you crazy, Jeanette. That's all it said. Ain't that some shit?*"

His hands stop moving. They just hang there, suspended in zero gravity with the moon cradled between his empty palms.

"Love *must* make you crazy," he says. "Where else would that kind of insanity come from?"

He wipes the invisible puzzle pieces onto the imaginary floor.

"I've seen some crazy shit happen in the name of love," Stella says. "That's for fucking sure."

"Same," I say.

God will forgive you, Jon—just come back! Only he didn't. My dad drove away, and the next morning she emptied every single thing out of our house. Furniture, clothes, food, it all went on the curb for someone else to deal with.

For a fraction of a second, the moonlight and starlight blink out, leaving us in complete darkness.

"I can't believe your dad killed your mom," Stella whispers, cracking into the drifting moonlight. "All my dads have been shitty to my mom, but . . . nothing like that. That's messed up."

"Yup. My life's a fucking true-crime show."

It gets quiet again for a while, except for the muted sound of B'Rad's granddad soapboxing from somewhere inside.

After a while, I hear Stella murmur, "We caught you cheating, by the way. You lit those last few matches against the box. Right, Daya?"

"Daya's not playing anymore," I say.

But Stella doesn't hear me. She's already asleep—I can tell by the rhythm of her slow, steady breathing.

I roll to the side to face B'Rad. He's wiping his eyes on the *Pray for America* shirt. It's the first time I've ever seen him with his glasses off.

"Your granddad," I say. "Does he do that every night?"

"Every night. Every day. Like he's stuck in a loop somewhere."

"It must suck, having to listen to that all the time," I whisper.

"Yeah, but . . . sometimes listening to the noise inside my own head is actually worse."

He pushes in close and stares at me for the longest moment ever. I can tell his eyes are red even though everything around us is washed in a silvery blue.

"I'm really sorry," I tell him.

181

B'Rad nods, closes his eyes, and rests his forehead against mine until his breathing becomes deep and regular.

I just lie there, letting B'Rad sleep while listening to his asshole granddad curse the moon and the stars and everything else in the universe.

Fifteen

THE GIRLS' BATHROOM

I don't know what time it is, only that it's wicked-early and I'd rather still be asleep than almost anything else in the world. But I'm also freezing, and I have to pee, and there's no way I'm dropping trou out here on B'Rad's pontoon boat. Unlike Stella, I have not mastered the art of peeing standing up.

B'Rad rolls onto his side and throws one arm over my waist. He's not exactly snoring in my ear, just breathing slow and deep, like maybe he hasn't slept this well in a while.

Sounds of his granddad shuffling around float toward us from inside the house: a slamming door, the TV coming on. It's *How I Killed Your Mother*—I recognize the theme music instantly. Joanna binged that show for two whole weeks last winter when she was stuck at home with strep throat.

The narrator's voice drifts into the yard, and B'Rad mumbles, "Man, I really hate that morbid shit first thing in the morning."

"What time is it?" Stella asks through a yawn.

"Six thirty," he says, sucking in his sleep drool. "The train to Phoenix just cut through town."

I look to see if Joanna checked up on me last night, but my battery's completely dead. I have no idea how much trouble I'm in, but

I'm guessing it's a lot. I'm guessing I'll know for sure as soon as I get my phone juiced again.

"Anyone have a charger?" I ask.

"Yeah, how do you power your shit out here, Be Weird?" Stella asks, sniffing her armpits. "I don't hear a generator running."

"I just charge my phone in the bathroom at school," he says, taking Stella's cue and checking his armpits as well.

"What about for other stuff?" she presses. "You must need electricity for *something?*"

"I siphon it off from the old man when I really have to. There's always an extension cord lying around."

"Cool, cool," Stella says, nodding. "So, how do you make breakfast without a burner, or, like . . . a microwave?"

Even under interrogation, B'Rad is as cool as a roll of Mentos.

"I have food," he tells her. "I just avoid keeping things on the boat that need to be cooked or refrigerated."

"Yeah, I bet shit goes bad fast out here."

"That, plus wild creatures."

"Ah. Good point."

I clear my throat.

"If you guys are hungry, I know where we can eat for free," I say, wiping my sweaty palms on the sides of my pants.

"I'm in. Let's go." Stella grabs her bag without asking for details, even though—as B'Rad likes to say—details matter.

He goes, "Hold up. No such thing as a free meal. Where is this glory hole of food, Daya?"

I swing between them a few times, long enough for the curtain to flutter and give Stella a glimpse at the reality behind it.

"Oh no," she says, holding up her hands. "No, I take it back. No way in hell."

"I knew it," he says.

"She's trying to rope us into going to that indoctrination meeting with her. The answer is no, Daya. It always *was* no. It will always *be* no. I'm not selling my soul for a maple bar."

I turn to B'Rad—all my hopes are pinned on him now.

"Sorry, Daya. You know Morales gives me the leftovers without making me sit through all that *in Jesus's name* stuff first."

"You guys suck," I tell them, but shame is still not enough to persuade either of them to change their minds.

For a second, he does look like he feels sorry for me.

He goes, "I'll save you one."

"It's not the same," I tell him as we roll up the sleeping bags.

Stella folds the aluminum foil blanket and hands it to him.

He says, "Don't be bitter, Daya. I'm still going to their prom thing with you. If that's not a sacrifice in the name of friendship—"

"Whoa, whoa, whoa," Stella says. She holds a flat-palmed hand in front of him but aims her question at me. "You guys are going to *Conversion Prom* together?"

I flash a look of panic at B'Rad, silently begging him not to spill our tea. Namely, that I'm going to Pure Prom so I can stroke my fantasy of being at prom with Beckett, and he's taking me because he wants a fun prom experience on the cheap.

"It's complicated," I say, as B'Rad adds, "I'm broke as fuck, but I really want to go."

Stella swings on me. "Please tell me you're not one of them now."

"Uh, never," I tell her. "This is nothing more than a good old-fashioned prom experience on a very lean budget. And, seriously, you *could* go with us—"

"My dudes, don't you get it? They want to *indoctrinate* you," Stella says. "Both of you. But mostly you," she adds, tipping her chin in my direction.

"I'm not that gullible. Besides, think about it like this. *We* could actually infiltrate Pure Prom, you know? Like moving the canned vegetables around at Fool City, only . . . better."

"Not on the coldest day in hell," she says as we head to the car. "Besides, I'll be at the *impure* prom, down at the country club, with Valentina."

"Wait, I thought you couldn't afford it."

"I couldn't," she says, climbing into the back seat, while I slide in up front. "But Valentina can."

"How?"

"I don't know, Daya. Maybe she got a GoFundMe. The point is, when the hottest girl at school tells you to just show up looking fly and not worry about a thing . . . what's a bitch supposed to do?"

I don't stand a chance in hell against whatever's burning between Stella and Valentina Orozco these days.

As we head to school, Stella pulls out her phone and goes, "Let's check out this whole Grace Redeemer situation. Y-O-U-T-U-B-E . . ."

"You're not going to find anything—" I start to say.

But Stella goes, "Are you serious right now—there's a *paywall*?

You can't even watch their videos for free? Since when did finding God become pay-to-play?"

"Grace Redeemer will set you free," B'Rad says. "But it'll cost ya."

Stella laughs.

"I get it," I tell them. "You're both hilarious."

"I don't think you do," Stella says. "Here, wait—I'm in."

She flips the video she found so we can both see it and turns up the volume. It's from summer camp last year. From the announcements at church on Sunday, camp is basically a two-week-long, nonstop concert with all the faith-based extras.

"That's fresh," B'Rad says. "Is that BTS?"

"Not unless BTS is singing about salvation these days," Stella tells him. "Look at all those hands in the air, Daya. Jazz hands for Jesus."

"It's called praise hands," I say.

"Man." She shakes her head. "This is some high-production-value brainwashing."

"I'd totally be their target audience based on the music alone," B'Rad says. "You couldn't tell me this was religious music, it's *that* subliminal."

"Come on, man," Stella huffs, mashing buttons on her phone. "Their stupid server keeps dropping me. What if I was having a deeply emotional religious experience, and I kept getting dropped?"

"Yeah," B'Rad says. "What message does that send?"

"Okay," I say. "I get the point."

"This is such a *joke*, Daya. Seriously, why don't you just go to prom with *us*? You can spend the night in style. Dinner at the boathouse.

Dancing at the golf club. Chilling with the life of the party—moi. Definitely not gonna be boring."

"Yeah, well . . . not everyone has a sugar mama."

The parking lot at school is pretty much empty when we get there. B'Rad takes the closest spot, sets the brake, and cuts the engine. He throws his arm over the back of the seat and turns.

"Hey, so . . . that matches game we played last night?" he says. "Let's just keep all that between us, if you don't mind."

Stella looks over at him, and says, "Sure, man. What happens on the boat stays on the boat."

He turns to me.

"You know I'm down," I say.

"Thanks."

"So," Stella says. "What's the hot Conversion Prom fashion trend this year?"

The question hits me like a blast of nitro. I look at B'Rad and he looks at me, and I go, "Shit, am I gonna need a *dress*?"

B'Rad pops the side of his head with his open palm as Stella spurts, "A *what*?"

"You guys. I don't have threads for something like this."

"What you need is a personal shopper," B'Rad says, and the three of us exchange glances like a trio of comic book villains.

Stella drama-shakes her head. "Nope. Not me. I am *not* that person."

I swing to B'Rad.

"I'll be real with you, Daya. I'm probably not your best option either."

"Please, B'Rad. I'm literally begging you."

"It's not a good look for her," Stella adds.

"It's Thursday already, I need *help*."

"Okay," he says. "No stress. We'll figure something out."

"Be Weird's picking you out a prom dress," Stella snickers as we hit campus. "Man, I can't *wait* to see those pictures."

It's still pretty early—just us and the custodians at school. I don't see them, but I know they're here because the bathrooms are already unlocked.

We say goodbye to B'Rad just before the 300 wing and duck into the girls' room to charge our phones and clean up a bit.

Stella pulls out a super-short cable and a splitter and plugs us in.

"How do you just happen to have a splitter?" I ask her, wetting some paper towel and wiping down as much of myself as I can.

"You'd be surprised how often girls' phones go dead, and no one ever has a charger." She throws me an emoji-smile.

"And the extra-short cable keeps someone you're interested in just close enough to get sweet on you?"

"There you go, Daya. Now you're thinking like a fuck-boi!"

"Okay, fuck-boi," I say, throwing my paper towels away. "Spill the tea about prom. How did this all happen?"

I hand her a few damp paper towels, drop my bag on the floor, and slide down the wall until I'm on top of it.

"It's no big deal. Me and Valentina were hanging out, and she was basically like, *Come to prom with me*. So. That's it. We're going to prom."

"I don't know, Stells. It's not your cousin Yoli's quinceañera, y'know? No one cared if *we* danced together that night because we were, like, eleven. And we had dresses on."

"Valentina will have a dress on. For a while."

I pull my hoodie up so I can tip my head back against the grungy wall without actually touching it.

"Prommin' for Jesus," Stella says with a snicker.

"Please stop," I say.

She goes, "Man, I'm serious, just go to prom with us."

"I really can't—"

"Yes, you can," she says. "You can always choose *other*. Man, if my mom said I had to go to something like that, I'd tell her to snort it."

"Your mom would never tell you to do something like that, because your mom doesn't think you're broken. Besides . . ." This is probably a huge mistake, but I've got to come clean with her, at least about this part. "Joanna's not making me go."

Stella's mouth jacks open. "You *volunteered* for Conversion Prom? Girl, did you hit your head or something?"

"I don't expect you to understand," I tell her.

"Well, good, 'cause I don't, and I never will."

"Fine. We don't always have to agree on everything."

"Praise the goddess," Stella says with a laugh.

"But you don't have to be all *like that* about it."

Stella takes a slow breath through her nose, then closes her eyes. When she opens them again, there's not even a nano-hint of a joke in them.

"Can I tell you how close I came to being forced into a summer camp for 'reprogramming'? By my asshole stepdad? Who went to Grace Redeemer?"

I stare at her with my mouth open, and she stares back with the weight of a newly told secret in her eyes.

"Why . . ." I try to corral my scattered thoughts. "Why didn't you tell me?"

She shakes her head, her mouth twisting up like she's fighting not to cry. "If a tree falls in the woods, and you pretend it never happened . . . did it?"

"Well, fuck," I whisper, laying my head on her shoulder just as my phone powers on. I check my charge to see how much juice I have now—it's enough to hold me till lunch, if I'm super careful. But there's nothing from Joanna. No voicemail. No text. That's not a good sign, considering I took off after a fight last night, never came home, and never told her where I was.

The bathroom door swings open and Lucy Davis strolls in. She stops hard when she sees me and Stella, looks down at us sitting on the bathroom floor. With a laugh and a shake of her head, she swings into the handicapped stall at the far end.

Stella bounces forward like she's about to jump Lucy right inside that stall, but I grab her by the arm and shake my head no. Neither of us needs to borrow that kind of trouble right now, not this close to prom. And besides, Lucy Davis isn't worth getting in trouble over.

Instead, I whisper, "Let's go."

She pops her charger out of the wall and we scramble to our feet.

On the way out, Stella kick-bangs the bathroom door open. The sound is definitely loud enough to startle someone's pee stream if they weren't expecting it.

She wanders off to wait for Valentina while I head toward room 333. It's weird showing up at Great Wait this early. No one's here yet, not even Nestor or Alexa. No Beckett. No buffer at all against the likelihood that Lucy Davis will be the next person to walk through the door, since I know she's already at school. I take a seat in the back, keep my eyes open and my attention sharp.

To my surprise, Beckett shows up first. Her smile breaks loose when she sees me. She slides in next to me, leans in close.

"Hi," she whispers.

"Hi."

"How are you?"

"Good. I mean, fine." Not really. But she doesn't need to know the real answer is *complicated*. I don't want to muddy the memory of how it felt in my room yesterday. When we kissed. When I kissed Beckett Wild.

When she kissed me.

She drops the volume another click and goes, "So, can we talk about what happened yesterday?"

Shit.

Shitshitshit.

I brace against what I know is coming. How she regrets kissing me. How she has second thoughts and wants to recommit to her purity. How her parents found out, and she's grounded for life, and she can't even go to prom now thanks to me. Wouldn't that be some shit? Me, going to Pure Prom and Beckett not even being there?

"I don't mean any disrespect," she whispers. "But your mom was a total bitch."

I hit pause on my own thoughts so they can catch up with what she just said.

"No wonder you started calling her by her first name," Beckett adds.

I'm reeling. I thought . . . when she said *can we talk* . . . it would be about the part where we kind of broke her purity promise.

She shakes her head again like she still doesn't get it, so I just go, "I'm not supposed to have people in my room when she's not home. I'm not supposed have . . . girls in my room. It makes her uncomfortable."

"So how much trouble are you in?"

"I don't know yet, honestly."

I leave out the part where, on top of getting caught with Beckett in my room, I also split, then spent the night with B'Rad and Stella. I have no idea what the fallout from all that is going to look like.

"But you're here," she says. "So does this finally mean . . ."

Her lips twitch like they're fighting a smile, the corners of her mouth lifting just so much. She kissed me the same way yesterday— smiling into it. Into me.

God . . . why does everything have to be so complicated?

"Does this mean you're actually coming on Saturday?" she whispers.

"Is it cool with you if I do?"

Her eyes lock on to my mouth, then drift away. But she's still smiling.

"Maybe I can show you around. There's this top-secret room where they keep—"

The door flings open, and more people start showing up now. Nestor. His VP, Alexa. A few others I sort-of recognize, even if I don't know their names. Beckett watches, smiling, as they file past. Only it's not a real smile anymore. It's a fake smile for a fake audience. For an invisible camera hidden somewhere that she's been conditioned to fake happy for.

Lucy pops up for the second time this morning, like an unwanted clown at a kid's birthday party. Just "there" enough to be terrifying.

"Hey, girl." She leans in and gives Beckett a peck on the cheek, which Beckett returns.

Then Lucy leans in close to me. So close I can tell what flavor toothpaste she uses.

She goes, "I don't see your friend here. Should we add her to our prayer list?"

Beckett toggles between me and Lucy a couple times before asking, "What friend?"

But I just go, "She doesn't need any prayers."

"Oh. Because it looked like she did when I saw you guys on the bathroom floor earlier."

Beckett watches us like she's trying to work out a math problem.

"Yeah," Lucy adds. "The last time I saw someone on the bathroom floor, it was Andrea Randall and she'd just OD'd, so. We prayed for *her*."

I kind of want to slap her right now.

By the time the band starts playing and Nestor comes forward to ask us to bow our heads in prayer, I'm all the way over playing nice with Lucy Davis.

"Lord, we pray that You help us honor our commitment to humility and purity, Father."

I can't do it. I can't sit here praying for humility after getting bathroom-checked by some bitchy girl who talks shit out of one side of her mouth and quotes the Bible out of the other. And I can't pray for purity with the echo of Beckett's lips against mine still pulsing all around us. Kissing her was the purest thing I've ever known.

As Nestor and Alexa go through the updates committee by committee, Cason and Javi whisper the play-by-play of their soccer game last night, and every few minutes Lucy tells them to shut up.

I can't keep my attention on any of the committee reports—not with Beckett sitting next to me, a modest hole near the knee of her jeans, the tease of skin just peeking through it. Clusters of freckles on her forearm that look like constellations. The fluid way she moves, like she's underwater. Not everyone moves easy that way. Some people go through the world like they're walking against a hurricane, but not Beckett. That's all I care about right now. Not whether Games and Activities went fifty dollars over budget.

And I really don't care if Lucy Davis wants to pray for Stella, much less if she feels threatened by me because she has some weird hetero-crush on her best friend.

I decide to skip the donut part of the meeting since B'Rad already said he'd share with me later. I do want to ask Beckett about getting together to work on our project, but definitely not with Lucy standing right there.

I slip away as everyone else pushes toward the piano, and text B'Rad, asking him to meet me right after homeroom.

The next forty-five minutes pass agonizingly slow, but luckily B'Rad is standing right outside the door after homeroom with the donut box already open. I take two.

"I was about to cut someone, I'm so hungry."

"Didn't you eat anything at the meeting?" he asks.

"Short answer? No." I go full Jaws on a maple bar, adding, "Dude, you're still glazed."

"Shit." He wipes sugar flakes off the corner of his mouth.

"So, are we on for dress shopping after school?" he asks.

I groan. "I mean . . . yeah? Just don't ask me where to go because I've never had to buy a dress before."

"Let's start with, where do you usually shop?"

"Savers. Or Value Village."

"So, you're looking for something vintage?" he asks.

"Dude, no. I'm literally looking for the cheapest dress possible, because I'm planning to ritually burn it the second it comes off. I don't even care what it looks like, honestly."

B'Rad snorts, and the tardy bell screeches from right above us.

"I'm having thoughts," he says as we scatter off to class. "Meet me in the parking lot at three."

I want the same forty-five-minute crawl of homeroom to last the rest of the day. Because the longer it takes for three o'clock to roll around, the longer I can put off spending the afternoon shopping for some hideous Daya-in-drag version of a dress.

But I can't.

Prom is in two days.

I'm literally out of time.

Sixteen

THE FREESTYLE EXCHANGE

"This isn't Value Village," I say as we pull up in front of #Smitten, the most overhyped clothing store in the universe, with its giant hashtag around the door frame and gimmicky cringe everywhere you look.

"Most of the high-profile thrift influencers do fashion dupes," he says. "That's where they find an expensive outfit they love and thrift a way cheaper version of it."

He turns when he realizes I've stopped walking, and goes, "What . . . ?"

"Did you just say *high-profile thrift influencers?*"

"I looked it up during Psych. We're going to find you the perfect outfit and dupe it somewhere else."

"This must be what hell looks like," I mumble.

When we get inside, B'Rad leads the way to the formals section, embracing his previously unknown alter ego: Captain Fashionista. I try not to gawk too hard at the clusters of shoppers at selfie stations all over the store, snapping their #trending outfits and uploading them to #Smitten's social media page in hopes of winning a shopping spree. This place is giving me serious Grace Redeemer vibes, only with a little more commerce and a little less Jesus.

This store isn't me at all. I'll take a really great thrift shop over this bullshit any day of the year. Hashtag budget friendly. Hashtag no selfie required.

"Here," B'Rad says, zeroing in on a tall carousel under a sign that says #Fancy.

"Seriously?" I say, pointing up at the sign. "Isn't that a little precious?"

"It won't be like that at the next place, I promise."

He immediately finds a bright purple gown with fake jewels all over it and holds it up for me to see. The top part has no sleeves or straps of any kind, and the bottom part has these swirly strips of fabric hanging all around it that look like jellyfish tentacles.

"That needs to be taken out to the lake and drowned," I tell him.

He puts it back, and a few seconds later pulls out another one. This time, he lets his face do the asking.

I let mine do the answering.

B'Rad gives me a look like I'm saying no just to spite him.

He goes, "What's wrong with this one?"

"Ruffles," I say. "Miles and miles of ruffles."

"Okay, maybe we can narrow down the parameters a little. Maybe by color? Or style?"

"B'Rad . . . no." I take the hanger from him and put it back on the rack. "You don't understand. I don't want to do a prom dress dupe. This dress is going to be a one-and-done. I just want to buy the cheapest thing that fits and call it a day."

It's a standoff, right here amid the waves and waves of lace and ruffles and bejeweled bra-tops and slits that go all the way up the leg.

"Daya," he says.

"Are you about to mansplain prom dresses to me? Please don't do that."

"Decades from now," he says, completely ignoring me, "we'll go to our high school reunion, and they'll have yearbooks out on all the tables, and people will wander around looking through them, and that's when they'll see it. You. In a dress that looks like a tablecloth your great-grandmother stuffed in the back of a closet. Hanging lifeless off your shoulders for no other reason than it was cheap and it fit. Is *that* what you want?"

The noise of #Smitten fills the air between us for a few moments as my gaze ripples outward from the racks. My brain is overstimulated by all the store announcements and canned instrumental versions of Eminem songs and the sound of shoppers giggling as they snap and upload their #selfies.

B'Rad pushes his glasses into place, runs one hand through his tuft of hair.

"If you don't care what *you* look like," he says, "at least think about *me*."

"What *about* you?"

"I'll be in the picture with you," he says. "For eternity."

I wish I could laugh, but this sucks too hard to find the humor in it.

"Just so you know . . . I will *never* go to a high school reunion," I say, dead serious, as he leads me out of #Smitten and back to his car. I don't say anything when we leave the city limits and continue east. A few miles farther, he pulls up in front of a store I've never heard of.

I go, "What's this?"

"The Freestyle Exchange. It's got a pretty cool vibe, and it's all secondhand." He gives me one of those looks like there's more to say about that, and then adds, "Sometimes Lucian buys some of my granddad's stuff off me."

I let out a breath. This is the first thing that's made sense all day.

The Freestyle Exchange is an acid trip, like crash-landing onto the mindscape of someone with both ADHD and OCD in the best possible way. Inside the once-abandoned warehouse, some guy named Lucian has assembled a collection of literally anything you can name in the universe. And he's got things weirdly organized so you don't have to wander around in a daze. If you want appliances, there's a section for that. If you're looking for trading cards or furniture or figurines, everything can be discovered in its own part of the Exchange.

"That's where I found my pipe," B'Rad says as we pass a whole rack of fondue pots. "This one chick, Amy—she doesn't work here anymore—but one day she set it down right there for some reason, and she was so stoned she forgot where she put it. No harm, no foul," he adds as he takes me to women's clothing.

I don't normally shop by gender, but at least there's something about this place that makes me feel less like I'm on an alien planet and more like this is a world I might be comfortable in. Except the part where we're standing under a sign that says WOMEN'S, staring down the barrel at several rows of formal gowns.

"I think I'll go look in men's," I tell him, pivoting in that direction.

"Whoa." He rushes me, blocks my path. "What do you mean?"

"I mean, maybe it'll be easier to find a suit I like than a dress."

"Daya . . ." He looks around the open space of the warehouse for a moment. "I don't know how to say this tactfully, but . . . we're going to prom at *church*. Do you really think we should both show up in a suit?"

"Yeah, but . . . I just want to be comfortable, y'know?"

He comes all the way over, places his hands on my shoulders, leans right into my face. "It's church prom. Comfort isn't really the point."

Right.

We go back to Women's, and I begin to methodically make my way through rack after rack. Every now and then, I glance up to see B'Rad the next aisle over, doing the same. The only sounds inside the Freestyle Exchange are the hum of a massive air-conditioning unit and the metal scrape of hangers sliding left to right in rejection after hideous rejection.

Ruffles—no.

Strapless—no.

Gigantic bows—hell no.

"Hey, Daya?"

I look up from a nightmare of 1980s satin and lace to see B'Rad lifting a hanger off the rack.

"Come check this out," he says.

I hear the excitement in his voice, but I don't share in his confidence as I join him the next aisle over.

I slip the hanger from him and hold it up.

He goes, "I've got some kind of feeling about this one."

I have to say, I don't hate it. It's not pastel, for starters. It's all black. Hangs straight down, no ruffles or puffs or pouf or lace, nothing glittery or shiny, and no bows. Just a long, slender skirt, a neckline that doesn't drop too low, and a slit that doesn't ride too high. The girliest thing about this dress is the sleeves, which look like someone draped some sheer fabric over the top of the arm, just enough to expose a teensy bit of shoulder. Not too daring, just a little more femme than I'm personally into.

"Try it on," he tells me.

I search for the price tag.

"Don't sweat it," he says, pulling the tag off before I can see it. "I've got some store credit from the last time I sold stuff to Lucian." He points out where to go and says, "You don't need to show me unless you want to."

I walk into the try-on room under the weight of dread. Just because I don't hate the dress doesn't mean I want to wear it.

The musty try-on room is more like an old broom closet with a curtain wrapped around it. I slip out of my jeans and tee and pull the dress over my head.

It feels weirdly nice as it falls down around me. Slick and cool. But I also feel naked underneath, with nothing but a pair of underwear between my bare skin and a couple yards of breezy fabric. I swallow hard and sweep aside the curtain that separates me from the humiliation of being seen by anyone, B'Rad included.

He turns, his gaze dropping agonizingly slow down the length of the dress. I wish he'd say something before I crawl out of my fucking skin.

"Wow."

I shake my head. "I'm gonna need more than that."

"You may not want to hear this, Daya, but you look sexy as hell."

"Oh God." I turn back to the mirror inside the broom closet and try to see myself through his eyes, or Beckett's. But I can't. All I see is a dress wishing it was a suit, and even if it looks great to the rest of the world, even if it feels cool and sleek against my naked skin, it does not feel anything like me.

"It's one night," he says.

Lucian finds a used-but-nice box with tissue paper inside to fold the dress into and tells B'Rad he'll adjust the balance of his store credit. I have no idea how much this thing cost him, and I don't want to seem ungrateful, but I can't help thinking that whatever he paid for it, it was a waste of B'Rad's hard-earned money.

On the other hand, at least that part's over now. I have something to wear to Pure Prom that won't get me kicked out.

We head home, but the closer we get to my house, the bigger the reality looms: I never went home last night, and I never told my mother where I was. And she never called or texted to see if I was okay.

"You all right?" B'Rad asks as we head down the Strip toward the Flats.

"Sure," I mumble, even though I'm not sure if I really am all right.

The closer I get to facing Joanna, the less sure I am about anything.

I peek through the back door window before going in. Joanna's standing at the stove, cooking the dinner I wasn't home to make.

Add another match to the flame.

I hold my breath as I step inside and softly close the door behind me.

"Oh good," she says.

Brace for impact.

"Dinner's just about ready. Are you hungry?"

I freeze. Of all the things I figured she'd say to me, *Are you hungry?* wasn't even on the list.

"Um. Not really. Thanks."

She turns, tongs in hand.

"Are you sure? I haven't made these in a long time, but they used to be your favorite. I even bought the good tortillas you like on my way home."

I am Dorothy, spinning inside the tornado right now, as she adds another pan-fried taco to a plate already stacked with tacos. She turns back to look at me like she's waiting for me to change my mind.

I shift, tuck the Freestyle box under my other arm.

"What's that?" she asks, pointing the tongs at it.

"It's my dress," I tell her, hugging the box a little tighter. "For Saturday. For prom at Grace Redeemer."

"You're going to prom at Grace Redeemer?"

I nod, and she shuts off the stove, motions to the box.

"Can I see?"

After everything she said last night, everything *we* said last night, all those hard truths . . . it doesn't make any kind of sense why she's being soft right now.

"You want to see my prom dress?" I ask.

She smiles, wipes her hands on a dish towel. "Of course."

"I thrifted it," I say as I lift the lid, as if that will be the key to whether she likes it or not.

She leans forward, looks inside.

"It's really nice, Daya. Simple. But . . . still elegant."

She reaches out to touch the fabric but pulls her hand back before she does.

"I don't want to get it greasy," she says.

I put the lid back on the box, and Joanna leans back and sort-of smiles.

"I'm so glad you're going," she says, almost like a sigh of relief. "That's just . . . it's great news."

I'm not sure what's happening here, only that I kind of want to jump in front of whatever might be coming.

"I stayed with some friends last night," I tell her. "In case you were wondering."

She takes a few steps back, slides over to the stove, gathers up the pan and utensils she's been using. She tosses the spatula into the frying pan, then the frying pan into the sink.

"It wasn't the girl from my room either, if that's what you're thinking," I add.

She still doesn't say anything, just brings the plate of tacos over to the table. Her movements are slow and fluid as she sits down. There's breathing room around her. I don't know why any of this feels easy, because it shouldn't.

I cautiously drop onto the chair across from her.

"You know . . ." She turns the plate around nervously, moves some of the tacos like she's styling it for a photo shoot. "It was pointed out to me last night that . . . you've never given me any reason not to trust you. You mostly follow my rules; you've never snuck out. Never had someone in your room until . . ."

We're in dangerous territory again.

Joanna seems to feel it too. She reroutes.

"I'm glad you're going to Pure Prom, Daya," she says.

"So . . . am I in trouble? For last night?"

She turns the plate again.

"I admit, I was upset. But I called Pastor Mike, and we had a really good talk. About us. About why and how kids rebel sometimes. We prayed over it. He helped me understand some things. That's when I . . . when I realized . . ." She clears her throat. "I'm just hoping this can be a fresh start for us. Yesterday was . . . unfortunate, but it's over. And I'm hoping we can just . . . move more toward the light."

I wait for her to explain what she means by that. I have no sense of what *moving toward the light* is supposed to look like. But she doesn't say anything else.

"Okay," I say.

"Good. I really think it will be good for you to spend the evening with other like-minded kids, Daya."

There's nothing like-minded about me and the kids from The Great Wait. But maybe it's best to keep that to myself.

I slide the box off the table. "I should probably hang this up."

"I'll set some plates out," she tells me.

In my room, I fire off a quick text to Stella.

My mom wants to "move our relationship toward the light."

The little dots pulse just long enough for her to type:

wtf?

I know, I write back.

She goes: **careful – that light could be the front end of a speeding train LOL.**

But I can't find my way to the joke of it, because that's honestly what I'm afraid of.

I want to trust my mom. I want to trust her softness tonight. When she said, *I'm hoping this can be a fresh start for us* . . . it gave me the exact same feeling I get when I listen to all that incredible music at church. Hearing her say that felt like faith. It felt like trust. It felt safe. It felt like having my mom back, the way she was before everything went bad.

I *want* a fresh start.

I want her back.

I want that light she talked about.

But I don't trust it.

I know what she said.

But all I can hear is the sound of an oncoming train.

Seventeen

SCHOOL, THE DAY BEFORE PROM

"I can't wait for this whole bullshit year to be over," I tell Stella.

She fishes a Pringles can out of her locker and pops it open.

"Preach it, Sister Daya!" She kicks me a look. "Sorry. Too soon."

"You just can't let it go, can you?" I mumble, stealing a Pringle out of her can.

She goes, "So, what's with your mom wanting to deep-share her feelings last night?"

"I have *no* idea. I thought she was going to lose her shit about me not coming home, but . . . she didn't, and now it feels like . . . I don't even know. Like Invasion of the Joanna Snatchers."

"Now that shit's funny."

We hit the commons, hop up onto a concrete planter box.

"Okay, so give me all the deets about this alleged prom dress B'Rad procured for you," Stella says.

"Uh-uh. I don't want to speak that entity to life. I just didn't think it all the way through."

"What part?"

"The having-to-wear-a-dress part? And now that dress is giving me serious regret vibes." I steal another chip. "Tell me about your plans with Valentina."

She shakes her head, makes fml-face. "Let's just say I was told it would be 'better for everyone' if I didn't show up at prom."

"Are you kidding?" I say. "They really did prom-block you?"

"They said it was because I have unpaid fees, but . . . *pfft*. I paid that shit."

"On the real—you never pay your late fees. But that's not why they blocked you, and we both know it."

I give her a look, and she gives me one back.

"Don't make me say you were right, Daya; you know how hard that is for me."

"Okay, but look. Your tux doesn't need to go to waste. You could still go with me and B'Rad."

Stella literally snort-laughs when I say this.

"First off, *hell no*," she says. "Second off, they'd never let my girl through the door in *her* smokin' hot dress that did *not* come from Church Proms R Us. Besides, there's a Fuck Prom party up in Oviedo for all us prom rejects and never-prommers, so. I think we're gonna hang out up there for the night."

"And your mom's cool with that?"

She makes face at me, and we both say "Mr. Zapata" at the same time.

"They do like their alone time," she adds, as if anyone needs to be reminded.

The courtyard fills in with students carrying paper boats piled high with Tater Tots and nachos, unwrapping tacos, diving face-first into cafeteria sandwiches wrapped in yellow paper. One hundred percent of the conversations walking by are about prom. Afterparties.

Hairstyles. Which nail salon they're going to.

"You know what I don't hear?" I ask.

"What?"

"I don't hear anyone else talking about being blocked from prom for wanting to take a same-gender date. Or getting kicked out for wearing what they're comfortable in. Or—"

We both spin at the sound of my name coming from across the commons.

It's Nestor Camarillo.

"Hey, Daya, you weren't there this morning, so . . . make sure you get to Grace Redeemer early tomorrow, okay? Everyone needs to be there by four to help set up."

I'm not getting there early *or* helping set up, but I don't tell him that.

Nestor turns to leave, but spins back around, fishes something out of the bag he's holding, and tosses it at me.

It's an *Ask Me About Pure Prom* T-shirt.

"Put it on," he says. "That's why we got them."

I'd sooner wear Stella's cousin Yoli's neon-pink quinceañera dress than this T-shirt.

He throws one to Stella too, before jogging off. She unrolls it, holds it up, looks at the bright yellow lettering, and goes, "Oh, this is too good." She flips it over. "*True Love Waits?* Waits for what? For your—"

"Don't say it," I warn her.

"Say what?"

"Whatever nasty thing was about to come out of your mouth."

"I usually like to put nasty things *in* my mouth. Hey, hold these."

She shoves the T-shirt and the Pringles can at me and dashes across the commons toward Valentina Orozco. She catches up, and they hug, and then Stella points at me and calls out, "Check you later!"

I lift the Pringles can like it's a glass of champagne.

"Cheddar sour cream," Beckett says, swinging around from behind me. "It's almost like you *knew* that's my favorite."

I keep eyes on her as she sits down next to me—as she reaches toward the can. I tilt it in her direction so she can get a chip out.

"I thought black licorice was your favorite," I say softly.

Her face goes red as she smiles.

"Missed you this morning," she says.

"Yeah, I slept in." I cross my fingers to ward off the bad juju of telling Beckett a little white lie. That after I committed and got a dress yesterday, the whole prom thing became a little too real. A reality I couldn't look directly into the face of. Not this morning. Not at that meeting, anyway.

She eats the chip, fanning herself by pulling on the collars of multiple layered shirts she's wearing.

"Are you okay?" I ask.

"I'm burning up."

"I see that," I tell her. "Why are you wearing a hoodie? It's, like, ninety degrees out here."

She lifts the hem of the hoodie a few inches and pulls down the bottom of the *Ask Me* T-shirt underneath.

"Nestor spent half the meeting today bitching about how the analytics on prom show attendance is lower than expected, and the shirts are supposed to be like advertising, blah blah blah. And since they printed half a billion of them, he gave everyone a new one and made us put it on right there."

I hold mine up and nod. "He just did a hit-and-run on me too."

She laughs a little, then squints across the commons, and I squint sideways at her, at the galaxy of freckled stardust swirling around her nebula eyes. Not to be a dork about it.

"Do you think we could meet to work on our project today?" she asks. "My parents are checking my grades online ten times a day, and . . . they're riding me pretty hard about that one."

I feel a quick hit of guilt, knowing we haven't done any work on it all week, beyond picking our important figure.

"Sure," I say.

We both reach for a chip at the same time, and our fingers touch. For a split second, they hook together, and I stare at the can, trying to figure out if she initiated the hook or if I did.

It doesn't matter. One minuscule touch from her, and I'm combusted.

I pull my hand away quick, and she smiles, and I can't stop myself from smiling back.

"Any chance we can go somewhere besides my house after school?" I ask. "Joanna . . ."

"Yeah," she says. "I figured."

She grabs her phone and taps something out on the keyboard. A few seconds later, a message pings back.

"We can go to my house," she says. "I'll pick you up at the flagpole after school, if you want?"

I ache with want.

I know kissing her the other day was a fluke and an accident and a mistake and it can never happen again. I get that. But the truth is, even though meeting at my house isn't an option anymore, meeting at her house is the only option, as I see it—the reality check I need to remind me about what's real and what isn't. Beckett isn't real. Crushing on a straight girl, even if she's confused, will never be anything close to real.

That's what makes Beckett's house the only safe place to go.

It'll stop us from doing the undoable again.

But it doesn't stop me from wishing we could.

As promised, Beckett is waiting at the curb just after three when I scramble out of sixth period to meet her. She's straddling that Vespa of hers like a fucking boss.

She hands me a helmet.

"Can we make a detour?" she asks.

Anywhere. I'd literally go anywhere with her.

Five minutes later, we roll into the parking lot of—

"Just a quick pit stop at Fool City," she says.

I notice the easy way the word *fool* rolls off her tongue this time.

"I'm dying for one of those deep-fried burritos," she tells me as she kills the ignition. "I know they're death, but my mom's probably going to make us some carrot sticks and hummus, and . . . sometimes I just want something a little bad for me."

I blink at her words, tell myself it's not some kind of secret code. Sometimes a deep-fried burrito is just a deep-fried burrito.

We shortcut down the canned foods aisle toward the sandwich counter in the back, and I pull a can off the shelf as we walk by.

"What's that?" she says.

I show her the label.

"Mexicorn?" she says with a smirk. "Really?"

"Really."

"It looks disgusting. Do you eat this?"

"You're wondering if I *eat* it, and not why it's called *Mexicorn*?" I ask.

"Good point." She laughs again.

"For the record," I tell her, "no, I don't eat this. Friends don't let friends eat something called Mexicorn. It's for an art project I've been thinking about."

She shakes her head, still smiling.

She goes, "Just like your grandpa, huh?"

I stop walking, press the can against my chest.

"How so?"

She stops too, traces the few steps back to me.

"I only meant . . . obviously I didn't know him, but from what you've said about him . . . and plus the way you draw all over everything . . . the whole world is art to you. Like you're always looking at it through his lens."

I'm surprised by the sudden ache inside my chest. She's right about my grandpa. And about how she sees me.

"Well, if it isn't Daya Keane."

I spin around, not expecting to see maybe-Naomi here, again, in the canned vegetables aisle.

"Hey," I say. The word bumps against my dry lips, trying to get out.

Her gaze flips sideways for a lightning-quick assessment of Beckett. Then, like the horror movie this suddenly is, she sticks her hand out.

"I'm Natasha," she says.

I realize too late that I'm the one who should be introducing them. If I had my way, they'd never meet at all. I'd keep them where they belong—at opposite ends of my social universe. They definitely don't belong in the same orbit together.

Beckett doesn't wait for me to jump in. She reaches out to meet maybe-Naomi's grasp.

"Beckett," she says.

The sight of them touching, even just shaking hands . . . it's like watching a black hole swallow up a blazing star.

Beckett's gaze washes over maybe-Naomi's magenta-tipped hair, splashes all the way down from her sporty warm-ups to her slick new Adidas. But from what I can tell, the only thing on maybe-Naomi's radar is me.

"Stella says you might make an appearance at Vanessa's tomorrow night," she tells me.

Beckett volleys between us, waiting to hear my response.

"Uh, no," I say. "I don't think so."

She makes a fake pout-face, and goes, "Bummer. I was kind of hoping for a do-over."

I kind of want to melt into the floor right now.

She takes one last look at Beckett and says, "Whatever you're doing instead, I hope it's worth it. Cuz that party's gonna be *amaze*."

I don't so much as twitch as she strolls toward the other end of the aisle. Just before she turns the corner, she spins around and flashes me a peace sign, and then she's gone.

My upper lip is dusted with sweat beads. I wipe them away, catch Beckett studying me like she's trying to solve a trig problem.

"Ex-girlfriend?" she asks.

I start walking in the direction of the deli counter in the back. That's the whole BS reason we came here in the first place—because Beckett wanted something a little bad for her.

"*Current* girlfriend?" she presses.

"Who, Natasha?" I say, clearing my throat. "Friend of Stella's."

"So . . . a friend-of-a-friend who wants a *do-over*."

I'm relieved to see someone waiting to take Beckett's order as soon as we approach the back counter, so we can get off the subject of maybe-Naomi. It's not like I keep throwing Cason in *her* face, even though it would be fair game if I did, since he's her *actual* boyfriend.

The distraction works. For the moment.

A few minutes later, standing next to her Vespa, Beckett pulls the burrito partway out of the white paper bag, peels the foil away, and takes a bite.

"Oh my gosh! I'm way too into this," she says, rolling her eyes in mock ecstasy. She hands it to me and damn, she's right. That deep-fried death burrito is everything.

Beckett stares at the burrito after I hand it back, then asks, "What kind of do-over was she hoping for?"

I finish chewing, force myself to swallow. "She wanted to dance with me at a party once."

Beckett looks like she wants to ask more, or know more—about the party, possibly about maybe-Naomi. But she just takes another bite instead and hands the burrito back to me. We swap it back and forth while the sounds of traffic and people talking and occasional music from a passing car fill up the space between us. It doesn't take long for us to demolish that burrito.

"So how come you didn't dance with her?" she says, wadding the foil and bag into a ball.

"She's not my type. But I think you probably know that."

The corners of Beckett's mouth lift into a smile as she tosses the trash into a nearby can, but she doesn't respond. She straddles the Vespa seat, and I slide in behind her. I study the minuscule stars on her shirt as she straps her helmet on. I think about stars as I put mine on. I mean, what are stars, anyway, but beams of light shining from billions of miles away. That's all I'm holding on to. Beams of invisible light, cast from stars so many light-years away that, even though they still look real, they may not even exist anymore.

I let that thought go in the wind as Fool City fades out behind us.

I don't want to think about burned-out stars right now.

I don't want to think about maybe-Naomi, or do-overs, or parties for girls who aren't welcome at either version of prom.

I want to work on our Spanish project.

And then get through prom night.

Once those things are in the rearview, the rest of my life can go back to normal.

Eighteen

THE COLONY

Beckett passes through the main part of Greenville, eventually turning right between a pair of tall stone columns that read The Colony in vertical wrought iron letters.

The Colony is a gated community of big stucco houses with balconies and stone walls. Trees and flowers grow in the yards, not just cacti. These Colony houses are a serious one-up on the houses in Justin Tadeo's neighborhood, and that's saying something.

One more left turn onto a cul-de-sac called Emmanuel Way.

There are only seven houses on this dead-end street. Beckett pulls up to the one at the very center, the biggest one, the macro-mansion with three mini-mansions flanking it on either side.

She parks out front, drops the kickstand, takes the helmet from me and slides it over the handlebar opposite hers. She doesn't lock any of it up, or put anything away, or take anything inside with her. But this is Greenville. Over in my part of town, you wouldn't leave your shoes out front if you still wanted them to be there later.

We cross the driveway to a massive front door, so big you could practically drive an eighteen-wheeler through it. As we walk inside, my line of vision goes vertical—up the sweeping staircase to the balcony that spans the length of the second floor. Our whole house could fit inside the space of this entryway with enough room to copy/paste a second one on top of it.

As Beckett leads me toward the kitchen, I see a common biblical theme in their home decor.

Her mom kisses her on the cheek when we come in, and Beckett goes, "Mom, this is my friend Daya."

"Welcome, Daya," Mrs. Wild says. "Make yourself at home."

"Thank you."

In my artist's mind, I was drawing Mrs. Wild as an older version of Beckett. And she is, sort of. The alt-universe version. Tall and lean. Sporty, like she plays a lot of tennis. Not artsy, which I guess kind of tracks too.

I turn at the sound of a metallic clink-clink coming into the room. A fluffy dog bounces straight over to smell my hand. I recognize him from Beckett's Insta page.

"This is Marshall," she says. "Who's a good boy?"

"Aw, he's sweet," I say, running my hand over the dog's thick, curly fur. "Marshall?"

"Named after our beloved Pastor Marshall," Mrs. Wild says. "May he rest."

"Marshall Mathers," Beckett whispers, squatting down to give the dog hugs and scratches.

I smile.

"Are you staying for supper, Daya?" Mrs. Wild turns to Beckett. "Daddy won't be joining us tonight."

Her mom's words are a blender-whirl of confusion. Staying for *supper*? *Daddy*?

"Oh, uh. No," I say. "I don't think so. Thank you, though."

"Can I at least get you girls a snack? I have carrot sticks and hummus."

Beckett raises an eyebrow at me.

"That's okay," she says. "We have a Spanish project we need to get to work on."

"Well, you have to eat something. Daya, do you like hummus?"

Beckett pops to her feet and blurts, "We don't want anything."

"Becky." The word comes out one part surprise, one part warning shot, and Beckett shrinks slightly under her mother's blistering gaze.

The room begins to fill with the worst kind of silence.

"I apologize," she finally mumbles. "Can we just . . . go now? We have a lot of work to do."

Mrs. Wild gives me a quick look, then turns back to Beckett. Her smile goes thin and tight.

"Nice to meet you, Daya," she says before turning her back on both of us.

The uncomfortable silence follows us as we head to Beckett's room, but on the way, I'm distracted by the vastness of this house. It feels like we're extras in a commercial for Sun Brothers Furniture Emporium in Phoenix. *A world of elegant and refined home furnishings*, the voice-over on the TV ad says. Every room in the Wild family macro-mansion could be its own Sun Brothers showroom. Everything shines like it's new. Everything's coordinated and ultra-matching. And unlike the secondhand picture frames at our house, the family photos along their fireplace mantel and up the stairway contain photographs of Beckett's actual family. I bet there isn't a single thing in this house that came to them secondhand, besides maybe a complete set of her grandmother's china.

My heart races as we climb the stairs. I've imagined being in Beckett's room a million times, but nothing could prepare me for the chaos of colors and textures as we walk inside. Macramé wall hangings, vintage glass lanterns dangling from the ceiling in clusters, pillows everywhere, some big enough to sit on. And Beckett's framed artwork on all the walls.

"Whoa . . ." I whisper, taking it all in.

"Is that whoa in a good way?" she says. "Whoa, as in, you like it?"

"Yeah." I take a slow spin. "I do."

She smiles, but her face quickly shifts from sunlight to shadow.

"My parents hate it. There's a shocker. They constantly threaten to bring in the interior designer and turn it into some urban farmhouse nightmare."

"What's urban farmhouse?" I ask.

"You know, all pastel and white, and just distressed enough to be trendy. I hate that whole vibe, y'know? There's no life in that. But . . . that's what they consider 'appropriate for a girl my age,' so."

Something in her laugh is dry and brittle as she nervously rearranges the pillows on her bed.

"Also, just so you know? Try not to say *God* in front of my mom, unless you're praying or praising."

I set my bag down on the seat of a vintage-looking velvet chair in the corner.

"Whatever you say. *Becky*."

Her cheeks do a slow burn, and for a beat or two, I wonder if she's actually mad. For all I know, Becky is her super-secret, family-only nickname, and she despises it, and now the painful truth has been revealed.

She moves in my direction, armed with a small pillow from her bed. She swats me with it.

"Is that supposed to be funny?"

"Yeah," I say, blocking with my arms. "A little."

"You're in *so* much trouble."

This time her laugh is not dry or brittle. This time, her laugh is as full and sweet as a ripe berry as she pushes into my personal bubble. I slide my fingers around her arms and pin them gently behind her to stop her all-out pillow assault on me, and we stand there in the middle of her room, eye-locked and smiling.

"I surrender," she whispers.

I let her go but she doesn't move away.

"Can I ask you one thing?" I say, low and soft.

"Okay."

I tip my head. "Did she really say: *Daddy* won't be home for supper?"

Beckett rolls her eyes. "They're from Texas. *East* Texas. It's an east Texas thing."

"Is that why you're blushing?"

"I'm not blushing," she says, imitating her mother's slight drawl. "That's just my natural peaches-and-cream complexion."

I shake my head. Smile. Drink in her light like sweet tea.

"What?" she says.

"You're like . . . a house with all these secret rooms."

She laughs. "What do you mean, secret rooms?"

"Like . . . I never know what to expect from you."

"So, what if I said . . ." She's blushing for real now. "What if I said *I* want a do-over."

Beckett pushes against me, and I want so badly to lean all the way in. I want her hair to fill the spaces between my fingers. I want her breath in my lungs. I want her lips, her tongue, her hands to be an answer instead of a million questions. But we're in her room. We're standing next to her bed where she probably kneels and says her prayers at night. I can't know if that's really what she does. But this? What's happening now, what happened the other day in *my* room? I'm one hundred percent sure this isn't what she really does either. And I'm one hundred percent confused about why she chose *me* for her first sapphic experience.

She slides her arms around my neck, and I close my eyes, waiting for the touch of her lips against mine. Her mouth lights me on fire everywhere it lands, flaring like the matches I threw at the moon the other night from the deck of B'Rad's boat. She dusts my jawline with kisses. The side of my neck. She pulls the collar of my shirt aside so she can run her tongue across my shoulder. My skin dissolves to nothing, turns me transparent. Everything inside me is out in full view for Beckett to see. The air in my lungs. The heart thrashing in my rib cage. The endorphins speeding through my bloodstream.

A sharp knock on the other side of the door zaps the energy between us into oblivion.

"How's it going in there?" Mrs. Wild calls from the other side. "I brought you girls some snacks."

I dash over to the chair in the corner, my heart thrashing with excitement and fear. I pray Beckett's mom won't notice the thickness of ache and want in the room.

Beckett checks herself in the stand-up mirror next to the door before opening it, and when she does, her mother peers inside, surveys the space. She lands on the velvet chair and puts a smile on when she sees me sitting in it. Then she steps inside, a wooden tray gripped in both hands, filled with little plates of cut fruit and vegetables and dips and two unopened bottles of bougie Italian soda.

"Let's keep this door open," she says, taking one last look around. "It's a little stuffy in here."

Neither of us moves a muscle or even exhales until the tapping of Mrs. Wild's footsteps disappears down the stairs. I wait a few seconds longer before I can work up the courage to finally look at Beckett.

All the light in her face is gone. The blood feels like it's drained out of mine as well.

"I don't get it," I say. I'm not whispering, but my voice is low enough to stay contained inside the room, even with the door open. "You can decorate your bedroom like this, dye your hair, paint your Vespa any way you want. But you have to keep the door open when you have a friend over?"

She sits down on the edge of the bed, unzips her backpack, starts taking things out one at a time.

"They worry about my choices." She slaps a notebook down on the bed. "Not like they let me have any." The pens she tosses next to her roll onto the floor. "I do everything they want. *My* choices are *their* choices." She turns her backpack upside down and dumps everything out at her feet.

"Okay, but . . . it's not like you locked yourself in here with Cason. You're just doing homework with a friend from school."

"Yeah." She drops the empty backpack on top of its contents and looks up at me. "Except I'm not."

My ears crackle the way they do sometimes when I'm in trouble, only right now I don't know who I'm in trouble with. Myself? Beckett's mom? Beckett? Is she the one lying to herself about who she is? Or am I lying to myself about who *we* are?

"What are you thinking?" she asks, cutting her eyes sideways at me.

I lean forward in the chair, weave my fingers together so she can't see them shaking. I want to tell her every thought I've ever had about her. About us. Every private moment we've shared in my mind. I want to tell her not to care what her parents think, but I can't even do that with my own mother. I want to say all the quiet parts out loud.

But when I open my mouth, all that comes out is, "I guess I'm thinking we should work on our project."

Beckett goes dark. Five minutes ago, she was full of light and fire. Now she looks like a match I snuffed out and tossed at the moon.

Nineteen

STELLA'S, ON PROM NIGHT

When I get to Stella's around five on Saturday, her mom is in the kitchen making lasagna and looking fly as hell in a pair of jeans and a nice kind of top. Mr. Zapata is kicked back on the couch with a can of soda in one hand and the TV remote in the other, like it's the most natural thing in the world for him to be here.

Like all of this is some version of . . . normal.

"Hey, Daya," he says. "Nice to see you."

He does seem more genuinely happy to see me than he ever was in geometry last year. Mostly he never seemed to notice I was there.

I lift a hand and go, "Uh. Hey, Mr. Zapata." It's all I can think to say back to my math teacher, when he's also the person getting busy with my best friend's mom on the regular. That's a mental image you can never erase.

"We're just about to watch a movie," he says. "Why don't you girls join us?"

"Oh . . . cool," I say, snagging a soda from the fridge. "I think we're good, though."

"It's prom night, Mark," Ms. Avila tells him sweetly.

"Oh. Right." He shoots me a wink, adding, "I knew that."

As I head back to Stella's room, Mr. Zapata quietly adds, "They're going to prom?" The note of surprise in his question follows me all the way down the hall.

Stella's on her bed when I bust in.

"Hey," she says, tapping away on her phone. "Gimme a sec. I'm working out the deets for tonight."

My stomach twitches at the word *deets*. Her deets for the night will be very different from my deets.

Stella throws her phone down when she's finished.

"You're here! Show me the dress!"

"It's not that exciting, I promise."

"I'll be the judge of that," she says, stretching out on her bed. "Come on, Daya. I want to know what a lesbian going to Conversion Prom looks like."

"You're really enjoying this, aren't you?"

"I dunno. I mean, *enjoy* is such a strong word."

She props herself up on her elbows and watches as I pull the dress out of my bag. I strip out of my jeans and T-shirt and slip it over my head as quickly as I can. It falls around me all cool and sensual—as if I needed any help feeling that way when all I have to do is think about spending the whole night near Beckett. Maybe sneaking off to the secret room she started to tell me about the other day.

"Dude!" Stella shrieks, sitting up again. "You look epic!"

"God, no, don't say *epic*," I tell her as she hops off the bed, grabs me by the wrist, pulls me out the door and down the hallway.

"Mamá! Look at Daya!"

Ms. Avila pulls off her oven mitts for some reason and comes around the kitchen counter to get a closer look. Mr. Zapata comes over too.

"Oh my goodness, Daya," Stella's mom says. "Don't you look lovely!"

"Dude, I'm serious," Stella says. "You. In this dress."

Mr. Zapata clears his throat.

"You really do look nice, Daya," he says. "But I understand how hard it can be to step outside your comfort zone."

He smiles and winks, then goes back into the living room. Stella's mom gives me a little squeeze and follows him. I mouth *what the fuck* to Stella, because I have no idea what kind of Nickelodeon-TV-family moment just happened here. Unless Stella's house is the magic portal to an actual alternate, Nickelodeon-TV-family universe.

Back in her room, she gets pulled into a last-minute text flurry.

"I thought you worked it all out already," I say.

"We did. My girl's just showing me what her prom dress *woulda* looked like if we were going. It was supposed to be a surprise."

She holds the phone out to me, shows me the selfie she just got. Valentina is smoking in some vampy, Jessica Rabbit–looking thing.

I go, *"Damn."*

Stella pulls her phone back. "Like I said."

She's still drooling over that photo when B'Rad texts me to let me know that he's getting off work.

just need to shower so I don't smell like a wiener. I should be at Stella's pretty quick.

don't ever say "smell like a wiener" to me, ever again, I text back with a wink emoji. I do it just to bug him. Unlike me and Stella, B'Rad hates the emoji-verse.

"Tell Be Weird I said *hey*," Stella says.

I stare at her like she's lost her lesbian mind.

"Why you sweatin' me about B'Rad?" I say. "Damn, woman, go get ready or something."

The joke is that *getting ready* takes each of us less than five minutes. I already have my dress on—don't need hair or makeup, no change of shoes since my dress is long enough to cover my sneaks. Stella just needs to change from her T-shirt to a button-down and throw a necktie around the collar.

"It isn't too late to change your mind," she says, fluffing up her hair in the mirror. "Girl, you know someone's gonna want to nail you in that dress, and it ain't gonna be Sister Mary Margaret. Maybe . . . Natasha?"

Not likely. Besides, maybe-Naomi is the last person I want anything from tonight.

"There's room in the car," she says, dangling the offer in my face like it's the keys to a Lamborghini. "It's not a sin to change your mind, Daya. And unlike prom, this party's free."

"My prom is free."

"No, it ain't," she says, shaking her head like she thinks I'm an idiot.

Her phone pings a message.

"Valentina's on her way. What about B'Rad?"

"Any minute," I say.

She hooks her arm through mine.

"Even though I'm a sinner, and you're going to the Good Place," she says, "I still love you."

"You're a jerk." I laugh. "But I love you too."

Right on cue, B'Rad texts to say he's out front, and Stella follows me out to meet him. On our way through the living room, Ms. Avila hops off the couch and gives us each a hug because this night is determined to be as awkward as fucking possible.

"You both look fantastic," Mr. Zapata says. "I hope you save me a picture."

Stella and I kick each other a look of confusion.

"Oh, no, Mark, they're not going *together*," Ms. Avila tells him.

Stella laughs out loud.

She goes, "Yeah, they wouldn't let me take a girl as my date, so I'm going to a lesbian anti-prom party instead. Daya's going to church prom, so she can tell her mom she found Jesus tonight."

I elbow Stella in the ribs, and she yelps in pain, but I don't care. She totally deserves it.

Mr. Zapata looks like he isn't sure how to respond, so he just says, "Try and have a good time," and Stella's mom gives each of us an air kiss as she scoots us out the door.

B'Rad is waiting in the car, but the minute the front door clicks shut behind us, Stella yells out to him. "*Dude.* Get over here and work your strut!"

He steps out, comes around to the passenger side, and spreads his arms like a freaking condor, rocking the funkiest plaid suit I've ever seen. It's . . . *shiny.*

"Damn, Be Weird!" Stella says, nodding her approval. "You look like you got hit-and-run by Christmas. I mean that in a good way."

I reach over, rub the lapel between two fingers.

"Not too shabby," I tell him.

"Man," she says. "Who'd you ice this suit off of?"

"Ignore her," I say.

"It's raw silk." He proudly pulls the front open to reveal a tag inside that means nothing to someone like me. "Check out the name on this label. It would have cost me a mint, too, even secondhand, except—" He holds his arms straight out in front of him, and now I can see that one of the sleeves is visibly shorter than the other. Not just by a little, but by several inches. B'Rad points toward his feet. "The pants are the same way. Lucian couldn't move the damn thing, so he gave it to me for a song, including this shirt and these shoes."

"You look dapper as fuck," I say.

"Just lean to the left and no one will be able to tell." Stella gives us both a nudge and adds, "Okay, well, you kids have fun tonight. But not too much fun, cuz you're at church prom, so." She starts to walk away, but then spins back. "*Wait*. Lemme snap a pic."

B'Rad throws two thumbs-up and a huge smile at Stella. The best I can do is pained half-smile.

"I love what you're wearing, Daya!" she calls out like she's paparazzi.

"Enjoy it," I tell her as I get in the car. "You'll never see me in a dress again."

As we pull away from Stella's, B'Rad goes, "What'd I tell you? You look amazing."

"So do you," I say. "Sincerely."

He turns the radio on and blasts the volume. We sing along to old-school hair-metal bands as we drive, head banging to Ozzy Osbourne until we're almost there. Nothing but Christian radio comes in clear this far into Greenville, but Ozzy keeps trying.

A click or two from the soaring steeples of Grace Redeemer, B'Rad suddenly reaches out and turns the radio off. "It just feels weird, y'know . . . the whole Satan-worship thing. *Here*," he adds, as if he needs to clarify.

"That's really thoughtful of you," I say.

We weave through the parking lot crowded with cars and prom goers, all dressed up fancy and walking toward the balloon-arched entrance. Two limos sit parked out front—one white, one black. I wonder who arrived in those.

B'Rad finally finds a spot, sets the brake, and cuts the engine.

"Don't move," he says, swinging his door open. "I'll help you out."

"Wait." I grab his sleeve so he can't move, and he slides back inside, closing the creaky door behind him.

He blinks at me. "What's wrong?"

I take a long look around the parking lot, swarmed by real Great Wait kids, kids who faithfully go to Grace Redeemer or churches like it. Who believe everything they're told here, not just the parts that feel right. Kids who think Pure Prom is the greatest thing since the Redemption Baptism Experience or whatever. I know I don't fit in here. I know I don't belong the way they belong, no matter what it says on Joanna's coffee mug.

"Tell me it's going to be okay," I say. "Tell me I don't have to be . . ." A cluster of Pure Prommers passes in front of the car. ". . . *that*. And I still get to have fun here tonight. Tell me no one's going to laugh at me for wearing a dress—"

"Look," he says. "I clicked the QR code on the ticket you sent me. You only have to wear the dress until midnight, okay? The dance part will be over then, and we'll get to change. Like Cinderella. Except here, it's nothing but fun and games till morning. And in the meantime? You get, like, all the free snacks your heart desires. And . . . you have . . . the *sexiest* prom date in the entire state of Arizona, in fact. And before you know it, it'll be over, and you won't ever have to do this again if you don't want to. It's gonna be fine."

I take a breath.

"I'm right here," he says. "I'll be right by your side the whole time. Leaning to the left."

That makes me laugh.

He grabs our bags from the back, then comes around and opens my door. I almost kill myself tripping over the hem of my dress getting out, but I guess a night that starts with a near-death experience can only get better from there, right? No need to take it as an omen.

I reach out, slide his arm through mine the way all these other guys do as they walk their dates across the parking lot. B'Rad squeezes my hand, and I suck in one more sweet breath of freedom before we cross under the balloon arch to go inside.

Twenty

GRACE REDEEMER

Nestor Camarillo ambushes us at the door.

"Daya—finally! We're going to need your people at the ticket station in about two minutes."

He gives B'Rad a quick sweep, but B'Rad is distracted by the ginormous neon *Make Room for God* wall, not to mention everything else that would freak a person out if they've never been here before.

"I don't remember you," Nestor says to him. "What committee are you on?"

B'Rad rappels his gaze down the towering neon wall. "I'm her plus-one."

Nestor seems too frazzled to process this information.

"Your group can tell you what to do." He turns back to me. "Have you seen Beckett?"

My pulse reverbs at the sound of her name.

"Uh. We just got here, so—"

"Well, if you see her, let her know we need to start taking tickets in, seriously, like, two minutes."

I'm not sure how this ticket thing got dumped in my lap when there's a whole committee for this that I never technically got added to. Nestor has already started to move on to something else when I remember the duffel bags slung over B'Rad's shoulder.

"Hey," I call out. "Where are we supposed to put our stuff?"

"I'll show you." The words sweep in from the side, brushing just below my ear.

I flame out as I turn.

Beckett shimmers behind me like the most beautiful mirage I could imagine.

Nestor calls out. "Beckett! We need your committee to get set up *now*."

But her eyes never peel away from me as she says, "Just let me show Daya where to put her stuff."

"I'll hang out here," B'Rad says, handing the bags to me. "In case he blows a fuse before you get back."

"You sure?" I ask.

B'Rad goes *pffft*. "I can handle him."

I can't take my eyes off Beckett as she leads me through the mini-mall-style foyer. But instead of going into the huge auditorium where they had services last Sunday, she takes me to what must be one of the side towers, if that's what those three looming facades out front are called. This section of the building is more of a sprawling meeting hall than an auditorium. Inside, a net has been stretched across the length and width of the room, keeping hundreds of balloons from floating all the way to the top. Their curling-ribbon tails drip down into the room like a wall-to-wall curtain of delicate tentacles. Meanwhile, a DJ in a booth up front is testing out his light show, the same kind of moving, strobing, multicolor lights they seem to use for every event at Grace Redeemer, from church service to youth group to concerts to summer camp. And now, apparently, prom.

Beckett keeps going, and pretty soon we're headed down a long hallway that leads to a small storage room, tucked into what must be the farthest corner of the building.

"They want everyone to put their things in the coatroom," she says. "But that's all the way on the other side. No one ever comes in here, so . . . I dunno. It just feels safer."

I nod like I understand what could possibly feel safer than already being in church.

I follow her into the room, and she turns, the strap of her duffel bag sliding off her shoulder.

"I wanted to text you last night," she says.

"Why didn't you?"

"My mom took my phone after you left, because . . . I guess I was being disrespectful to her." She hesitates, then turns and tucks her bag under a metal table stacked high with books. I toss our bags under as well. She doesn't stand up right away—she stays crouched, looking through her stuff. I use the moment to absorb the details of her without anyone else around. My drifting gaze lands on her back like the first snowflake of winter up in Flagstaff, tumbling across her shoulders, catching on the sequins and sparkles of her pale pink dress, then up again, into the braids and spirals of her done-up hair. A hundred different kinds of ache press against my chest.

Beckett stands up suddenly, tucking a phone into a pocket hidden in the fluff of her skirt.

"They still have mine," she explains. "This one's a burner."

I lift my hand to my mouth, clear my throat a little, hoping I can get out some of what I've been wanting to say to her since yesterday. To ask her about what happened with her mom. About why her parents are so worried about her so-called choices. Why her mom was so intent on leaving the bedroom door open. It's not like she was in there with—

"So . . . where's Cason?" I hear myself ask instead.

His name makes the air in the room feel dirty.

"He'll be a little late—they made a pit stop first." A look crosses over her face, like she just got caught in a lie. She goes, "Honestly, he was like, *If we have to be locked up with no in-and-out privileges, I'm gonna burn a few before I'm stuck in there all night.*"

"Gotcha." I look at the floor, try to think of something else to say, since I can't seem to say what I want. "How come you didn't go with him?"

"It's not my thing. Sometimes I wish it was, though."

I'm pretty sure that by *sometimes* she means tonight.

She leans against the metal table like we have all the time in the world. Like the two minutes Nestor gave us before we have to start taking tickets haven't already passed, plus several more after that. Like Nestor won't lose his super-organized shit if we don't turn up soon. Like people won't talk, or even wonder, about us if we stay here one minute longer than we've already *been* here. The sheer layers of Beckett's skirt float around her, little specks of silvery thread shining through like sugar stars in one of her coffee-cup galaxies.

"What are you thinking about?" she asks, and just like that, I'm out of my head and back inside the storage room at Grace Redeemer Church.

"Me? Nothing. Why?"

She shakes her head like she's trying to keep from saying something, then blurts, "You look unbelievable, Daya."

I know she means it. I can tell by how she's looking at me, by the way my body responds, that she means it. But there's something else there that I can't shake loose from. Like she *wants* me to look incredible so I can fit into this world—*her* world. Like she wants me to belong, when it's pretty agonizingly obvious that I don't.

We both start talking at the same time.

"You go first," I say.

"No, it's just . . . we should probably head back, that's all."

Yeah. I guess she's right. But I leave the storage room hoping that's *not* all. Aching for more time alone with her, however I can have it.

I follow Beckett back to the ticket station, to the long tables covered in black stretchy fabric, set up for us to scan everyone who comes in.

When we get there, B'Rad is sitting next to Cason and Lucy, with Lucy's date, Javi, on the end. I'm not sure why they need six people to do tickets, but it's not my place to crit, since I made zero contributions to this committee.

Before long we get into a kind of rhythm—Beckett, B'Rad, and I scan each person's e-ticket, while Cason, Lucy, and Javi attach the vinyl club-style bands to everyone's wrists. But the brainlessness of the task does nothing to water down the vibe at our table. Not the unignited heat sparking between Beckett and me. Not the buzzed horniness of Cason Price, spewing like a shaken beer can over every girl who comes to the table. Not Lucy's loyalty toward Beckett that's strung like a wire cable between the two of them.

Half an hour in, give or take, someone makes an announcement that it's time to get the party started, and a few minutes later, they announce that they've locked it all down. Nestor comes by to tell us we can go into the dining hall with everyone else.

I stay where I am for an extra moment, to avoid the crush of all those people moving in the same direction at once.

Beckett floats by, two steps behind Cason. "You two coming?"

B'Rad and I bounce a look off each other, and we get up in unison, following loosely behind Beckett.

The dining hall is set up in the third tower section, where most people had to walk through to put their overnight bags in the coatroom. Round tables are set up all around the room, with eight chairs at each table. The lights in here are low but not dim. It smells like food even though there's no actual food on the tables yet. The whole thing has this incredibly surreal filter to it.

I look over at Beckett, laughing at something someone must have said, but all I can see is us kissing in her room and in mine.

Not surprisingly, we end up at a table with Beckett, Cason, Lucy, and Javi. No one sits in the other two seats. On one hand, I'm relieved to be at a table with just them, since they're the only people here I really know. On the other hand, the only person I like besides B'Rad is Beckett, so that's not super helpful.

A college-aged-looking dude with an in-ear microphone stands in front of the sweeping window that makes up the front of the tower from the outside. He's wearing a powder-blue tux with a white T-shirt underneath that says something on it, probably True Love Waits, and navy-blue Chuck Taylors with no socks.

"Good evening, brothers and sisters . . . welcome! I'm so glad you're here. I'm Pastor Ben, the youth pastor here at Grace Redeemer." A huge cheer rises into the dining room. "It's amazing to be in this room tonight, in this mood tonight, with love and light all around us. *Are you ready, Grace Redeemer?*"

More noise from the Pure Prommers.

Pastor Ben laughs. "Well, we're gonna feed you first, so let's take a moment to praise Him for this opportunity. Lord, we thank you—"

I close my eyes, my hands twisted in a sweaty knot on my lap, until Beckett nudges me under the table. I shoot her a look of panic as she reaches for me, until B'Rad also fumbles for my hand on the other side, and I realize this is what's happening all around the room. I give him a stealth eye roll and shove my hand into his. We both hold on for dear life.

"Father, we ask that You bless this food to our bodies and our bodies to Your service."

Beckett's hand is soft and warm. There's no agenda in the way her fingers thread through mine, no expectation in her clasp, not even a reminder of who she is or what we've done together. I'm the one who can't seem to forget.

"Lord, You've promised us salvation. You've promised us eternity, and all You ask in return is for us to commit to You." His voice builds to a crescendo. "All You've asked is for us to remain *pure* and *ready* to fulfill Your perfect plan for us, and Lord . . . we're here to commit to that tonight."

Beckett flinches at the word *pure*.

"We ask these things in the name of Jesus," Pastor Ben says. "Amen."

A small army of parents and siblings pours out of the kitchen, carrying prepared plates of chicken, and mashed potatoes, and mixed vegetables that look like they're from a can.

Beckett leans close and whispers in my ear.

"Mexicorn?"

I smile, and she laughs a little, and a puff of her breath tickles the side of my cheek. I catch Lucy watching and instantly back away.

Cason Price is chewing on B'Rad's ear like they're bros from all the way back in the day. I'm pretty sure if Cason wasn't stoned right now, he wouldn't be bro-crushing on B'Rad so hard. I kick my foot out to the side and tap it against his foot. He looks over at me, his eyes going comic book huge behind the thick lenses of his glasses.

Help me, he mouths, and I mouth back, *I'm so sorry*.

Cason doesn't seem to notice. He never seems to notice anything that doesn't directly involve him. Every time I start feeling guilty about kissing his girlfriend, he does some jerky thing that makes it hard to go all the way there.

Dinner is quickly becoming a hellscape of awkwardness. I have no one to talk to, since B'Rad is currently being held hostage by Cason, and Beckett seems to be splitting her attention between Lucy and Cason and whoever else orbits around her. But her smile isn't real. It's that fake smile I've seen her put on before, so that no one can see she's having some real kind of emotion that isn't grateful or joyful or blessed. I wonder which one of a thousand things her fake smile is a cover for tonight.

Finally, Pastor Ben's voice explodes into the room.

"Grace Redeemer! Are we ready to *Praise God all night long?*"

Cheers from the Pure Prommers, who spring out of their chairs, leaving the dishes and chicken bones and uneaten Mexicorn-wannabe for their parents and siblings to clean up. Everyone rushes to the dance hall on the other side of the building.

The music is already bumping when we get there. The DJ puts one hand on his oversized headphones, the other in the air.

"How's everyone doing tonight?" he shouts into the room as we swim through a sea of colored lights and all those ribbons hanging down. He gradually dials the volume down, and the bass-heavy song eases into something more gentle and aching. It plays in the background as he talks.

"Father, we're here tonight to give You praise. Hold these young hearts in purity and light tonight. Remind us where we belong, and to Whom we belong." The crowd begins to call out and cheer. "Remind us that our joy . . . lies *not* in the flesh . . . but in the *spirit!*" A small cluster of nearby girls look my way when he says this, I don't know why. *"Let us praise His name with dancing!"*

And with that, the room erupts in cheers as everyone starts jumping up and down in time to the music.

My gaze wanders across the dance hall. No one would ever know this wasn't any other high school prom, in any town, anywhere. Except for all the praise hands in the air. And the deliberate lack of PDA. And the sudden realization that every single prom dress here is some variation of a pastel. I spin a slow circle so I can verify this. No one's wearing red. There are no jewel tones, no deep blue, or emerald green, or royal purple, and for sure no silver or gold. I'm wearing the only black dress in the room. I'm also showing the most skin of anyone else here, which, given the minuscule expanse of my exposed shoulder, is saying something. None of the gowns are strapless or even sleeveless, and all of them have necklines that don't come close to revealing collarbones, much less cleavage.

Beckett floats up beside us, her cotton candy gown swirling around her. I bet her mom picked it out. Beckett hates pastel-anything.

She points to B'Rad's tux, and because it's too loud to hear anyone talking, she gives him a thumbs-up and he gives one back to her. Cason grabs Beckett's hand and pulls her onto the dance floor like a caveman dragging his woman by her hair.

Cason. Price. *Disgusts*. Me.

B'Rad taps me on the arm and dips his chin toward the dance floor. He makes sure I know it's a question by the look on his face. But I don't feel like dancing. I don't want to stay in this room if it means watching Beckett and Cason do whatever heteronormative purity ritual they're doing right now. Not when all I've been thinking about all night is going back to the storage room with Beckett, even just for a minute or two, if for nothing else so I can breathe her in.

I tip my head toward the door leading out to the mini-mall. That's where prom photos are being taken. Where the selfie station is. Where the gift shop is still open for those last-minute prom purchases, whatever those might be.

B'Rad and I leave the dance hall, walk over to a bench under the MAKE ROOM FOR GOD sign. At least out here we can almost hear ourselves think.

"You don't look like you're having any fun," he says, adding in a whisper, "Must be hard watching her get manhandled by you-know-who."

"I guess I don't have my game face on."

"You mean, your praise face?"

I bump him with my exposed shoulder. "You're as bad as Stella."

He looks around. "This is wild, man. You should have warned me."

"You never would have believed it," I say.

"No," he snickers. "I wouldn't." He looks over at the selfie station. "I've sold bud to a bunch of those guys."

"Go ahead and get baked," I say, "as long as you're celibate while you do it."

"Right? There's . . . a . . . *lot* of talk about purity tonight. But show me where it's written *Thou Shalt Not Burn One?*"

"I think that's in Cannabis 4:20."

We both laugh.

"We're going to hell for that, aren't we?" he whispers.

"It's not the only thing, but yeah. Probably."

B'Rad pretends to notice the massive neon sign behind us for the first time. He drama-flinches from it, and even though it's not that funny, we both giggle hysterically.

We sit there a while longer, watching as people take selfies or prom pictures, listening as the music reaches out to us from inside the dance hall. I know at some point, B'Rad will want to take pictures, too. I just want to get through this night with the least amount of damage to my heart as possible, since things are already going sideways and it's not even midnight yet.

"You look like you're a million miles away," he says. "Where are you?"

"Honestly? That party up in Oviedo. I'm starting to think I just should've gone to that instead."

"That bad, huh?"

"It's not the company." I lean into him. "It's just . . . right now . . . anything would be better than sitting here . . . stupidly wishing I could be Cason Price for one night." I say this last part right against his ear, in a whisper so soft, no one else could possibly hear. I know it's wrong for me to say it out loud, in this room, under a neon sign that says Make Room for God. Maybe worse than saying Cannabis 4:20.

I look up from whispering in B'Rad's ear to the sight of Beckett headed our way.

"I wondered where you went." She pushes back a strand of hair that worked its way loose. "Are you guys out here to take pictures, or . . . ? Because I can text everyone to come join us."

I'm not sure how to tell Beckett that I really don't want to take prom pictures. I don't need a souvenir of this dance, or this dress, or these people, once tonight is over. I don't need a nonstop reminder of Beckett's purity promise. Or that the person I want to be with more than anything is only okay if she's flirting with me in my teensy corner of the world, because who am I kidding? This church is her *whole* world, and even though this world is massive enough to contain a trillion secret rooms, there would still never be room for us to hide here.

B'Rad leans in and tells me, "I'm gonna hit the bathroom real quick. I promise, I'll be right back."

I try to stop him, but he vaporizes into the crowd coming out of the dance hall.

"Maybe we should go get in line," Beckett says. "Looks like it's moving kind of slow."

I follow her to where the photo area is set up. She takes her phone out, and not long after, Lucy and Cason and Javi are headed our way. Cason's trying to drink a cup of punch he brought out with him, and Javi keeps pretending he's going to bump his arm and make him spill it. I hope he does, to be honest. I hope Cason spills bright red punch all over his pale pink tuxedo.

Beckett and I don't say much as we stand in line, but I can't stop remembering. Her hair in my hands when we kissed. Her lips curved into a smile against my mouth. Her body on mine. My body on fire. And it still is. Even now. Even here. Standing in line for pictures. Aching to be alone with her. Still wondering how to manifest that impossible fantasy in this unforgiving space.

Some girl calls Beckett over to join their group photo.

"I'll be right back," she says as Cason chucks his empty cup into a trash can and scuds right for me.

"Dude!" He drapes himself across my shoulders. "Where's your weird friend?"

"He's not weird," I say, but Cason doesn't hear me.

And he smells nasty.

Lucy goes, "Get off her, Neanderthal."

Only she's not defending me, if that's what I'm thinking. As soon as he moves away again, she visually dissects me from head to toe.

"Classy," she says.

I don't give her the satisfaction of a response, and now that Beckett's back from making a cameo appearance in that other group's prom pictures, Cason switches from pawing at me to pawing at her.

"Get off me," she whispers to him.

"It's prom night, Becks," he says. "Jeez. Loosen up."

I panic-search the mini-mall for B'Rad.

"Come on, Becks." Cason nuzzles the side of her neck. "I thought we were gonna have some fun tonight."

"What's *wrong* with you?" she whispers, shrugging him off.

Javi jumps in and goes, "Man, let's just chill and take our pictures," which catapults Lucy into Beckett-defense mode, and the volume starts dialing up, and one by one, people turn and stare.

Too much drama. I'm out.

I start to walk away, but Beckett comes after me.

"Wait, where are you going?" she says. "It's almost our turn for pictures."

"I'm just gonna go find B'Rad," I say, looking in the direction where I think he might have gone.

She goes, "Okay. But. Do you want us to wait for you?"

"You don't have to," I say.

"Daya—"

"Don't worry about it," I call out over my shoulder. "It's fine."

"Daya!"

I pick up the pace, not stopping to look behind me. I duck into the prom hall, weave my way through dancers and balloon ribbons and music that sounds like an excited heartbeat filling the room. It does not sound like a heart that's breaking.

Beckett catches up to me when I'm halfway down the long hallway leading to the storage room and wraps her fingers around my wrist.

I whip around.

"What?"

She doesn't say anything. She just stands there, holding on to me.

I pull out of her grip, but I can't pull away from her eyes. They're searching for something in mine.

"I can't do it," I finally say, blinking away the tears I've been fighting. "I thought . . . I thought we'd have a chance to . . . But obviously, that's not why you're here, and I can't do this."

"Do what?" she asks.

Her confusion confuses me.

"I can't sit here for the next ten hours, watching you through some blurred window and pretend I don't feel things for you. I can't watch you sidestep your drunk boyfriend all night and not want to punch him in the fucking face." I sniff, wipe tears away. "And I can't put on a dress and fake like I'm straight to make everyone else think I belong here. And I sure as hell can't spend all night wondering whether *you're* faking straight, or faking like you're into me, and . . ."

She blinks and tears spill down her face too.

"I don't know what I'm doing here," I say. "That's all. And I just . . . I can't do it anymore, so. I don't think I can be here."

The fluorescent lights overhead buzz against the ceiling, casting a yellow glow into the hallway.

"Then let's go," she says, wiping her tears away with the tips of two fingers.

"What?"

"Let's get out of here. Go . . . somewhere. I don't even care where."

My head tips heavy to the side. "Beckett . . ."

"I'm serious, Daya."

Why don't we head out to nowhere, girl . . .

"Hey!"

I spin around, beyond elated to see B'Rad jogging down the hallway toward us.

He looks flustered.

"Where've you been?" I ask.

"In the coatroom, looking for our stuff," he says, keeping his voice low. "I was afraid someone was gonna come in there and bust me for trying to steal shit."

"Our bags aren't in—*were* you trying to steal shit?"

He makes a face at me. *"No."*

"Then why were you—?"

"They keep the service door unlocked," Beckett cuts in.

We both turn to face her at the same time, and for a few breaths, no one says anything.

She goes, "It's literally right there. All we have to do is grab our stuff and go."

I turn back to B'Rad, and we lock eyes. A whole conversation transpires between us in the next few silent seconds. At the end, I give him a minuscule shrug, and he pops one back, punctuated by a microscopic nod.

Minutes later, we're on the expressway, putting as much distance between us and Grace Redeemer Church as humanly possible.

250

Twenty-One

OVIEDO

The Fuck Prom party is at the end of an unpaved road on the outer edges of Oviedo, at this girl Vanessa Manrique's house.

I kick Stella a text when we roll up.

You're not gonna believe what's out front.

Stella shrieks when she sees us.

"Dudes!" She catches me in a hug like a half nelson. "What the fuck is *this*?" she shouts. "You really did it—you escaped! Be Weird . . . you drove her up here?"

He starts to answer but she jumps on him next and hugs him within an inch of his life.

"You know what you are? You're James-freaking-Bond, that's what!"

She turns to Beckett.

"Church Girl!"

"It's just Beckett," Beckett says.

"*Pfft*, I know your name. I'm just so stoked you're all here!"

As we turn toward the house, B'Rad goes, "Okay, so . . . I'll come get you guys in the morning."

"What are you talking about?" Stella calls back to him. "Get your ass over here!"

"I . . . okay . . . I thought this was a girls-only party?"

"We'll just tell everyone you're team mascot," she says. He still doesn't move. "Look, as long as you understand you've got pretty close to zero percent chance of getting laid tonight, you're gold."

He jogs to catch up with us. "If I knew I was gonna stay, I woulda changed when these two did."

Stella goes, "Don't sweat it, man. You know you look fly as hell."

As we walk toward the house, Stella tips her head in Beckett's direction and whispers, "How'd you pull *this* off?"

"We can share those stories later," I whisper back. "Right now, I just need to chill out for a while, cuz it's been intense."

"Okay, but just so you know? This reads like 'recruitment' to the people down the hill."

"You're high," I laugh.

"Whatevs." She takes the short flight of steps out front two at a time. "Right this way, bitches. First stop: beer and grub."

"I thought it was *wine and women*," I joke as we follow Stella into a room low-lit with all kinds of cool lights, past the open French doors of a side room where one group is watching *Carrie* around a giant-screen TV. The living room is full of girls dancing and more colorful lights pulsing from a pair of tower speakers. There's a game of what looks like full contact foosball going on at the back end of the room, but Stella keeps us moving—past the couches and reclining chairs where a few girls are making out, through the kitchen littered with chip bags, and warehouse store–sized tubs of candy, and drink cans, and bottles of alcohol. She opens the back door, and we pop out onto a wooden deck, then down a few steps to a fire pit behind the house.

The air out here is full of starlight and music. Someone strums a guitar and others sing along, and bubbles of laughter pop here and there in a breeze that's so warm and sweet I could drink it. For the first time all night, I feel like I can exhale. For the first time in a long time, I don't feel like an apology.

"Who's the dude?" some girl asks from across the fire pit as we squeeze in where we can. She's wearing a soccer jersey with the number 15 on the front.

Stella goes, "That's B'Rad. Say hi, B'Rad."

B'Rad lifts his hand as someone jokingly asks, "Is he the MC?" and someone else goes, "Nice suit." The words instantly evaporate inside the crackling flames of the fire.

"What's your poison, MC?" number 15 asks B'Rad, but it's maybe-Naomi who answers from right behind me.

"I've got it covered," she says, stretching forward, passing a can of hard cider so close to my face I can feel the cold pulsing off it.

She rests her hand on my shoulder after B'Rad takes the cider can from her.

"Thanks," he says.

I inch away from her to give myself a safety bumper, not that maybe-Naomi understands boundaries.

"You're here," she says, kneeling beside me. "I thought you weren't coming."

I look directly into the fire to avoid making eye contact.

"Unexpected change of plans," I tell her.

Beckett leans across me. "Natasha, right?"

The heat coming off her could blister a person's skin if they weren't careful. It catches me a little off guard.

Meanwhile, maybe-Naomi acts like she's trying to remember how she knows her.

"Oh, yeah," she says. "From the other day. Hey."

"Yeah, hey."

But maybe-Naomi turns her back on Beckett like she's a side note.

"So, Daya. This is great, right? We can finally have a do-over on that dance from last time. I feel like we stopped before things got interesting."

"I think I'm just going to hang out here," I tell her.

She looks from me to Beckett, carving a visual path down the length of her.

"Your call," she says. "But in case you're wondering, I operate on the three-strikes plan."

She pulls herself to her feet.

"One to go," she adds with a wink.

It isn't hard to watch maybe-Naomi walk away—it's definitely a relief when she disappears inside the house. Across the fire pit, Stella and Valentina are kissing on a swing bench. Around the circle from them, the girl with the guitar is showing the girl next to her how to shape her fingers into chords, and number 15 is now deep into a theoretical conversation with B'Rad about the nature of the universe as interpreted by various animated characters.

I look around the circle of faces, and I'm so fucking happy, I can hardly contain it. I finally feel like I'm somewhere I don't have to hide. Like I can stand still instead of being a moving target. Like my feet can hit the ground without eggshells underneath them. No one here makes me feel broken, or like I need to be fixed, or like I can't show up and just be who I am. For the first time in as long as I can remember, I feel ease. That's all I need tonight.

Just one perfect moment.

Beckett tilts forward.

"Hey, is that a pool back there?" she asks.

I lean around her to see what she's looking at.

"I think so," I say.

She stands up, holds her hand out to me.

I take it.

I follow her.

For a split second, I look back at Stella. She's all eyes. She gestures between me and Beckett, like, *How the hell did this happen?* but all I can do right now is throw her a peace sign as we kick down a handful of steps and around a row of hedges to the pool area.

Beckett and I stretch out side by side on a lounge chair, letting the shifting blue light from the water lap over us. Starlight pours through the sky like sugar crystals, vanishing as it hits the arc of city lights in the distance. The guitar notes floating over from the fire pit are like summer's version of a snowdrift.

Beckett shivers, and I feel her relax into me. I can't believe I'm here. I can't believe *she's* here. With *me*. Staring into a flawless sky, searching the stars for constellations, attuned to every subatomic shift around us—the soft breeze that picks up a few loose strands of her hair and brushes them against my face. Her foot, tipped to the side so the toes of our shoes are touching. Her fingers reaching for mine.

"I like your hands," she says. "I feel like they know things."

My head spins the way it did on the pontoon boat that night, when I had a little bit of weed in my system.

"My hands know things?" I say.

Her laugh comes out in this soft puff of almost-embarrassment. "Yeah. I think they do."

"Like what?"

She lets her fingers weave between mine. In. And out. And around.

"Like the shape of things. The way lines can move. When to keep them still. The saturation of colors." She laughs again. "I don't know. It sounds weird, but . . . I think artists know how to find the stories in everything."

"You're an artist," I say. "What's telling *you* a story right now?"

She takes a deep breath, and goes, "The air."

I wait to see if she says any more about it, but that's all she gives me.

In a whiff of laughter, I go, "Were you going to elaborate, or . . ."

She rolls toward me, tucks her head into the curve of my neck. Our fingers are living a life of their own and I'm barely breathing through it.

"It's like . . . every time the water ripples, or a cricket chirps, or . . . your heart beats?"

"You can hear that?"

"Yeah. With every beat, waves of energy lift into the sky. And they keep rippling that way forever, because sound is infinite. Y'know?"

Everything is infinite right now.

Our fingers wind together, touch fingertip to fingertip, stroke soft, then not so soft, but I keep bumping against her promise ring.

She slides it off, slips it onto my pinkie this time. I don't know how to feel about the fact that it fits.

Nothing about her purity promise fits what I'm thinking.

"Your heart is beating so hard," she says. "I can feel it all the way into my body."

"Yeah?"

"Yeah." She shifts again. "Can I put my hand on your chest?"

I guide her to the space just above my rib cage.

"Wow," she whispers. "What are you thinking about that's got your heart beating so fast?"

"Truth?" I ask.

"Definitely."

"I'm thinking about kissing you," I say. "I've been thinking about kissing you all day."

She rolls so she's half on top of me.

"What's stopping you?" she says.

I can't hold her close enough, kiss her deep enough, touch her soft enough or hard enough to feel like anything I'm doing is good enough. I don't know where to go, what to do. I don't want to suck at this.

I ask her, "Is this okay?" and she says yes again, and again, and I can't keep up with the infinity of her yes. I kiss her like kissing her makes absolute sense. I kiss her like kissing her puts the planets into alignment. I kiss her like I will lose my soul if we don't kiss, if I don't take the clips out of her hair, if my hands don't get lost in the curls that hang loose around both our faces, if her hands don't explore my throat and my chest, if our fingers don't discover each other's breasts, if our breath doesn't fill the sky, if our lungs don't swallow the stars whole so they can go supernova inside us. I kiss her like I'm not terrified, like I'm not confused as hell about being both terrified and electrified by kissing her.

We surface with her face still in my hands, and I search her eyes—back and forth, over and over. Is this real? Is this okay? Does it matter what happens tomorrow as long as this can happen tonight?

I lift my hand to stroke Beckett's face, and the lights all around us glint off her ring on my finger. I want to throw that ring at the moon like I did with the matches. I want to set fire to the idea of purity that says it's better to get groped at a church dance by a drunk boy than for two girls to lie under the stars in a perfect moment, asking if it's okay to kiss and touch.

Beckett says, "You look really intense right now."

"This feels really intense," I tell her. "Doesn't it feel that way to you?"

"Well, sure . . ."

"No, but I mean . . . doesn't it freak you out at all? Being here? Like this?"

She presses into me, as if her lips, her tongue, her breath are the only answers to the questions I can barely hold inside me. I'm desperate to know how this can make sense, how it can be real, how I can trust that it won't evaporate into dreams and mist by sunrise.

She swings one leg over me, straddles me as she bends forward to kiss me again and again. She moves against me, and as I lift up off the lounge chair, she leans back and pulls her blouse over her head, and my mind can't process how perfect she is.

"It's okay to touch me," she whispers, sliding my hand inside her bra. I'm shook by how soft she is, how connected and lit up I am. How being with her like this is so good, it's almost painful.

I press into her soft and easy, the way I'd catch snowflakes on my tongue. I ask her, "Does this feel good? Is this okay?" She moans and whispers her answers to me.

A couple of girls stumble tipsy and laughing down the stairs leading to the pool. I panic for a moment, hold my breath, hoping it's dark enough that they can't *see us*-see us.

"Oops," one of them says. "I guess this spot's ocupado."

She giggles again, but the other girl goes, "This whole house is ocupado—*damn*."

They leave, but they never really feel gone after that.

This isn't the first-time vibe I've fantasized about all these years. I always pictured a candlelit room, and bubbles spilling gently from a fancy tub, and rose petals, and something sparkly to drink that isn't champagne. I wanted that with Beckett. I wanted her first time to be perfect, too.

"You're so beautiful, Daya," she whispers against my mouth.

I kiss her, because I don't know how to respond. *Beautiful* is a word reserved for girls who look like her. But I *feel* beautiful, being with her like this.

She takes my hand, guides it to her pants, helps me unzip them. When I slip my fingers inside, she makes sure they go where she wants them to.

Her smile melts into my kiss as her body melts into my hands. She tells me what feels good, whispers where to touch her, where to kiss her. Every sound she makes detonates inside me.

"I want you to feel good," she says.

I want that too. Wanted it for so long . . . thought about it . . . fantasized . . .

But in the privacy of my room, things feel different. There isn't a crowded fire pit a short distance away, no drunk never-prommers stumbling into our space. And having someone touch me is a lot different from touching myself—that's something I wasn't expecting. I've never had to tell myself what feels good, what I like, what I want.

"Are you okay?" she keeps asking.

"Definitely," I say. And it is, all of it. It feels amazing. She feels amazing.

But also, I think I've psyched myself out a little.

We touch and kiss deep into the night. By the time she falls asleep, I'm pretty sure she came at least twice.

She's apologized at least that many times because I couldn't quite get there, even though I don't think that's something anyone needs to apologize for.

For a long time after she falls asleep, I lie still, watching the Milky Way swirl around us. I lost my virginity tonight. With Beckett Wild. And she lost hers to me. In what universe does that get to happen?

I hope she's right, though. I hope that sound waves do ripple into the universe forever. Because that would mean that every breath and heartbeat of this night is already eternal.

Twenty-Two

WITH BECKETT

I hear my name drift through space again and again, until I finally open my eyes.

B'Rad is standing next to us, three overnight bags strapped across his shoulders.

"We gotta go," he tells me, adding, "I didn't see anything, I swear." He points to his glasses on top of his head.

It's all good. We're mostly dressed anyway. Not much to see but our arms and legs tangled together under a blanket of clothes.

"I'll give you a minute to . . ." He doesn't finish, just turns around.

I wake Beckett up with a kiss, hand her the parts of her clothes that didn't quite make it back on in the middle of the night.

We follow B'Rad through the misty yard, into the house littered everywhere with empties, and half-eaten snacks, and sleeping girls, past a couch where maybe-Naomi is out cold, her long legs wrapped around a redhead in a SpongeBob T-shirt. I don't see Stella and Valentina, but I know they're here somewhere.

Beckett and I curl into each other in the back seat of B'Rad's car, still breathing each other in, our hands stroking and caressing the same way we did last night.

After a while, she says, "Let me see your phone."

I pull it out of my bag and hand it to her. She puts my contact info in her burner so she can text me.

hi

hello, I text back.

I can smell you all over me, she writes.

I throw a quick look in B'Rad's direction. No wonder she wanted to text instead of just talking.

I send her back a blushing emoji, adding:

I hope last night was ok?

it was perfect. well . . . almost perfect.

I look up at her, confused. Type three question marks and wait for her response.

I meant, for your first time. She looks at me after she hits send, and I stare at her for a few seconds after I read it.

I write: **what do you mean?**

it would have been perfect if you could have . . . y'know?

I shake my head. **what do you mean, for my first time? it was your first time, too.**

Her expression goes blank, fingers freeze-hover over the keyboard, eyes freeze-hover on mine. She finally peels away, starts typing again.

"That wasn't your first time?" I blurt.

Beckett checks to see if B'Rad heard. Of course B'Rad heard, he's driving the damn car. He's just too polite to show it.

She goes, "Daya—"

"You had sex with Cason?"

A massive wash of red pours over her. "It's not . . . I didn't . . ."

We are one click away from Grace Redeemer.

I'm reeling.

"But you said . . . I mean, who else would it be? It's not like you had sex with—"

There it is. The whole truth. Splashed all over her face.

". . . with Lucy . . . ?"

We swing into the church parking lot and B'Rad goes, "Oh, *shit*."

A police car with its lights silently flashing is parked next to the sagging balloon arch out front. A crowd of people is pooled on the steps: some of the kids from last night. Pastor Ben and Pastor Mike. Parents. Cops . . . all gathered in front of the church.

"Drive around back," Beckett tells B'Rad in a panic, but the phones have already come out. All those cameras, pointed straight at us.

"Hurry," she says.

"Why?"

"Because that's where the unlocked door is."

"It doesn't matter. They've already seen us."

"Just *go*—"

"It's too late," he says, slamming the brakes to avoid hitting Beckett's dad, who sprints down the steps toward us.

"Shhhhhhit," B'Rad hisses, tracking Mr. Wild to the back of the car.

Beckett visibly flinches as he throws the door open and leans in.

"Get out," he tells her.

She's frozen. We're all frozen.

"Get out of the car," he says again.

Her turn is quick, the look on her face a blast wave of fear in my direction as her dad reaches in and yanks her bag through the open door.

"Now, Beckett."

He crushes the words between his teeth, shoots me a look like he wishes he could crush me, too.

B'Rad stares straight ahead, trying to be invisible. But there's no escaping her dad's rage as he presses right up to the open driver's-side window.

"Be grateful," he says, "that all you are is fired."

B'Rad blinks hard against the shock of those words as Beckett scrambles out of the car and follows behind the long, heavy stride of her father. He escorts her to a white sedan and throws the door open, and she dissolves into the back seat. Her father doesn't get in right away. He returns to the crowd of worried Pure Prommers and parents who have been watching everything from the steps, now looking like a hornets' nest that just got poked.

I turn back to the white car, search the rear window for any glimpse of Beckett. All I get is the ghost image of her face through the tinted glass, lit up every few seconds with blue and red from the police car parked a few feet away.

I bend forward to get a better look at the steps, wondering where Joanna is in that swarm of people.

It doesn't take more than a few seconds to realize she's not there.

"Let's get out of here," I beg B'Rad, and he cuts away quick from the front of the church.

Every beat of my heart feels like I'm being body-slammed to the pavement.

Once we're headed out of Greenville, I unbuckle and climb into the front seat.

I feel him turn, feel him stare at me, feel the air fill with questions he's too nice to ask. He doesn't try to talk me out of crying, not even when crying turns into full-body sobbing. At a red light, he reaches over and opens the glove box, pulls a Hound's Tooth napkin out from under the rolled-up *Pray for America* T-shirt, and hands it to me. It smells vaguely of pot as I blow my nose into it, but the tears just keep coming.

"What do you want to do?" he finally asks.

"They'll kill her for leaving last night." I have a hard time catching my breath. "And if they find out what we did . . . ?"

B'Rad goes, "I know—"

"No, you don't." I take another napkin out, blow my nose again.

For a long time, he drives around, letting me cry. How can he still be so nice when it's my fault he got fired?

"I'm sorry you lost your job," I say.

"It's not your fault."

"You need that job."

"I need *a* job. I'll find something else—"

"*Fuck. Him,*" I shout.

He looks at me for so long, it gets uncomfortable. I turn away, watch the road roll then disappear beneath us. Follow the pale morning light as it seeps upward from behind the distant rocks.

"Can you just take me home?" I ask.

B'Rad doesn't answer right away. We pass a couple restaurants and a gas station before he says, "I mean, yeah, but . . . why would you want to go *there*?"

"Whatever's gonna happen, I just want to get it over with."

We silently weave through town, past the businesses on the nicer side of Escondido that won't be open for a few more hours, and the ones that don't open at all on Sundays, toward the shops and stores on the south end of town that are boarded up now, never to open again. It seems like nothing in the Flats stays for long. Businesses come and go. People come and go. And yet, I feel anchored. Not the kind of anchor that holds you steady—but the kind that keeps you from going anywhere.

When we pull up in front of my house, B'Rad sets the brake and turns toward me.

"Are you sure this is really what you want?" he asks.

What I really want imploded on the way home from Oviedo.

What I really want can never be found at Grace Redeemer Church.

What I really want didn't even bother to show up on the steps with the other worried parents this morning.

So, actually, what difference does it make what I want?

B'Rad looks at me like he's deciding if he should let me out of the car.

"You know, you can sleep on the boat just as easy as you can here. Probably easier."

Definitely easier.

"Seriously, Daya." He looks over at the house. "Is it even safe for you to go inside?"

I shrug. I don't know. I don't know anything.

"You're not . . . I hate to ask this, but . . . you're not thinking about hurting yourself, are you?"

I dry-laugh, and shake my head no.

"Look, I know it's going to be pretty thick with your mom too, so . . . I mean . . . what kind of friend would I be if I just . . . let you walk in there by yourself, with no backup?" He waits for me to answer.

"I guess . . . the kind who trusts."

I skim a glance off him. He looks hurt. He looks like a guy who's trying to think of another, better argument to keep me from getting out of the car. But there isn't one. I'm in choice. I'm choosing to face this.

After a while, he opens the door and gets out. I hear him pulling my bag from the back seat.

"I'll wait here for a few minutes—"

"You don't have to." I lift the bag from him.

But he watches me walk up the gravel driveway and around the side of the house, where I jiggle the back door handle to pop the lock. As far as I know, B'Rad's still at the curb when I go inside.

For a flash, I regret not asking him to stay, just in case. I have no idea what I'm about to walk into.

I wonder, though. Joanna may not even know what happened. Maybe that's why she wasn't at the church with the other parents. Why *wouldn't* she be there, unless she had no idea we left last night?

Maybe she doesn't know.

I keep this thought on repeat as I navigate the pitch-dark house toward my room.

Twenty-Three

HOME

I tiptoe down the hall, careful to avoid the floorboards in the middle that squeak. Ease my bedroom doorknob all the way to the side so the door doesn't make even the tiniest click when it opens, then shut it all the way behind me before turning on the light.

The sudden brightness startles us both.

Joanna sits up on the side of my bed with the folds of my pillowcase embedded in her cheek and my grandfather's Adelita statue clutched against her chest. I want to grab it away. But I can't. All I can do is stand against the door and stare at her.

Her question pierces the air between us.

"Where were you?"

If I thought it would change anything, I'd answer.

"They were about to file a *missing person's* report on you, Daya."

"You were worried?" I ask.

She flinches like I slapped her. "Of course I was worried."

"Then how come you weren't down at the church this morning with all the other parents, making sure I was okay?"

Joanna slides off the bed.

"Because I've been sitting *here* all night. Worried for *you*. Waiting for *you*. Praying I was wrong."

She wrings the Adelita between her hands.

"Wrong about what?" I ask.

I track her movements, the way she tosses the Adelita on the bed, the way she bends down, picks up my sketchbook off the floor, flips through the pages. That's when I notice the mess that wasn't here when I left yesterday. Like my room has been ransacked.

"You went through my stuff?"

She doesn't answer, she just holds the sketchbook open to the page where I drew images of Beckett's face on repeat.

I dip forward, swipe it out of her hands.

"What gives you the right to go through my stuff?"

"You sat there in that kitchen," she says. "Knowing what you were going to do. And you lied to my face."

It takes a beat to realize what she's accusing me of.

"Wait, you think I *planned* it?"

"What did I say to you? *You've never given me a reason to doubt you, Daya. You've never snuck out.* You sat there—"

"I didn't plan it."

"You . . . the drug dealer—"

What . . . ?

"—and your girlfriend."

Oh my God.

Joanna's eyes dart around my room. At my broken desk chair, at my dresser, at my photo collage, my artwork on the walls. At my bedspread. Maybe she thinks the answers to what went wrong with me are hidden in those things and maybe she doesn't. But at least by looking at them, she doesn't have to look at me.

"It was one of the ladies from SHIMMER who called me first," she says. "Some kids were missing from prom, she said. I got in the car. I was ready to race up to that church."

Memories of those last days with my dad click through my head. The fighting. The pleading. The sudden emptiness of our house, filled with nothing but Joanna's guttural pleas to God to fix it back to how it was.

"Pastor Mike called just as I was leaving. Told me that three kids were missing, and that one of them was you. I just sat there . . . in the driveway. For hours. Praying I was wrong."

She finally turns to me, and her eyes spill over with tears.

So do mine.

"I knew you weren't missing, Daya. I knew you were with her."

I know you were with her, Jon; that's why you took the job in Memphis, isn't it? To be with her. Tell me . . . please. Just tell me how long you've been planning this.

I was only seven. I didn't fully understand, but I felt the weight of it. I remember.

"I'm not him," I tell her.

She doesn't hear me.

"This isn't the same," I say even louder. "I'm not doing this to hurt you. I'm doing this because it's who I am. *Me*. Your daughter."

"If you only knew the ugly things people are saying about my *daughter*. About my *daughter* and that girl."

"That girl has a name. And me and Beckett are not him and her—"

The slap of her open hand against the side of my face registers as a sound before I ever feel it. My arm goes up in case she decides to do it again, as the sound waves echo to infinity inside my room.

The sting of that slap spreads through my entire body.

"Dad didn't just leave you," I say, still holding my face. "He left *us*.
I lost him too. And then I lost you. I've done everything you wanted,
everything I could think of to keep things peaceful. So you'd be okay.
I *want* you to be okay. But I can't keep pretending just to make you
happy. Why can't you love me for who I am?"

"God doesn't accept this," she whispers.

Her words echo around us, exactly the way I remember her saying
them to my father.

"You're wrong," I say.

"*I* don't accept this."

"But *you* have a choice—"

"Not when He commands us to bring those who stray to the truth."

I recognize the words. From last Sunday at church. Not her words.
Pastor Mike's words. Words she's just regurgitating from his sermon
and trying to force-feed down my throat like a faithful mama bird.

"Do you believe God loves me?" I ask.

"You couldn't even stay at that dance and give your *life* back to
Him!" she screams. The words fall around us like broken bits of glass.

She takes a few breaths to restore her calm and self-control.

"You refuse to see His truth, and you refuse to repent your sin . . .
but that's the price of living in this house. Now *you* have a choice."

She leaves me, shock-frozen and alone, in the middle of my room.
I swallow over and over again to stop crying, rubbing my face to tame
the burn she left with the full force of her open hand.

My duffel bag from last night is still strapped across my shoulder.

I grab a nearby T-shirt to wipe tears and snot off my face, then pull a few clean shirts and some underwear out of the dresser and stuff those inside too. I kick through the clothes and books and junk on the floor, snatch up my sketchbooks and pens. I grab the Adelita from where she dropped it on the bed, wrap it in a hoodie, close the zipper on my bag to protect what's inside. To protect everything I have in this world.

I don't know what else to do . . . except leave.

At the end of the block, I drop to the curb and pull my phone out. I can barely see through my swollen eyelids, but I open my messages and try writing to Beckett, if my hands would stop shaking long enough. I send it to her burner, so I know she'll see it.

> hey r u ok?
>
> i know things are bad, but can you call me when you get a chance?
>
> or text
>
> we need to talk
>
> i don't want to wait till monday to see you
>
> i don't care about you and lucy right now
>
> i only care about you
>
> can we talk?
>
> please?
>
> i hate this

By the time I send my last text to Beckett, my battery is almost dead—enough charge left to ask someone to come get me, but maybe not enough to hear back if they can.

I'm just getting ready to hit Stella up when a text pings through from Beckett, and my hands shake so hard, I almost can't get it open.

This is Beckett's father. Do not attempt to contact her again.

I stare at the message, read it over and over again like it's written in some other language, like my brain can't make these lines and shapes fit together.

Her father has her burner phone.

He read my messages.

About me and Beckett.

About Beckett and Lucy.

He knows everything.

I lean over, throw up into the gutter, then text Stella to tell her where I am and beg her to come get me.

Her **brt** comes back a nanosecond later.

I'm still sitting on the curb when she and Valentina roll up.

"Hey," she says, hopping out of the car.

"Hey," I sniff.

She goes, "Girl, you look rough," and waves at Valentina, who comes around the other side to open the door for me. She helps me into the back seat, and I wrap my arms around my duffel bag like it's a life raft.

The ride to Stella's blurs out completely.

When we pull up in front of her place, she gives Valentina a quick kiss before helping me out of the car.

"Seriously, Daya," she says as we head up the walk. "Are you okay?"

"No."

She opens the door, and we freeze for a beat at the sight of Ms.

Avila and Mr. Zapata standing in the kitchen, cooking breakfast.

"Good morning, m'ija," she says, giving Stella a hug. "How was the party?"

"Y'know. Cool," Stella says. I catch her throwing her eye-line in my direction.

Ms. Avila comes over to me. "You look like you can use a hug too, m'ija. Is that okay?"

I nod, and Ms. Avila pulls me in the same way she just did to Stella. "I don't know all the details of what's going on," she whispers in my ear. "But you can stay as long as you need to."

"You girls hungry?" Mr. Zapata asks. "I've got pancakes going, and some chorizo and eggs. And coffee. Stella, your mom tells me you like coffee. How 'bout you, Daya?"

I'm swallowed into a black hole in one of Beckett's coffee-cup galaxies, but Mr. Zapata takes my shaking head to mean *no*.

Stella goes, "We're gonna go put our stuff down. We'll be out in a few."

Her mom and Mr. Zapata go about their business like every part of this morning is situation-normal, while Stella ushers me down the hall into her room. She closes the door behind us, slides the duffel bag up over my head, eases me onto the bed. She plops down next to me, and I sink against her and ugly-cry. She doesn't try to talk me out of it, doesn't seem triggered or even upset by any of it.

She starts to ask, "You want me to——?" but I nod because I already know what she's going to say. I did it for her after Duke crushed her heart.

Stella wraps her arms tight around me to keep me from shattering into a billion pieces, and we stay that way, not moving or talking, until it seems safe for her to unwrap herself just a little. I keep my head on her shoulder while she strokes my hair and dries my tears, the way you'd comfort a little kid who's scared of the monster in their closet.

After a while, she goes, "Okay, bitch. Three deep breaths."

I wipe my nose on my sleeve.

"You know I don't believe in that Deepak Chopra, zen bullshit," I say, struggling to stop the endless flow of my tears. But I do the three deep breaths anyway.

Lying there, face-to-face with Stella, I know I should tell her everything. But how do I do that when telling her everything would mean trying to fit the entire universe into the space of an atom?

"I messed everything up," I whisper.

"Messed up how?"

"Joanna knows what I did last night—who I was with—"

"Oh shit."

"Beckett got caught too." Something about saying it out loud shatters me. I force the words out between sobs. "I kept texting her about it, but her dad had her phone. I didn't know—"

"Breathe," she says.

I stop for a minute, take a shaky breath, then another.

"I really fucked up, Stells."

"Can I ask you something?" She brushes the hair away from my eyes. "Whose idea was it to leave prom?"

I don't want to say it, but I have to.

I clear my throat and say, "Hers."

"That's right."

"But I *chose* to go."

"Daya, listen to me, I'm dead serious about this. You had every right to leave that dance. And so did Beckett. I don't care if they made it look like Happy Fun Prom. That lock-you-in-at-church bullshit is so meta, it's not even funny."

I nod. Swallow to put out the flame in my throat.

"And I don't even know what to say about Joanna. I hope she enjoys the Kool-Aid."

"I can't go home," I tell her.

She wipes away a few of my tears. "I know."

"No, I mean, I *can't*. She kicked me out. And I'm not going to Tennessee, either, even if my dad and Cindy say I could."

"Would you even want to?"

I shake my head.

"You know my mom doesn't care how long you stay, right?"

"What about Valentina—won't she feel weird about me being here?"

"*Daya*. Stop worrying about what everyone else thinks. You deserve to be okay. Lay that shit down, let people take care of you for a minute. Fuck."

I nod and it gets quiet between us, and Stella hates quiet, so she goes, "You know I texted my mom when we were coming down from Oviedo. In case you were wondering why they were scrambling eggs and shit when we got here."

"I figured."

"I just wanted to avoid the awkwardness of walking in on them doing it up against the entertainment center."

"Don't ever say that to me again," I whisper, and she smiles, and I kind of smile back, but in that tilted way of someone who's not sure she's done crying yet.

"I know what you're trying to do," I add.

She goes, "I'm just saying, it was almost as awkward to walk in on them in the kitchen like some 1960s TV couple. Aprons on, flipping pancakes. Sweet baby Jesus."

I go, "It could be worse."

"Oh yeah?" Stella pushes away some hair that keeps falling into my eyes. "How?"

"They could've been squeezing fresh orange juice."

"Gross!" She laughs, but the laughter dies out quick, and the room goes quiet again until Stella finally says, "Are you hungry?"

I shake my head no.

"Okay, but . . . even an ugly crier needs to eat, right? You can eat and cry at the same time."

I shake my head again. "I think I'm done crying for now."

"Bitch, lemme bring you some food. You don't even have to eat it. You can just . . . smell it, or whatever."

She stands up, makes it to the door, turns around. "Hey. We got this."

"I know," I tell her. "I'm just tired."

"Then sleep. Those pancakes aren't going anywhere."

The door clicks shut behind Stella, and suddenly the room feels like a still-life painting. Everything so quiet, almost static. Window open, curtain fluttering softly. I try to imagine myself painted on to this canvas, but I'm not sure how I'd pose for it. Am I tragic, broken, emptied out from crying? Or sleeping peacefully against a nest of pillows with the breeze lifting my hair?

The soft sound of voices drifts in from down the hall.

Stella saying, "I think her mom's having another breakdown."

Mr. Zapata mumbling something too low to hear.

"I'll call her mother," Ms. Avila says. "We'll work something out."

I drift, never settling on how to exist in this still-life moment.

Because within seconds, I slip into the deepest sleep of my life.

Twenty-Four

THE PAST

Walking the hallways at school Monday morning is like walking an electrified plank of weekend prom gossip, and eyes cutting sideways as I go by, and fragments of doctored rumors passed off in whispers as gospel truth.

The Gospel According to Escondido. So it has been written. About me . . . and Beckett.

It all hurts. The guarded whispers. The not-so-guarded whispers. People in class watching dozens of videos of us, recorded Sunday morning from in front of the church. All over Instagram and TikTok, even YouTube—all just a click away. Watching, then looking up at me like they know something.

They don't know anything.

At the beginning of lunch, Cason Price circles me at my locker with a stare that's part challenge, part threat. Every time he comes around, he gets closer.

SOS, I text to B'Rad.

He's there in a minute, ushers me out to his car, shuttles me away from campus, away from Cason and Lucy and everyone who went to Pure Prom and everyone who didn't but watched those videos after.

He swings into a little taco stand just out-of-the-way enough to feel safe from all of it for a few minutes.

"What can I get you?" he asks, like he's taking my order at the Hound's Tooth.

The thought makes my chest ache with regret.

"I'm not hungry," I say, following him up to the window.

He orders me two tacos anyway and hands the woman a ten.

"At least let me pay," I tell him.

"No, I got it."

I tip my head. "Dude . . . come on. You lost your job because of me."

"Is that how it's gonna be from now on?" he says. "*You lost your job because of me—let me give you my kidney.*"

I roll my eyes.

"You're not in great shape either, you know," he says as the taco stand woman calls out our number.

"Besides"—B'Rad takes the foil-covered paper plate from her—"the old bastard had a Mac Classic sitting out in the yard under a tarp. Can you believe that shit? Fully functional. I sold it online for . . . well, enough to buy a few hundred street tacos, let's just say that."

"I thought your days of selling off his shit were over."

He holds my gaze for a long beat.

"It was a *Mac Classic*, Daya," he says, and I lift my hands in surrender.

We sit in the back of his car with the hatch up and our feet dangling. B'Rad hoovers the three tacos he got for himself while I pick away at mine.

I go, "You have every right to be pissed at me for what happened."

He pushes his glasses back up by the nosepiece, looks out across the gravel parking lot as he chews.

"For a long time . . ." he says, wiping his mouth with the back of his hand. "Like, a *really* long time, I was afraid that . . . y'know, that whatever drove my dad to do that to my mom . . . ? It might be . . . I mean, nature versus nurture and everything."

"B'Rad . . ."

"Because the thing is, it wasn't just my dad. It's my granddad too, right? He's a whole skin-bag of nothing *but* anger."

He squints, finishes the last bite, wipes his face on a napkin, wads the napkin up with the foil, and throws it in the back seat.

"But I figure, most things aren't worth being angry about," he says. "That shit's lethal. And it sure as hell isn't worth getting angry over losing some basic job at a crappy hot dog stand, y'know?"

I feel a little love-rush for B'Rad just then. I'm not sure I could be so generous in his position.

After lunch, in Spanish class, my gaze keeps sliding to the space where Beckett's hand would usually be—raised to ask a question, minuscule gold band that's no longer on her ring finger because she gave it to me on prom night. I touch the chain Stella loaned me to keep it on, run the slender ring across it the same way Beckett fidgeted with her gold cross at Justin Tadeo's party on a night that seems forever ago, even though it wasn't.

Señora Muñoz calls Beckett's name for roll and someone at the back of the room says, "She transferred." The person behind me says, "No homos," low enough for Señora Muñoz not to hear. But I hear. The words ripple forever, because sound is infinite.

After Señora Muñoz offers to help me find a new partner, I sneak-text Stella about it under the desk, and she's waiting for me outside the door at the end of fifth period.

"I'll have my mom write us a note," she says, edging me off campus. She hooks her arm through mine as we walk home, so I can cry and not worry about crashing into anything.

"Fuck the haters," Stella says. "Seriously, fuck them. They eat people."

"It's not just that," I try to tell her. "It's . . . everything."

"I know," she says. "I get it."

Honestly, I'm not sure she does. When she and Duke broke up, Duke was still walking around school. Stella could see who she hung out with and what parties she went to. Duke didn't just disappear, which meant Stella didn't have to make up stories about her. She didn't have to wonder. It would be easier to be mad at someone, to move on even, if you could see *them* moving on. But I don't know if that's what Beckett's doing. I don't know if she's okay. If she wants to talk to me again or not. I don't know if she hates me, or if her parents sent her for deprogramming, or . . . anything. Not knowing is actually harder than knowing something bad.

At least I can deal with something bad. Process it. Move through it.

I don't know *what* to do with a heart full of nothing but broken pieces.

The shade doesn't ease up much as the days drag on. Being low-profile queer in this town was nothing compared to what it's like being "the dyke who got caught defiling Escondido's queen of purity." It's completely irrelevant what the truth of the situation actually is.

Stella puts up with my nightly check-ins, where I ask if she's heard anything about Beckett, and she tells me she hasn't. She rolls with it, as long as she can stream old *Veronica Mars* episodes on TV while I interrogate her. She calls teenaged Kristen Bell her TV crush.

That's what we're watching on the last Monday night of the school year when out of nowhere she goes, "What about Be Weird?"

"What *about* him?"

"He's got shop class with Cason, doesn't he? Can't he get intel?"

"They've iced him out too," I tell her. "Guilt by association. They're calling him Kingpin now. Can you believe that?"

"Why, because of the pot thing?"

I nod. "I think that whole drug-dealer rumor broke the sound barrier."

She nods. "Right? Like, who do they think people like Cason Price get their nugs from, anyway?"

"Seriously." I reach into Stella's bowl of popcorn I told her I didn't want any of and steal a handful. "All her church friends are on complete information lockdown too."

"How about social media?"

I shake my head. "Her accounts have all been deleted."

"Damn," Stella says. "So maybe it's better not to know, y'know?"

"Maybe." I lean my head on her shoulder. "It's not going to stop me from wanting to, though."

In private, I acknowledge this is only a half-truth. I want to know everything about Beckett. Everything but the part about Lucy. I never want to know the whole truth about Lucy. What they were. What they did. I don't want those images living in my head.

Sound isn't the only thing that's infinite. So is pain. Pain and memories.

On Tuesday, Stella has detention after school for the fight she got into with Valentina in the science wing, and B'Rad's going job hunting, and suddenly I have no one to walk home with. They've been really careful about not leaving me alone—a coordinated but unofficial effort to keep a safety net under me. They think I don't know, but I do, and I love them for it.

The truth is, I'm not sure which is weirder—being alone for the first time in nearly two weeks or realizing I'm alone for the first time in nearly two weeks.

When I hit the Strip, I detour left instead of going straight. Straight would take me to Stella's. Left leads in the direction of the mortuary.

Joanna's car is parked in the back lot. I stand on the other side of the street, looking at it.

I could go inside that building right now, if I chose to. I could cross the distance between here and there, open the door, and walk inside. But then what? Would she talk to me? I don't think so. I think she'd rather talk to the dead. I think she believes they deserve something I don't. Tragedy is Joanna's safe space. It's where she's most comfortable. She's designed her whole entire life around it. And she made it more than clear when Stella's mom called her . . . I don't belong in that space with her.

I'm worse than dead.

I'm unredeemable.

By the time the last day of school comes around, things at Stella's mom's house have settled into a freakishly normal routine, whatever normal is. Mr. Zapata out back grilling burgers or carne asada. Ms. Avila laughing in that way women do when they're happy. I don't think I ever heard Joanna laugh like that.

A call hits my cell as I'm setting out paper plates for our celebratory, last-day-of-school dinner. The sound is jarring—I almost never get actual phone calls.

"Guess who just got a job bussing tables at O'Ring?" B'Rad says, and I can almost see him pointing to his own chest with both thumbs.

"Awesome!" I say. "How'd that happen?"

"The owner took one look at my work history and hired me on the spot."

"*What?* Did he just have a gut feeling about you?"

"That, plus check this out. The guy had a horrible experience buying a scooter at none other than Wild Rides Vespa last year. He left a scathing Yelp about it, but . . . he's still burnt over it after all this time."

My heart plunges when he says the name Wild Rides.

"Daya, for real, when Ulises heard I was fired from the Hound's Tooth by Dennis Wild himself, it lit him on fire. I'm telling you . . . I think you need to capitalize on this."

"*Me?* How?"

"I mean, create a fake work history showing your very brief stint at the Hound's Tooth."

I wait for him to laugh it off as a joke, but he doesn't.

"Are you sure you're not stoned right now?" I ask him.

"I'm not, I swear. Come on, it's not a *total* lie—you did work there that one night. Look, just come in tomorrow and talk to him. I'll put in a good word for you. You know we make a great team."

I don't tell Stella about it that night, but I spin the idea around my head a few billion times. In the morning, I head down to O'Ring to talk to Ulises, and after an interview lasting two minutes and some change, B'Rad's new boss becomes my boss too.

I hurry home to share the good news, but I'm not sure who's more excited—Stella or her mom.

"Good for you, m'ija!" Ms. Avila says. "That's fantastic! We should celebrate!"

Stella cuts right to it. "Can I use your employee discount?"

"Jesus, woman," I say. "I don't even start till Monday. Hey, so B'Rad's taking me to the Freestyle Exchange after his shift today so I can get some work clothes. Wanna come?"

"Nah," she says. "I'm helping these two power-wash the back patio. But there's a party at Cara's tonight and we"—she flips her finger between us— "are going. So if you see something fly on the racks—"

"Yeah, I don't think so," I tell her.

"Come on, man. You can't lay around being morbid all summer. We're seniors now!"

"I really can't," I say. "I'm not ready. It's just . . . it's hard, y'know?"

"I know, but . . ." Stella heads to the fridge, grabs two Cokes, and hands one to me. "I mean, it wouldn't be fair for me to have *all* the fun this summer, right?"

I don't take the bait. I'm not ready to joke this part away.

She goes, "Look, I just don't want you to be alone."

"I won't be. I'm hanging out on the boat tonight with B'Rad."

"Okay. Well." She sets her Coke down so she can slip on a pair of rain boots. "Here's the deal. You get a pass tonight, but that's the last one. Next time, you have to roll the dice and come with me, no matter what."

"Uh-uh." I shake my head. "That's too much power for one lesbian."

"Dude, I won't make you go skinny-dipping in a public fountain or anything. I promise. Just pinkie swear you'll do it?"

"I don't feel good about this."

"Come on," she says. "There are so many great parties happening this summer, and *pity party* isn't one of them. Walk away from that, Daya."

She stands up, tucks her hair into a ball cap.

"And quit listening to Cassie Ryan," she adds. "That shit'll make you tragic."

"If I say yes, will you finally stop talking?"

"You have to pinkie swear."

"Fine, *I pinkie swear.* Are you happy?"

It turns out that what Stella actually meant by *next time* was the Fourth of July.

"Time for re-entry," she announces the second my eyes open at the crack of early evening. I swear, opening shift at O'Ring is gonna do me in.

I pull the blankets up around my head and roll over on the trundle. "What time is it?"

"I just told you."

"What *actual* time is it?"

She throws a pair of her pants at me—plaid, with random buckles down the leg—does an all-teeth smile, and goes, "Time to head to Los Escondidos."

I sit up and make face back at her. "The fair? Seriously?"

"So many girls, Daya."

"I've already told you. I'm not interested."

"Bitch, not for *you*. For *me*."

"Okay, but . . ." I swing my feet onto the floor. "What if you run into Valentina and what's-her-name?"

"You mean Puta?"

"I think it's pronounced Paula."

"Either way, I don't care. See? This is me, not caring who Valentina wants to see. Come on, Daya. Let's go do the Fourth at Los Escondidos. They'll have fireworks!"

Stella widens her emoji-smile, and I cave. I find a cleanish T-shirt and a pair of jeans shorts to slip into, because there's no way I'm wearing her weird Hot Topic buckle pants to the fair in ninety-seven-degree heat.

Half an hour later, I squeeze next to Stella in the tiny back seat of Mr. Zapata's dinky car, with her mom up front, riding shotgun next to him.

"Sorry about the tight quarters, girls," Mr. Zapata says. "I took your mom's car to the shop for servicing. I just didn't know it would take this long to finish."

Stella elbows me. I elbow her back.

"How old are you?" I whisper.

"How old are *you?*"

We have to turn away and look out our own windows, so we don't send each other into the mother of all giggle fits.

When we hit the fairgrounds, he drops us off at the gate before parking and promises they won't *harsh our vibe* while we're there.

"You have the weirdest expressions," Stella tells him.

"Here," he says before we get out of the car. "Have a good time. No kissing boys."

Our hands stop midway to taking the money he's holding out to us.

"Hashtag dad jokes," he says in his own defense. "Not funny?"

Stella goes, "Your timing's off."

Ms. Avila adds, "Just needs a little tweak."

"Yeah, I'll work on that," he says.

"Okay, well. See you folks later." Stella slips the cash out of his hand before leaning forward to kiss her mom on the cheek.

"Thanks, Mr. Zapata," I say, sliding out behind her.

He goes, "Hey, you know you can call me Mark, right?"

"Too soon," I say, shutting the door.

Stella and I buy our tickets and push through the turnstiles.

"Where's Be Weird?" she asks. "I thought he was meeting us."

"He's just leaving work."

She goes, "Tell him to let us know as soon as he gets here."

"Dude. Chill. I'm working on it," I say, firing off a text to him.

hey, hit us up when u find parking

be there soon, he shoots back.

also, don't text and drive, I add.

We're cruising the souvenir circuit when another text pings through.

meet @ baby animal pens

He's standing by the goats when we find him.

"Dude!" Stella calls out, pulling him into a bro hug.

"I thought you were going to text from out front," I say, but B'Rad is so stoked, he steamrolls right over me.

He goes, "For real? I've been waiting all day for this. Let's go eat something greasy and disgusting. First round's on me, no strings attached."

We spend a few minutes debating between giant turkey legs or pizza or shave ice or tacos. Eventually, we agree on The Battered Ram so Stella can get the nachos she wants, and B'Rad can have the corn dog he's been craving, and I can get my personal favorite: funnel cake. If it can be dipped in breading and/or deep-fried, The Battered Ram will sell it to you.

B'Rad steps up to the window to order first, and just about then, Stella notices that the girl hanging out the window taking orders is kind of cute.

When it's her turn, she gives that girl in the window The Smile, and asks, "Which would you recommend—the nachos or the smothered fries?"

"It's not Chez Panisse," I tell her. "Just pick one."

Stella ignores me, and the girl in the window uses her tongue to play with the diamond stud pierced into her lower lip. She takes her time, gives it some careful thought.

"Honestly?" she says. "The smothered fries are one of our best-sellers."

Stella nods like she's assessing the rec. "Okay."

"Besides," the girl says, dimple-smiling down at Stella. "They're kinda sexy."

"I guess we have a winner, then," Stella says. Man, that girl can charm the paint off a car.

I edge her out of the way so I can order my funnel cake, then step aside to let B'Rad pay, and that's when someone says, "Hey," from so close behind me I jump at the sound of it.

Maybe-Naomi takes a few steps back once I turn. Her smile is about half of what Stella's is right now, still getting her flirt on with the Battered Ram girl.

"Hey," I say back, not sure where to go conversationally after that.

"Happy Fourth of July," maybe-Naomi says.

"Yeah. You too."

Some middle schoolers stagger past us like a bunch of drunk college freshmen on spring break, completely on fire about whatever ride they just got off. I watch them until they disappear around the back of the merry-go-round, and then I pick out one of the horses, the purple one, and track it as it comes back around.

"Funnel cake?" I hear from the window, and B'Rad taps me on the arm and hands it to me. Stella is in the process of asking the girl in the window what time she gets off.

"Wanna go for a quick walk?" maybe-Naomi says. "I won't keep you from your friends too long, I promise."

I look over at Stella, who's faking like she doesn't notice us. She's still flirting, but she's also keeping a close eye on whatever's going on with me and maybe-Naomi right now.

I ask B'Rad, "Hey, where are you guys gonna be?" and Stella goes, "Just meet us at the entrance to the stadium. The fireworks are gonna start soon."

Maybe-Naomi and I wander off with no real destination, at least not in my mind. I use the flimsy plastic fork they gave me to wrestle off a piece of funnel cake and eat it, relieved she's not watching as I shove it into my mouth.

"Bite?" I offer, holding the plate out to her.

"Sure." She takes the fork, twists off a piece, then puts it in her mouth without touching the fork to her lips. "I wasn't sure if you were, like, a germophobe, or . . ." she says around the bite before stopping to chew. She wipes her mouth with the back of her hand in case there's any rogue powdered sugar left behind and hands the fork back to me. "I just didn't want to make you uncomfortable."

I don't say anything, because the truth is, maybe-Naomi has always made me uncomfortable.

"My friends tell me I do that sometimes," she says. "Come on too strong? So. I'm trying to do better."

I nod, working to pry off another bite of funnel cake but failing miserably.

"I'm losing the fork," I say with a laugh, and maybe-Naomi laughs too and says, "Good call."

We walk past the game booths, past the fast-talking carnies waving at us to come try our luck, past the rows of vinyl blow-up toys and rainbow-colored plushies hanging on S-shaped hooks inside the game tents. As we walk, we take turns pulling off pieces of funnel cake and licking the powdered sugar off our fingers. Out near the go-karts, I hold the plate out to her.

"Last bite?"

She shakes her head. "Nah, I already ate your whole thing."

"I offered," I tell her, picking up the last piece between two fingers and dropping it into my mouth. It makes me laugh for some reason, and when I do, a puff of powdered sugar micro-explodes from between my lips, and that makes us both laugh. But once the funnel cake is gone, I have no idea what to say or what to do with my hands. Maybe-Naomi takes the plate from me and throws it away and we keep walking, dodging the crush of bodies moving in the direction of the stadium.

"I guess they're getting ready to start the fireworks," I say.

Maybe-Naomi stops and turns.

"Look, Daya . . . I just want to apologize for . . . everything. For being a dick, especially that night in Oviedo. I wasn't cool, and . . . yeah. I'm sorry."

It's weird hearing her mention Oviedo. That night feels like it happened light-years ago, or like it happened to someone else. But I'm not going to do that thing girls do, myself included. I'm not going to tell her it was okay when it totally wasn't.

A loud *boom* cracks the sky, and we turn to look up. One long spiral of smoke and sparks rockets high above the fairgrounds before bursting red, white, and blue into the sky. The crowd cheers as the explosions start coming fast and relentless, strobing color and light across the sea of upturned faces. I sneak a look at maybe-Naomi, watch her face flash purple, then gold, then green.

"I should probably go find Stella," I tell her.

"Cool," she says, taking a step back. "Thanks for the walk. And the funnel cake."

"I mean . . . I don't think they'll care if you want to hang out with us?"

"Yeah?" maybe-Naomi says, a look of surprise across her lit-up face. "Sure. For a little while."

We find Stella and B'Rad just outside the gates of the stadium. I have to shout to be heard over all the noise around us.

"B'Rad, Natasha," I say. "Natasha, B'Rad."

He mimes drinking the hard cider she brought him that night and gives her a thumbs-up. She throws rock-star fingers back at him and smiles. B'Rad and Stella lean into each other as they look toward the sky, and then Stella throws an arm around me and hooks me into a hug.

I look up at the bursts of flame and color breaking loose above us, and hope that somewhere, Beckett's watching it too. That it reminds her of something real, or something that could be real. If not for me *and* her, then at least for me. And her.

All around us, kids squeal and couples kiss and people *ooh* and *aah* and the breeze chases itself through our hair and the air smells like smoke and grass and hot dogs and sugar and the sky fills with flash-bursts of color.

And for right now, everything is perfect.

Acknowledgments

With love and profound gratitude to young readers. You are the hope seekers, the truth tellers, and the mirrors that reflect the best of ourselves to the rest of the world.

Supreme gratitude to my agent, Erin Murphy, for your patience as I tunneled my way to the heart of this story.

Huge thanks to my editors: Kristen Pettit, for your keen vision; Clare Vaughn, for including me in every step of the process; and to the entire editorial team at Harper Teen, who had faith in Daya's story right from the jump.

To our heroic librarians, educators, and booksellers, who face unimaginable challenges in uncertain times, yet continue to do the real and transformative work of championing literacy.

Early readers e.E. Charlton-Trujillo, Pat Z. Miller, Joanna Marple, and Melany Joy Beck, your notes, thoughts, and suggestions were everything I needed to reach Daya's inner and outer world. She, and I, are the better for it.

To cover artist Beatriz Ramos, for capturing the heart and soul of this story in such stunning fashion.

To my Mamacita—part mom, part sister, part friend, and wholly unconditional love.

To Jennifer Salas, mi hermana para siempre, cheerleader and sage adviser extraordinaire. The day you threw your arms around me and cried "I'm so happy for you!" was the day I was able to breathe again and take my first step toward an amazing life.

To Jorge Salas, Designated Cruise Director for all those amazing fiestas.

And to Alicia and Adriana Salas, world's greatest kitty wranglers. Additional thanks for being down to read anything I've ever put in front of you.

To Elly Swartz and G. Neri—if not for that pep talk of yours in Atlanta, Daya would have languished at the bottom of a drawer forever.

To Patti Ashwell—in my moment of darkness, you uttered the most transformational words ever: "A year from now, you'll look back and be astonished at how different your life is." You were right then, as you have been every single year since.

To Amy King, who will go to the ends of time and space to honor, celebrate, protect, defend, listen to, *and* hear kids. *Everybody's* kids.

To Naheed Hasnat, whose badassery knows no bounds, and to Doug Marshall, whose generous heart does the same.

To Cindy Vela; Dave, Tanya, and Mel Bartlett; Eva Goins; Hannah Moushabeck; Helen Read; Jenny Cameron Paulson; Kelly Silwani; Kimberlee Wheeler; Kimberly Woods-Bonéy; Leigh Purtill; Mary Dodge; Sally Derby; the Struyf family; and carrying with me the memory of Karl Miller, Feven Mebrahtu, and Margaret Speaker-Yuan.

To the memory of author Julie Anne Peters. *Keeping You a Secret* was the first queer YA book I ever came across. What a revelation! I say this with confidence, that *The Redemption of Daya Keane* may never have come to be without the influence of Julie's writing on me.